"This Southwestern cozy comes with a spicy Tex-Mex flair. Its delightful characters and clever mystery will have you stomping your boots for more."

> —Mary Ellen Hughes, national bestselling author of the Pickled and Preserved Mysteries

"Adler's debut sizzles with West Texas flavor and a mystery as satisfying as a plate of fresh tamales. Slip on a pair of cowboy boots, pour yourself a margarita, and kick back to enjoy this Texas-sized delight."

> —Annie Knox, national bestselling author of the Pet Boutique Mysteries

"Rebecca Adler's *Here Today, Gone Tamale* is a much needed addition to the cozy mystery genre. Terrifically tantalizing . . . and as addictive as a bowl of chips and salsa. Settle in for a mystery fiesta you won't soon forget."

> —Melissa Bourbon, national bestselling author of the Magical Dressmaking Mysteries

"What a tasty idea for a new series! In *Here Today, Gone Tamale*, Rebecca Adler merges the warm and vibrant West Texas town of Broken Boot with a clever murder mystery that kept me guessing until the exciting finale. Josie is an engaging hero who must solve the mystery while helping her delightfully quirky family and balancing trays of steaming tamales!"

> —Kathy Aarons, author of the Chocolate Covered Mysteries

Cinco de Murder

Rebecca Adler

BERKLEY PRIME CRIME
New York

BERKLEY PRIME CRIME
Published by Berkley
An imprint of Penguin Random House LLC
375 Hudson Street, New York, New York 10014

ISBN: 9780425275955

First Edition: April 2018

Printed in the United States of America
1   3   5   7   9   10   8   6   4   2

Cover design by Judith Lagerman
Cover illustration by Ben Perini
Book design by Laura K. Corless

For my mother,
Mildred JoAnn Wallace Woodall

Acknowledgments

As always, big hugs to my family and friends for their patience and encouragement.

Thanks to Pat French and B.L. Brady, precious friends, whose loving prayers and home-cooked meals warmed my soul during the writing of this book.

This story was made into a much better book through the efforts of my editor, Rebecca Brewer; copy editor, Randie Lipkin; cover artist, Ben Perini; publicist, Tara O'Connor; and the many fine folks behind the scenes at Berkley Prime Crime and Penguin Random House. Many thanks to you all.

As always, heartfelt gratitude to my agent, Kimberly Lionetti, and BookEnds Literary Agency for always having my back.

To the One who created the Chihuahua Desert, the Chisos and Davis Mountains, and the rugged beauty of The Big Bend, thank you for your countless gifts and tender mercies. They are beyond compare.

Chapter 1

▰▰▰▰▰▰▰▰▰▰▰▰▰▰▰▰▰▰▰▰▰▰▰▰▰▰▰

Folklórico Rehearsal

On such a gorgeous May morning, what could be better than a power walk to Cho's cleaners with my long-haired Chihuahua, Lenny? The morning sun had tossed a wide blanket of gold over the Davis and Chisos mountains, awakening the piñon pines and the weeping junipers from their slumber, illuminating the bluegrass and scrub so they looked like desert jewels. The plan had been to retrieve my *abuela*'s *folklórico* costume and burn some extra calories. And though we made good time—considering the length of my canine sidekick's pencil-thin appendages—the morning sun galloped down Broken Boot's cobbled streets while I paid Mr. Cho with a crumpled five-dollar bill and a coupon for a dozen free tamales.

"Yip." Lenny lapped from the pet fountain in front of Elaine's Pies, soaking his black-and-white coat.

"¡Vámonos, amigo!" If we were late to the final dance rehearsal before the Cinco de Mayo parade, God only knew

when Senora Marisol Martinez, our matriarch, would permit me to call her *abuela* again.

During my first few months back home, I was elated to find I could accomplish tasks in far less time than in the crowded thoroughfares of Austin. Almost a year later, I was forced to admit the slower pace of our dusty little town didn't aid me in my quest to check things off my list. It merely encouraged me to meander.

On that happy thought, Lenny and I raced down the sidewalk toward Milagro. Suddenly I tripped over the plastic clothes bag, nearly kissing the pavement with my face. "Whose great idea was it to rehearse this early?"

"Yip."

"That's what I was afraid of."

When we barreled through the front door of Milagro, the best, and only, Tex-Mex restaurant on Main Street, I expected the *folklórico* rehearsal to be in full swing. Instead my best friend, Patti Perez, glared at me, which only made me smile. I was wise to her marshmallow center, in spite of her ghostly Goth appearance.

"Sorry," I mouthed. After all, it had been my idea for all of us to join the local *folklórico* troupe—my way of embracing life back in good old Broken Boot, Texas.

"About time," she chided as I draped Senora Mari's costume over a stack of hand-painted wooden chairs. In my absence, the other dancers had cleared the dining room to create a dance floor on the beautiful Saltillo tiles.

"I would have called," I began.

"But I was trapped in a dead zone," we said in unison. Service was so bad in Broken Boot and its outlying communities that folks were slower here than in the rest of the country in ditching their landlines.

"Where's Anthony?" When our headwaiter offered his newly formed mariachi band to play for our first performance, I didn't have the heart to say no. Beggars can't be choosers, or look a gift band in the mouth.

"Tsk, tsk." Across the room, Anthony's new fiancée placed her hand over the bar phone's mouthpiece. Though christened *Lucinda,* we'd quickly dubbed her Cindy to avoid calling her Linda, my aunt's name, and vice versa. "He *says* his truck has a flat tire." She scowled at whatever Anthony said next and responded with a flurry of Spanish.

"Who doesn't keep a spare in the desert?" Patti, whom I referred to as Goth Girl if for no other reason than to hear her snort, delivered this line with a deadpan expression and a flick of her rehearsal skirt.

"Yip," Lenny said, chasing after her ruffles.

Goth Girl snapped her head in my direction and gave me the stink eye. "Tell me you replaced *your* spare."

"Uh, well, not yet, but I will after Cinco de Mayo." Money was a bit tight, what with the loss of tourists during the winter months.

To my right, Aunt Linda, a stunning middle-aged woman with warm chestnut hair, modeled her bright-colored skirt better than any fashionista in Paris. "That's what you said about Valentine's Day." She was my late mother's older sister. She might look great in her Wranglers, but she and rhythm had never been introduced.

"And Saint Patrick's," chimed in Senora Mari, executing a double spin. This morning she wore a rehearsal skirt of black-tiered lace along with her Milagro uniform of peasant blouse, gray bun at her nape, and large pink flower behind her ear. No matter how much I rehearsed, none of my moves could compare to her sassy head turns and flamboyant poses. Who knew my seventy-something, four-foot-eleven *abuela* would turn out to be the star of our ragtag troupe?

A sharp clapping interrupted our chatter. "Let's try it on

the counts," cried Mrs. Felicia Cogburn, mayor's wife and self-appointed dance captain.

"Yip," Lenny agreed.

"Why is that dog here?" Mrs. Cogburn demanded, her hands raised in mid-clap.

"He has a key role, remember?" My *abuela* smiled, an expression so rare on her dear weathered face it made folks uncomfortable.

Mrs. Cogburn blinked several times. "Of course." Before she could begin, a small truck landed at the curb with a bed full of musicians, trumpets and guitars in full serenade. The band stopped playing long enough to hurry inside.

"*¡Ay, Dios!* Senora, I had to borrow a spare. Mine was flat." Anthony waved his friends into a semicircle just inside the door.

Senora Mari thrust a finger into the air. "So you say." She snapped her head dramatically to the side. "Play."

With a worried look, Anthony counted off, and the group of dark-haired men and boys began to play the *jarabe tapatío*, the Mexican hat dance. I spied a familiar face on trumpet. Anthony's little sister Lily gave me a wink and a nod.

As the trumpets and guitars played, Mrs. Cogburn called out, "And one, two, three, four."

"Where's your skirt?" Patti asked as we twirled first right and then left.

"Ah, chicken sticks." I dodged the dancers, ran up the stairs to my loft apartment, and retrieved my long skirt from a chrome dining chair.

"Yip, yip, yip," Lenny cried from the bottom of the stairs.

"Sorry." I found his straw hat on the yellow Formica table and made it downstairs without mishap. "Here you go, handsome." I perched the hat on his head and tightened the elastic under his chin. As we danced, Lenny would spin in place on his back legs, melting the hearts of the crowd faster than fried ice cream in August.

"Yip."

I hurried to my place on the back row next to Patti as the band launched into their next number, "El Mariachi."

"Josie, stand up straight," called Mrs. Cogburn. "Linda, you're turning in the wrong direction."

After running through our routine six times without a break, we collapsed into the dining room with refreshments. I was removing Lenny's straw hat when the cowbell over the front door clanged.

A middle-aged man with a gray buzz cut and white coveralls stepped inside. "Howdy." He checked his clipboard and gave us an expectant smile. "I'm looking for Mrs. Cogburn."

"That's me." With a hand to her hair, Mrs. Cogburn stepped forward. "As long as you're not from the IRS." She giggled, her cheeks flushing a soft pink.

Aunt Linda marched to the front door. "We have plenty of parking on the *side* of our building." She pointed through the doorway to where a white cargo van, emblazoned with FILLMORE'S FIREWORKS, stood double-parked. "Why don't you use it instead of blocking traffic?"

Buzz Cut's eyes narrowed. "Maybe I'd forgotten how ornery and downright persnickety small-town business owners can be."

A tense silence followed as he glared at her and she glared at him. Suddenly they burst into laughter and hugged. "Frank, what are you doing here? I thought you'd moved to Marshall or Longview, somewhere out in the Piney Woods."

With a self-conscious smile, he ran a hand through his hair. "I did, but business still takes me out this way a few times a year."

Patti and I exchanged glances. I had never seen my

business-minded aunt react so warmly to any man except Uncle Eddie.

With a glance at our curious faces, Aunt Linda presented Buzz Cut like a sequined model presenting a heavy-load truck to a mesmerized crowd at the El Paso Car Show. "My prom date in high school, Frank Fillmore." With a flourish, she swung her arm wide. "And this is everybody."

"Nice to meet *all* of y'all." His eyes widened as he took in the large group of dancers and musicians. His grin revealed a wide space between his two front teeth. *"Hola, ¿cómo estás?"*

"Fatal," Senora Mari muttered. "Are we going to dance or chatter like squirrels?"

"Senora." His eyes twinkled with good humor. "Would your cooking be the source of the amazing, mouthwatering aroma of this place?"

She shrugged. "It's my kitchen, so it must be true."

"And I bet it's *your* way or the highway."

After a moment of hesitation, she honored him with a careful smile. *"Sí.* Of course."

"My wife, Felicia, was the same way." His expression softened. "Had to be in charge of the kitchen, didn't want any help. Didn't even trust me to wash a dish."

"Come back after lunch and we'll set you up with all the dishes you can handle," I said. If the dishwasher didn't show up, me, myself, and the busboy were screwed.

Everyone laughed. Even Senora Mari added her abrupt ha-ha-ha.

"This young *lady* with the sassy mouth is my niece, Josie Callahan." Aunt Linda raised an eyebrow and gave me a look of gentle reproach.

"Miss Callahan."

"Frank, we'll have to catch up later. Glad you're back this year for Saturday's big show."

Mrs. Cogburn clasped her joined hands to her chest. "Mr. Fillmore, please accept my apologies. I should have recognized you from the last time you participated in our Cinco de Mayo festivities, regardless of your new hairstyle."

"No need to apologize." He gave her a brief smile. "But I do need someone to follow me to the fairgrounds. The mayor wanted a bigger show; and it requires a different setup."

Aunt Linda took Mrs. Mayor by the arm. "Senora Mari will take them through their paces, won't you?" She raised a brow at her mother-in-law.

My *abuela* studied us like a drill sergeant studies his rough recruits. "*Sí*, I will lead."

"I wish my husband was here. He would make it plain as day."

"I can go," I said.

"Jo Jo, you stay." Uncle Eddie entered from the hallway, dressed in his usual attire: pressed jeans, plaid Western shirt, and leather vest. "You and I need to go over the last-minute details for tomorrow. I don't want no International Chili Association official to tear a strip off my hide." A tourist at Two Boots dance hall, our other establishment, might suspect Uncle Eddie of wearing a costume. Little did they know, he wore the same outfit day in and day out.

"I'll be glad to help out." Aunt Linda threw an arm around Mrs. Cogburn's shoulders.

I waited for my aunt to introduce Frank Fillmore to my uncle, but the introduction never came.

"*¡Vámonos!* Don't stand around gawking." Senora Mari took her place front and center while the rest of us darted into position and the band started to play.

After a word to Fillmore, Mrs. Cogburn returned to her charges. "And one, two, three, four."

Uncle Eddie made for Milagro's office just as Frank Fillmore opened the front door for my aunt. She caught my eye, glanced toward her husband's retreating back, and, with an impish grin, lifted a finger to her lips.

Two hours later, my *abuela* threw her copy of the *Broken Boot Bugle* onto the counter. "*¡Suficiente!* Who cares if you break one or two rules?"

Senora Mari was not my grandmother. Technically, she was my Aunt Linda's mother-in-law, but since I'd been raised in their home after the car accident that claimed both my parents, she often allowed me to refer to her as *abuela*. But if Lenny had been under foot or barked too loudly in the morning, she would remind me that Senora Mari was her rightful title.

"*Mamá.*" Uncle Eddie lowered a fresh glass of sweet tea without taking a sip. "The town council is watching me like a hawk, just waiting for me to screw up." My uncle's dark hair was slicked back in his usual style, light puffs of gray at his temples. His broad, honest face was tense with worry, deepening the wrinkles the West Texas sun had furrowed across his forehead.

"You're imagining things." I took the International Chili Association cook-off planning binder from his hands. "It will all fall into place, you'll see." And I gave him a pat on the shoulder. "We've reviewed every detail from beans to trophies."

"Yip." Lenny stood on a wooden chair so Cindy could complete his costume fitting.

"Okay, okay, little one. Soon. I will finish soon." Her small, delicate hands had created a darling pair of white satin pants and jacket to match what the members of Anthony's mariachi band were wearing.

"Where's his sombrero?" asked Uncle Eddie.

"I have it here." From her sewing kit Cindy retrieved a

white satin hat with gold detailing and placed it on his head.

I squealed with glee. "Isn't he adorable?"

"Humph." Senora Mari thrust her hands on her hips. "If you think a long-haired rat dressed like a human is cute, you are loco."

"Is it not right?" Cindy asked.

I glared at Senora Mari behind the young woman's back. "It's not you or your beautiful costume." I smoothed Lenny's white jacket and rubbed him under the chin. "She would say the same if he were dressed like Our Lady of Guadalupe."

Cindy turned her wide brown eyes on Senora Mari. "You would?"

"I would."

Cindy smiled. "Then he is perfect for tomorrow's parade."

"Let's try it out." I lowered Lenny to the tile floor. "Stand," I commanded. Without hesitation, he lifted his front legs and pawed the air.

"So adorable." Cindy clapped her hands.

"Turn," I continued.

With the grace of a ballet dancer, Lenny hopped in a full circle until he was back where he started, paws still high.

"Good boy." I scooped him up and kissed his head.

"Yip."

"Yes, yes, very handsome." I paid Cindy on her way out, even though she insisted the beautiful costume was a gift.

When I returned, Senora Mari was waiting. "Where are you?" She tapped the paper with the tips of her fingers. "You said you wrote a story."

"Page ten. The article about the fifty head of Herefords blocking Highway 90."

With a grunt, she found the page and read the article. "This is," she held her thumb and index finger about two inches apart, "smaller than a *cucaracha*." She lifted her chin. "Why?"

"That's how much my editor trusts me." In fact, he probably trusted a cockroach more.

Uncle Eddie wiped his brow with a handkerchief from his pocket, still nervous as a cat on a porch full of rocking chairs.

I grabbed two lime wedges and a salt shaker from behind the bar. "Even if we could rattle off all the ICA rules in our sleep, we're bound to forget something on the big day." I salted both lime wedges, handed him one, and we both took a bite. "Truth is, if we make a mistake, the judges will be there to smooth things out." As one, we both made a sour face.

Senora Mari shook her head in disgust. "What power does this IGA—"

"ICA. The IGA sells sweet tea and chicken nuggets."

She glared. "Why must we bow to this ICA?"

"Let's see." I counted off on my fingers. "One. They sponsor hundreds of chili cook-offs worldwide each year. Two. They raise millions of dollars for charities and nonprofits. And most importantly, the town council insists the cook-off be an ICA-sponsored event."

"Humph."

"If Uncle Eddie wants to earn the town council's respect, he's got to make sure this soiree goes off without a hitch." I wasn't about to admit how much I longed to throw the ICA's rules and regulations binder into the nearest ditch.

She drew herself up to her full four feet, eleven inches. "He should not have to work so hard to earn the respect of other men. Which one of *them* owns *two* successful businesses, like my son?"

"You don't understand." His shoulders and chest deflated until he looked like a droopy cactus. "If I screw up again, the town council will tie me up faster than a rodeo calf *and* run me out of town on a rail."

"This cannot be true."

With a growl, he picked up the *Bugle* from the counter and quickly flipped through the pages. "How can I ever live this down?" He stabbed the photo that accompanied my story and began to read. "Dozens of Herefords were scattered across Highway 90 Monday afternoon, creating a traffic backup that lasted several hours."

Gently I took the paper from his hand and threw it behind the antique oak bar. "How were you to know the photographer didn't know how to close a cattle gate properly?"

"Tell that to Pratt. It took him and his hands over an hour to round up his herd."

"He can't force you off the town council. It wasn't your fault!" Rancher P.J. Pratt, long-time council member, had lined up one of the *Bugle*'s photographers to take my uncle's official portrait on Pratt's ranch.

"No, but his friends can." Senora Mari placed a hand on her son's forearm. "He's the richest guy in three counties; he can do what he wants."

I gave her a look. "They'll do no such thing." I threw my arm around his shoulders. "You'll prove you deserve your seat on the council tomorrow when the cook-off goes as smooth as cold butter on hot corn bread." I fired off a silent prayer that this good man's bad luck would change.

As if reading my thoughts, Senora Mari crossed herself and brought her thumb and forefinger to her lips. "Amen."

Our prayers must have worked. A few minutes later, Uncle Eddie hit the road, a spring in his step and hope in his heart. I hit the stairs, a hope in my belly that the leftover chicken in my fridge hadn't spoiled.

"Where do you think you're going?" Senora Mari was like a Mexican ninja.

"To raid the refrigerator." I glanced longingly up the stairs.

She led me into the kitchen instead. "Ballet *folklórico* is a good idea. You and your friends embracing my heritage." She spun around to stop Lenny with her foot. "No dogs in the kitchen."

With a soft whine, he trotted off, making a beeline for Aunt Linda's office and the doggie treats hidden in her desk drawer. Lenster was no fool.

"I won't be good company if I'm hungry."

From the bottom rack of the oven, she pulled out an aluminum pie plate covered with foil. "Here. Eat."

Beneath the foil, I found two breakfast tacos, each containing egg, potato, cheese, and salsa. "Gee, thanks!" I was suspicious of her motives, not an idiot.

"Last night . . ." Slowly she walked to the window and gazed out into the alley as if in a trance. "I had a dream."

I swallowed. "Was it scary?" My *abuela* took great pride in her dreams. She believed they held great significance for the people in our community.

"I'm thirsty." She found a tamarind-flavored Jarritos soda in the fridge. "You listen. This one has meaning for you." She grabbed a knife from the counter and flipped off the bottle cap.

Fighting a smile, I raised my hands in protest. "You know I don't believe in dream interpretation." Heck, I didn't even read my horoscope.

She wiped her mouth with her pinky. "That is because you went to college. Forget all that and listen."

"Okay." I sighed. "Go on."

She shook a stubby index finger at me. "God's prophets interpreted dreams in the Bible." She jabbed her finger into her chest. "Why not me?"

I could have said many things, but I remained as quiet as a pillar of salt.

"Last night I was eating chili." She folded her hands in her lap.

"I thought you had tilapia."

She glared. "In. My. Dream. I was eating a perfect bowl of chili." Tapping her chest, she lifted her chin. "I made it. That's why it was perfect."

"Of course," I said with a wave of my hand. "Continue."

She leaned in closer. "After I finished, bits of ground beef formed a pattern in the bottom of the bowl."

"Like tea leaves. Well, I don't believe in those either."

"Shh. The bits of beef created a symbol."

"A question mark or a cross?"

"Shh. A lightning bolt."

I frowned. "Like Thor?"

"No." A deep frown line appeared across her forehead. "Like power."

I leaned back against the industrial sink. "What do you think it means?"

"I am not sure." She slid from her stool. "Lightning is powerful. Like you." Softly she laid a frail hand on my shoulder. "You don't think so, but you *are* a Martinez."

I blinked away unexpected tears. "*Gracias, Abuela.* I've made some dumb mistakes."

She patted my cheek. "So have I. Remember?" She claimed she stole some goats and spent time in the local jail when she first arrived in Texas—but I wasn't convinced. She raised up on tiptoe and took my face in both hands. "You lost your important job and your fiancé. So what? We solved two murders."

"*We* did?"

"*Sí.* You, me, and that smelly *chucho.*"

I disengaged myself, swiping at the corner of my eye

with my sleeve. "Don't say that in front of Detective Light-foot or Sheriff Wallace. They might throw a hissy fit."

"Humph." Abruptly she removed a container filled with skirt steak and marinade from the fridge and fired up the stove-top grill. "So you can't cook." She thrust her index finger into the air as if leading a charge. "It's never too late."

"Hey, what's going on?"

She grabbed her purse and the large black-and-white golf umbrella she used as a parasol from the broom closet.

"Finish the skirt steak." She marched into the alley, opened the umbrella, and nearly fell over from the force of the wind. One strong gust and she'd fly into Parker County like a Latina Mary Poppins.

"But where are you going?" I called as she charged toward the street.

Stopping long enough to glance over her shoulder, she responded, "To teach the town council a *powerful* lesson!" She narrowed her gaze and lifted her chin. "If I'm going to win tomorrow's cook-off, I need to set my hair."

Chapter 2

❦❦❦❦❦❦❦❦❦❦❦❦❦❦❦❦❦❦❦❦❦❦❦❦❦❦❦❦

The First Annual Charity Chili Cook-Off Reception

After posting Lenny's daily remarks on his Little Dog Blog and sprucing up my look, I strutted downstairs. The First Annual Broken Boot Charity Chili Cook-Off reception was now in full swing and Milagro was overflowing with contestants, council members, volunteers, ICA officials, and the usual Thursday-night regulars. As the town council members and other locals had arrived, they all looked to my *abuela*'s empty stool as if the world had tilted on its axis.

Coach Ryan Prescott warbled a familiar drinking song from behind the bar as he fired fresh fruit into the blender and let her rip, filling the air yet again with a refreshing burst of lime and an earsplitting whir.

I stole a good hard look at his tan profile. In spite of losing his frat boy smugness and sleep-deprived lassitude, he'd kept his lean, athletic frame and wavy hair, not that you could tell with it hidden under his cap. I might not drink from the holy grail of football, but Ryan had won the hearts of rabid West Texas fans by leading sweaty, testosterone-dripping, heat-addled young men into battle day after day, week after week.

"What?" He rinsed his hands and bent to turn off the faucet with his elbow. "I'm doing it wrong . . . again?" With a quick flick of his wrist, he snapped me with the hand towel that seconds earlier had rested on his shoulder. "What'd I do now? Add too many limes? Not enough mix?"

"Yip," Lenny called.

"Are you trying to get me fired?" I scurried around the bar and found my handsome Chi hidden under the sink.

"Yip, yip."

"Uncle Ryan's an old softie, huh?" I chucked Lenny under the chin. "If Senora Mari hears about this, it's pistols at sunrise—and I don't own a weapon."

"Women don't understand how hard it is for us to be cooped up, do they?" Ryan placed Lenny in his crate in the storage closet. "Keep the faith, man." Ryan lifted a fist to the side of Lenny's crate, and the Chi met the fist with his paw.

Ryan joined me at the bar sink. "I've never known Senora Mari to be sick."

"If she's sick, I'm a rodeo clown."

"I was wondering why you were wearing makeup tonight." Ryan ducked my swing.

"Three frozen, one salt, one sugar, one bare as a baby's bottom," Aunt Linda called through the window between the bar and the kitchen.

"Mrs. Martinez, where's Senora Mari?"

She threw her hands into the air. "Don't ask." She waited until Ryan began filling her drink order. "All I know is those judges from the International Chili Association better hold on to their clipboards."

I was walking back to my post, ready to greet any late arrivals in my fashion: wide smile, warm gaze, and a heartfelt *howdy*, when the door catapulted open on a gust of wind so strong I thought the Four Horsemen of the Apocalypse had developed a hankering for Tex-Mex. In the distance, lightning danced on the horizon near Big Bend National Park, and two older gentlemen in cowboy duds stepped through the doorway.

"Is this here the chili cook-off reception?" A tall, white-haired man with a luxurious salt-and-pepper mustache thumped his naked chest, which was bare except for a jungle of curly white hair, freckles, and a small leather medicine bag that hung around his neck. He was at least six feet tall, but I swear his ten-gallon hat made him ten inches taller. And if I didn't know better, I'd bet good money that he and his friend stopped at a costume shop on the way, one specializing in singing cowboys like Roy Rogers and Gene Autry.

"Uh, sir. You can't come in here without a shirt on." I pointed to a hand-painted sign behind the cash register. NO SHOES? NO SHIRT? NO TAMALES.

"Pay up, you old goat!" His stocky companion didn't laugh as much as he brayed like a donkey. "Heee . . . haw!"

"I ain't never" The tall man's cheeks flushed bright red above his mustache.

"Only every single time you enter a new chili cook-off." His friend, who wore his lank, black hair parted in the middle and pushed behind his elephantine ears, stuck a plump hand in his friend's face. "Hand over my five dollars and button your dang shirt."

The tall dude cut his eyes at me. "Hold your horses, Whip." From the bag around his neck, he withdrew a roll of bills, peeled off a five, and flung it at him.

Before it could hit the floor, his companion plucked the bill from the air. "Don't pay him no mind. He insists on going around half-naked no matter the occasion."

The *he* in question fisted his hands at his sides. "You'd better watch that lip, boy. Lucky's Naked Chili has won more cook-offs than anyone else in this entire salsa-swigging casita." Muttering rude comments under his breath, Lucky buttoned every last button, threw a bolo tie around his neck that he fished out of his pants pockets, and tucked in his shirt.

"Howd—"

"Answer the blipping question." Lucky, the formerly shirtless of the two, lunged closer. "Is *this* where the chili contestants are meeting?"

"Yes, sir." I plastered on a smile and gritted my teeth. "All contestants and their posses are welcome."

The two exchanged puzzled glances. "Was that a requirement?" Whip, the shorter one, smoothed a strand of lank hair behind his ear. "To bring a posse?"

"No, and neither is ordering. Would you like menus? Or are you here for the meet and greet?"

"Menus, if you would be so kind, senorita," said Lucky, taking his hat in his hand, spreading his manners on thick when thin would've impressed.

"Don't mind my friend. That's Lucky Straw and I'm Whip."

"I figured that out." I handed each a menu. "Gentlemen, welcome to Milagro and Broken Boot's First Annual Charity Chili Cook-Off."

Whip drew a deep breath and sighed. "Whatever smells so divine, that's what we want, darlin'." He was making serious eye contact as if I held the power to declare the winner of tomorrow's contest in my hot little hands.

Carrying a tray of margaritas, Aunt Linda hurried past. "Come on in, fellas. Let's get you signed up." One glance at her beautiful face and figure, and they trailed behind her like two lovesick calves.

I followed along to where Uncle Eddie sat alongside a leathery-skinned woman with shoulders as wide as his own.

"What are your names, boys?" Bridget Peck wore a neon yellow ICA visor over her cloud of gray curls, and a matching golf shirt. If it were up to me, I'd burn her headgear for failing to do its job. Her skin was red and sun-beaten, and unfortunately, starting to peel. God forgive me, her skin made me think of the side of a barn left too long without a paint job. And if anyone within a mile radius had a doubt she was the ICA official on duty, she flashed her yellow and red badge and whipped out her official letter of introduction from the president of ICA.

"Bridget, cut the snuff. We've only attended two dozen of these here cook-offs," Lucky said, smoothing his mustache with a bronzed knuckle.

For a long moment, she studied the two chili cooks from their boots to their eyebrows. With a dramatic sigh, she shook her head as if bewildered. "Nope. Don't know you. Show me your IDs and I might return them." Her high-pitched laugh squeaked like a rusty door hinge.

With matching scowls, they retrieved forms of identification, Whip from his wallet and Lucky from the medicine bag inside his shirt. "Bridget Peck, four years is too long to hold a grudge."

Her face turned a pale pinkish color. "Seems to me that four years might not be long *enough*, considering what the other person did to land a body in jail overnight, which caused her Thunderbird to be towed and her prize chili pot to be stolen out of the backseat."

Lucky swallowed hard. "Now, Bridge, it's not my fault you didn't pay your tickets in Highland Park. Those high-falutin cops don't play."

"Was it or was it not *you* who told the police officer that my registration sticker was out of date in an attempt to keep me from entering the Highland Park Presbyterian Chili Cook-Off?"

"How was I to know they'd throw you in jail overnight?"

Her jaw clenched so hard I thought she'd start spitting teeth. "Not to mention, the police also took possession of my daddy's Colt .45 from under the front seat, where it lived since the days when my daddy drove that Thunderbird back and forth to Texas Power."

"He made it home to the missus one night too many, if you ask me," Whip muttered.

"I heard that, mister. Don't think I've got wax flowing from my ears."

Bridget made a big production out of poring over their pictures before eventually locating them on the list of registered chili contestants. She retrieved their preprinted application forms from her plastic file box and tossed them on the table. "Welcome to the provisional ICA Broken Boot Charity Chili Cook-Off. Make sure to sign at the bottom, and don't skip any lines."

Uncle Eddie handed each man a black pen with a pair of boots on top, his idea of a promotional tchotchke. "Keep the pen, boys, and check out Two Boots while you're here, the best dance hall in Big Bend County." My uncle told the truth. We owned the best and only dance hall in three counties.

As his friend signed his waiver, the short fellow named Whip pulled a pair of frameless glasses from his pocket and studied the assembled cooks. "Quite a turnout you got here. This your first time outta the gate?"

"Yes, sirree." Uncle Eddie stuck his thumbs in the straps of his leather vest and puffed out his chest. "Next year we'll have even more."

Bridget Peck adjusted her visor. "The *committee* will

review your event and make the final decision on whether or not you will be allowed to proceed in the future as a sanctioned ICA event." She lowered her readers and leveled Uncle Eddie with a look I associated with prison matrons, wearing steel gray hair buns.

"Looks like you're the last of the bunch." Without acknowledging Bridget Peck's remark, Uncle Eddie peered at the list over her shoulder, a deep furrow appearing between his eyes. Poor man should've been wearing his glasses, but he was too vain. He could no more read the checkmarks on that page than I could dance the flamenco.

"Don't give me one of your icy stares, Bridget Peck. Lucky was the one who just had to say good-bye to Becca for a good fifteen minutes before we could leave." Whip glared at his friend.

"Oh, honey, I'll miss you," Whip said in a sweet falsetto. Along with the high voice he added a drawl right out of Georgia. "Give me another kiss, you big, strong handsome man."

Lucky slammed the pen to the table. "Course I did, and you would too if she were still your woman . . . which she ain't."

He pressed a cell phone into my hand, and I immediately understood that he fit his moniker. His screen saver was a gorgeous blonde with fashionable inky roots, bright red lips, and light blue eyes like cornflowers in the sun. He was obviously Lucky in love and proud of it.

"Give him back his phone before he has a conniption fit." Whip gave his friend a long-suffering look of amusement. "Can't stand to go a moment without keeping her in full view."

"She's something, all right." I returned Lucky's phone. I was embarrassed for the shorter man. His friend needed a lesson in humility or simple good manners.

"When are you going to let us set up, Bridget?" Whip asked. "Lucky and his iron skillet are primed to take the win."

"Eight o'clock tomorrow morning," she answered, poring over the two men's applications. "Same as every other event you've attended," she said under her breath.

Lucky straightened his shoulders. "Now, Bridge, how do we know you didn't bend the rules for this flyspeck town?"

I resented that remark. It didn't matter that we had only three thousand or so residents—we had a hundred entrants.

"Bending the rules in my business can endanger the lives of animals and humans, not to mention the natural beauty of protected areas like the Chihuahuan Desert." Frank Fillmore, the fireworks guy, had wandered over unnoticed. "Why not play by the rules and keep everyone safe?"

"Any of you know this joker?" Lucky, sneering, asked the rest of us.

"What do you think would happen to these fine folks and their houses, cars, businesses, and whatnots if I fired off my rockets and missiles at will?" Frank's gaze narrowed on Lucky like a mountain lion tracking a desert cottontail. "You think I can shoot off rockets in any direction, anytime, day or night, and on any day of the year without following the guidelines set in place by the Texas fireworks code?"

"Hey there, Frank," I said with a bright smile, hoping to distract him from his tirade. "Glad you could make it. Are you hungry? Would you like some quesadillas?"

"Thank you kindly." He rubbed his hand back and forth across his forehead. "I apologize. It's been a long day and I have a thunderous headache."

Bridget Peck handed Lucky and Whip their lanyards and welcome packets. "No irregularities. Move along."

With a glare at the ICA official and a curt nod to Frank,

Lucky moved to a vacant booth, and Whip trailed behind, eyes wide behind his nearly invisible lenses.

"If you're hungry, I've got the cure for what ails you." I gestured to the buffet tables filled with flautas, quesadillas, and warming trays overflowing with fajita fixings: sautéed onions and peppers, savory chicken, and fajita skirt steak.

"How much?"

"All of the chili cooks eat from the buffet. It's included in their entry fee." We'd lose money, but it was our first rodeo—so to speak—and Uncle Eddie and Aunt Linda wanted to make a lasting impression. "For you, seeing as how you're Aunt Linda's prom date, it's on the house."

He cast a furtive glance around the room. "The state fire marshal nearly shut us down."

"Good Lord! What was he doing here?"

"The mayor's office set it up."

"Why?"

"Every fireworks display site has to pass inspection."

If we canceled, that would put a hole as big as the Grand Canyon in our weekend. Visions of angry tourists seated on blankets at the fairgrounds filled my head. Faces, young and old, looking up into a dark sky to a big fat nothing. As if the tooth fairy, Easter bunny, and Santa Claus all forgot to visit on that special morning.

"But we're good to go? You passed?"

He sighed. "Yeah, after separating several launchpads and moving the whole platform one hundred more feet from the parking lot."

My heart sang with relief. "But you passed with flying colors!" I would've offered him drinks on the house, but a hungover fireworks engineer—or whatever they called themselves—didn't sound like a safe idea, especially if a state inspector was lurking around town.

Frank gave me a wan smile and headed for the grub.

"Each and every event must be run the same way." Bridget Peck was frowning at Uncle Eddie. "Doesn't matter the size or shape. It's best for the hosts to learn the rules at the very beginning."

She checked her watch and scurried to the center of the room. "May I have your attention?" Her voice took on a melodious tone, which projected to the far corners of the room. The volume slowly lowered until only one or two voices could be heard in the back.

"My name is Bridget Peck. I'll be your lead official and head judge at this event. On behalf of the International Chili Association, I want to welcome each of our entrants and their friends and family to the Broken Boot Charity Chili Cook-off." Warm applause followed along with a couple of whistles. "Now, I don't want any of our more serious cooks out there—Lucky, I'm looking at you—to worry about any irregularities that might keep you from qualifying for the nationals in Boise. We've worked closely with Eddie and Linda Martinez, the host of our event tonight, to guarantee a well-organized, official contest."

"Where's Sam?" asked a female voice from the back. "I thought two officials had to be here."

"Mary Jane's having her third boy, bless her heart." The room erupted in applause. "But Sam'll be at the fairgrounds tomorrow."

The cowbell clanged. "Wait for me," a too-familiar female voice called. Hillary Sloan-Rawlings hurried into the room in five-inch heels, a fur vest, and enough bling to feed a small country. The locals in the crowd applauded and my heart sank. Six years after almost winning Miss America and she was still Broken Boot's biggest celebrity. Hang it all.

Bridget frowned as the beauty queen made a production

of hugging a few folks along the way to an empty seat at a front table.

"Looking good, Hillary," a local rancher called from the back.

"Who said that?" The beauty queen stood, hands on hips. "You are too sweet, P.J. Pratt. Does this mean you're going to sell me that piece of property I've been begging you for?"

The crowd laughed. The battle between the two sides had carried on for the past twelve months. Hillary wanted to extend her own acreage, but despite his drought-related problems, Pratt refused to sell.

"Uh, hem." Bridget's smile faded as she waited for Hillary to take her seat. "As I was about to say, everything you need to know is spelled out for you in your registration documents. If you have any questions, this would be the time."

A dark-haired woman wearing red-framed glasses stood, giving the crowd a nervous glance. A small girl and two young boys munched on chips and salsa at her table, all three children wearing wire-framed glasses. They wore clean, well-worn T-shirts and matching sneakers. "Will we have our own water hookup?" The little girl clamped two hands around a large red tumbler and slowly maneuvered it toward her mouth while the boys stuffed already-full mouths with tortilla chips until their cheeks were as round as a sow's belly.

"That's my understanding." Bridget Peck turned toward another raised hand.

"Last time," the dark-haired woman interrupted, "I had to share with Lucky." She extended her arm and pointed a finger at him, like Dickens's Ghost of Christmas Future. "And he only let me use it once." Without taking her eyes from his, she reached down to help her daughter hold her drink.

Lucky laughed, but no one joined in. "That's not how I remember it. If you needed water, Dani O'Neal, you should have spoken up loud enough for me to hear you."

She kept her fervent gaze locked on Bridget Peck. "You're positive about the water?" Dani's bottom lip trembled.

"Eddie Martinez, come on over here." Bridget waved to my uncle. "Why don't you set the woman's mind at ease?"

With a nervous smile, Uncle Eddie wove his way through the tables and chairs. "That's right. I spent a couple hundred dollars having the hookups added so we would meet the ICA standards." He smiled wide. "So keep on drinking and I'll make that money back in no time."

"Will do," someone hollered. Laughter followed.

A heavyset man with long, wavy hair staggered to his feet. "Why don't you tell Lucky's lapdog to keep his hands off other people supplies?"

"Let it go, hon," said the red-headed woman seated next to Grizzly Adams.

Whip jumped up. "Russell, I didn't take your bowls in Laredo." He looked to the crowd for support. "Is it my fault he can't count?"

For a giant, Russell was fast. He was in Lucky's face before you could say *chile rellenos*. "You, my *friend*, always weasel spices, gear—heck—even meat off other folks who can't afford to share!" The crowd murmured in agreement. "What happened to your fat pension?"

"That true, Whip?" Bridget Peck asked.

With a worried look, Whip adjusted his leather vest. "Maybe once or twice, but I'd never steal from someone, only borrow."

Russell bowed out his chest. "No, but you'd steal someone else's recipe."

Eyes round as a couple of cue balls, Whip stepped forward. "Ain't that the pot calling the kettle black?"

"Boys, boys." Bridget Peck's voice demanded their attention. "Go on back to your seats and order some grub. It's been a long day and I bet you had to put in a full day's work before you hit the road."

Russell nodded and, with a swift glance at Whip, trudged back to his seat. The shorter man watched him go, eyes narrowed and neck stretched forward like a rattler.

"It's not *all* about the winning." Bridget Peck grinned. "It's about the food."

"You got that right," someone shouted from the back.

"So go out and make chili like your mama taught ya and don't forget to have fun!"

As enthusiastic applause changed to excited chatter, Uncle Eddie joined me behind the counter. "I thought for sure, Jo Jo, we were about to have a sparring match, right here in front of God and the ICA."

"Night, folks." I waved to a group of customers still chattering about their recipes.

"Mommy, I have to go potty." Something jerked my apron. Below me stood a miniature person with glasses, only three feet tall.

"Hey, honey. Where's your mommy?"

"Kayla." Suddenly the woman called Dani appeared with one of the young boys in tow. "I told you not to talk to strangers."

With a whimper, she buried her head against her mother's leg. "I have to go potty," she wailed.

"Come on," I said with a smile. "It's right this way." Luckily, the *niñas'* room appeared to be unoccupied.

Dani opened the door, prodding the girl in front of her. As she tried to bring the boy inside, he dug in his heels. "Not going in the girl's potty. I'm a big boy."

The exasperated mother rolled her eyes. "Not now, Keith," she muttered between clenched teeth.

"We'll wait out here." I gave him a wink.

And he reciprocated.

After a quick study of my face, Dani accompanied her daughter inside.

"Keith, huh." I didn't know what else to say to a seven-year-old. "Like Urban?"

He rolled his eyes. "Heck, no. Toby Keith. He's a red-blooded American."

Before I could defend the handsome Aussie, the mom and daughter reappeared, singing "Courtesy of the Red, White and Blue."

"I promise, Uncle Eddie's as good as his word." I grinned. "You'll have all the H2O you need."

Dani lowered her voice. "It's not him I'm worried about. If Lucky can rain down havoc on his competitors, by God, he will."

"Sounds like a real nut job." *Nut job?* I sounded just like Uncle Eddie.

The cords in her neck stood out. "I swore I'd never be on welfare, and here I am. Why else do you think I entered this contest? Because I like chili?" She grabbed the hands of her two children and hurried away.

I hurried to the bar and found two margaritas and a Coke. "Who are these for?"

"Table six . . . I think." Ryan had his thumbs raised to type a text. "What time is this shindig over?"

"Thirty minutes ago."

As he typed, a faint smile appeared.

"Big plans?"

Wiping away his smile, he pocketed his phone. "You'd better deliver those before I have to remake them."

"Good point." I loaded my tray and turned, nearly slamming into Lucky Straw.

"Whoa there, gal." With nimble hands, he steadied my tray as Coke splashed over the side of a red tumbler. He smelled of cinnamon candy and salsa.

"Oh, wow. Are you okay?" I stepped back.

He pasted on a charming smile. "Is one of those mine?" With a long arm, he reached for a glass.

"Sorry. Table six."

The smile evaporated along with his smarmy tone. "You've yet to bring me and my buddy Whip our free drinks." After a deep breath, I replied in my best friendly-yet-firm manner, "The drinks aren't free tonight. Only the Cokes and iced tea."

Narrowing his eyes, he studied me as if I enjoyed cheating him out of his due. "Seems to me, you've been avoiding me and my friend. We're tired of waiting on you to take our order."

I glanced around the dining room, filled to capacity with smiling faces and cheerful conversation, until I located Anthony. "There's one of our other waiters," I said, gesturing with my chin to the corner. "That young man will help you straight away while I take care of these drinks." Inwardly, I groaned. The glasses were sweating and the ice had begun to melt. I could hear Aunt Linda's rant in my head.

Mouth turned down in disapproval, Lucky paused. "Better than waiting for you to get around to it." He marched away two steps and spun again. "And by the way, I have special dietary needs, which you would know if you read the comments section of my registration."

Oh, great. Had I forgotten any dietary requests in the dozen or more comments we'd received? My stomach plummeted. I vaguely recalled setting aside a registration to discuss with Carlos, our lead cook. Something that required creating an additional item or two for the evening's menu.

Lucky pulled the corners of his mustache. "Just as I thought. You're dumbfounded."

I found another two inches in my spine. "Who says we didn't get your request?" I prayed my nose wouldn't start to grow. "Wouldn't you prefer it fresh? Not sitting in a warmer growing spongy?"

Again with the mustache, only this time he curled the ends. The corners of his mouth curved as well. "Prepare away, my taste buds are buzzing with anticipation." I watched him barrel his way through a group of chili cooks conversing and blocking the aisle. "Excuse me. Watch out. Coming through."

"Is he bothering you, Jo Jo?" Uncle Eddie asked, joining me.

"Do you remember anything about a special dietary request?"

He grabbed the brim of his hat with two hands. Uncle Eddie never wore his hat when working the restaurant, not unless he was putting on the dog for the tourists. "It's on the bulletin board in the kitchen."

"Did Carlos see it? Did you two discuss it?"

Slowly he shook his head, like a three-year-old caught with a crayon in his hand next to a dinosaur drawing on the living room wall. He took the drink tray from my hands. "Why don't I deliver these for you? That way Linda can yell at me if they complain."

"Table six," I called above the din as he started off in the wrong direction.

I hurried toward the kitchen, dodging Lily as she bolted from the kitchen with a platter of quesadillas. "Carlos!" No sign of him. With my right hand, I grabbed Lucky's registration from the bulletin board, and with my left, took a pan from the stove.

"What are you doing, Josefina?" Senora Mari stood at the back door. In the alley beyond her, Carlos was staring at me, jaw gaping, cigarette in midair.

"I'm leaving it in your capable hands." I handed Senora Mari the pot and Carlos the form before she insisted I prove my negligible cooking skills. Fifteen minutes later, I sent Anthony to the kitchen to retrieve the desired dietary delicacy for Lucky. If that crotchety chili cook said one more cross word to me, I would spit in his eye.

After an hour, folks finally headed out. Lily was busing the last of the tables with the help of her older brother. With a quick sip of soda water and lime, I braced myself for the final push of the night. "I got it." I handed her an empty rubber tub and grabbed the full one. I hauled the dirty dishes to the kitchen and delivered them to the dishwasher. When I returned to the dining room only Whip, Lucky, and Bridget Peck remained. They all turned toward me.

"Did you find a small leather pouch?" Lucky grabbed his shirtfront.

"Sorry," I said. "I'll keep an eye—"

"Inside was a card about this big." He held his thumb and index finger two inches apart. "And a topaz the size of your thumbnail."

His jaw clenched, his chest rose, his hands fisted.

Whatever was in that bag meant a great deal to Mr. Lucky Straw. "We're about to clean up. If it's here, we'll find it." He was a thorn in my side, but I was skilled at recovering lost treasures—keys, earrings, cell phones, and especially dog leashes.

"Give her your number, man." Whip pointed to his own cell phone.

With a grunt, Lucky trudged over to the cash register, grabbed a to-go menu, and scribbled his digits.

"I've told you a hundred times, Lucky." Bridget Peck removed her visor, rubbed her temples, and plunked it back on her head. "Use the ingredients you submitted to us. No last-minute changes. No whims. The health department is not shutting us down to please your muse."

Instead of heading for the door, the tall wannabe cowboy hunched his shoulders like a Brahma bull. "You can quote the dad-burn ICA rules until you're blue in the face, but you can't cook chili to save your life!" With a long, bony finger, he caught the inside of the rulebook and flipped it to the floor, pages spread open like the wings of a wounded bird.

I expected Bridget to respond in kind, but she surprised me. Her eyes narrowed and an angry smile spread slowly across her weathered lips. "Son, you better pray not one page of that book is damaged."

With a quick glance at Lucky's clenched jaw, Whip carefully lifted the binder from the floor, his dark hair falling in his face. He handed the rules and regulations to Bridget. "Come on, Lucky," he murmured, grabbing his companion by the arm. "Don't get kicked out over something stupid."

I held my breath, waiting for the two chili slingers to fling more vitriol. Instead, Lucky gave his friend a nod, and the two sauntered out as if already holding the championship trophy in their ill-natured hands.

Chapter 3

❧❧❧❧❧❧❧❧❧❧❧❧❧❧❧❧❧❧❧❧❧❧❧❧❧❧❧

Let the Games Begin

The dusty-colored coyote merely stared as we approached, his mouth open in a welcoming smile. Without the wag of his tail, he was a dog-shaped cactus. Or a friendly stray . . . if I didn't know better.

As my Prius entered the weedy car park at the edge of the Big Bend County Fairgrounds, another canine nose slipped through the long grass. No smile on the muzzle of that one. Only when I turned off the engine with a sputter and shake, did the coyotes disappear.

"Yip, yip, yip." I scooped up Lenny and placed him on the dash, the better to see his opposition. He smashed his nose against the front windshield as if the harder he pressed the more likely he was to apprehend his long-lost cousins.

"Don't mess with those two unless you want to lose a leg." Coyotes might seem friendly and nonthreatening due to their size, a mere twenty-four inches from the ground to their chest; but they would bite and tear and rip without a growl.

"Yip."

"A wheelchair would definitely impede your dancing, my friend." And after a close call with a clipper-wielding killer a few months back, I was keeping my crime-solving partner close.

A loud squawk erupted from the police scanner I'd stuffed below the dash. "Dispatch?" Deputy Pleasant's voice pierced my eardrums.

"Yip," Lenny howled.

I lunged for the volume control. Lenny had most likely bumped it with his tail again.

"Go ahead." The young female dispatcher responded, smacking her gum.

"Taking a 10-10." Even though Deputy Pleasant was the only female officer in Big Bend County and the tri-county area, she wasn't embarrassed to communicate her personal needs.

"Roger that."

Sumter Majors, my enigmatic editor at the *Broken Boot Bugle,* had insisted on giving me a police scanner to help me in my pursuit of local crime stories, which lay thin on the ground, like frost on the desert in February. I hadn't learned all the radio codes, but I knew a 10-10 meant the female deputy was taking a fifteen-minute break. Why she bothered to use the code was a mystery. Even a civilian like me could figure it out.

Once out of the car, I slowly turned in all directions, carefully looking for our four-legged friends among the ocotillo plants and shin-dagger agaves along the edge of the parking lot. Those coyotes should've run from us, but I could hazard a guess as to why these two wanted to play with our shiny metal vehicle. Food. Someone had fed them or left savory trash behind, transforming this remote location into a canine epicurean market.

Once on his leash, Lenny bounded first in one direction and then another. I gave him only six feet of lead, but still he leapt the full length, pulling and straining, growling a warning to the coyotes that the big dog was in town—all six pounds of him.

It was barely six thirty in the morning, but I'd shot up like a rocket at five o'clock. Downstairs, Uncle Eddie had foisted coffee and cinnamon rolls into my hands and hurried me out the door. It was my job to check the location of each chili cook on the fairgrounds one last time before they began their savory battle of beef and spices to make sure nothing—no wind, no varmints, no vandals—had messed with the electricity, water hookups, or Uncle Eddie's chance to impress the other members of the town council.

Two dozen RVs had parked behind their assigned plots. No lights were on. In one giant RV with a tan and brown landscape painted on the side, a screen door appeared to be the only barrier between the great outdoors and the sleeping contestants inside. In the far distance, I spotted a white truck with FRANK'S FIREWORKS emblazoned on the side and a platform covered with boxes and odd-looking gizmos set up just beyond it. Our pyrotechnical wizard had made the most of his location. The crowd would park in the lot, set up their chairs and blankets nearby, and enjoy the bright lights and loud bangs from a good half mile away.

"Yip."

"Don't wake anyone or I'll never hear the tail end of it."

The first two pop-up canopy tents we approached were both cockeyed. No longer upright, they swayed in the wind like drunk cowboys on a Saturday night. I straightened them both and retrieved their tent numbers from the grass. The power and water appeared to be in order, so I moved on. At each tent, canopy, or shelter, I placed a check on my list that water and electricity were in working order and that the contestant number and set of ICA rules were attached to the electric pole with an extra-large rubber band. I'd decided on the rubber bands the previous afternoon after the first dozen sets blew across the parking lot and into the scrub faster than a jackrabbit on speed. Fortunately, my uncle had thought of everything and handed me a full bag of rubber bands as I headed out the door. He knew a thing or two about outsmarting the winds of the high desert.

When my Chi and I reached the last setup, a high pitch tent with side flaps zipped shut, I was stumped. But it was early and my brain was foggy. It was only after marching Lenny around the tent two times that I realized the owner had erected the harem-style shelter over the electric and water supply.

"I have not injected enough coffee to handle this . . ." I waved my hand in the air.

"Yip."

"Accident waiting to happen! That's exactly what I was thinking. But someone's got to go in there and check it out, and you and I, my friend, have drawn the short straw." About twenty feet beyond the tent in question, near a copse of bent mesquite trees and prickly pear cacti, rested an RV of epic proportions—a fifth wheel—if I had my terminology correct. I was 98 percent sure the owner would rather sleep in that luxury double-wide than the modest polyester shelter before me, but I'd tread lightly. Three panels were part mesh and from where I stood I could make out various shapes that looked like kitcheny stuff: coolers, a generator, and plastic tubs.

"Hellooo." I knocked twice on the side of the tent, which was like trying to lasso creamed corn. Then I tried the zipper and found it unlocked. "Here goes nothing." A band of gold now hugged the horizon, banded by a rippling sea of periwinkle clouds into the mile-wide sky. This welcoming light infused the east side of the tent, while the remainder lay in shadow. I gathered Lenny into my arms, gingerly unzipped the brown and tan panel, and stepped inside.

I immediately tripped over a nest of rattlesnakes coiled on the tent floor. As I jumped to my right, kicking my feet as fast as mixer blades in a blender of poisonous reptiles, I realized I'd been attacked only by lifeless extension cords.

"Yip."

"Sorry, buddy," I said.

I noted a folding table covered with spices, a cutting board, and some very sharp knives—a perfect place to leave the contestant's number and set of rules—but whoever belonged to this tent had better watch themselves or they would do themselves an injury. I attached the rules to a knife on the table and turned to go. The wind caught the unzipped panel, fluttering the canvas like a flag on the Fourth of July, driving sunlight into the dark recesses between the containers and coolers.

Something under the table caught my eye, and the air flew from my lungs like a clay pigeon from a trap. I couldn't breathe. Then realization dawned as I recognized Lucky Straw.

Of course, it was the strident chili cook's tent. It was filled with too many supplies, yet organized from top to bottom like the cereal aisle in a Walmart—all except for the extension cords. "Sorry," I whispered. His eyes remained closed in a deep sleep. I turned to go and paused for a second look. He was wearing a chef's apron with no shirt underneath. I felt my cheeks warm until I realized he wasn't completely naked. A hand lay over his heart as if he'd fallen asleep saying the Pledge of Allegiance to the Texas flag.

From our earlier encounter, I gathered he was a health nut, but he was obviously a rugged outdoorsman if he slept without sleeping bag, blanket, or pillow. Suddenly, the blood drained from my face, my head floating like a stringless balloon. Maybe he'd suffered a heart attack. I retreated far enough to tie Lenny's leash to a tent spike, returned to Lucky's side, and drew a deep breath before kneeling down beside him. I held my breath and lightly placed two fingers on his wrist. His skin was neither warm nor cold. In the dim light, I thought his chest rose infinitesimally, but I wouldn't have staked my life on it.

No pulse. But I was lousy at the pulse thing. I forced myself to relax and tried again, this time at his neck. I waited several seconds. Nothing. I fumbled for my phone, lifting to my knees to yank it from the depths of my pocket.

I dialed 911 and prayed I was wrong.

"Yip, yip."

My gaze drifted from Lucky's cold body and across the fairgrounds as I filled in the dispatcher. Uncle Eddie was leaning against his truck, talking fervently with someone on the phone. He was going to be so upset. He'd worked so hard.

"Miss, miss!" The dispatcher's voice held irritation.

"Yes, I'm sorry."

"Do you know CPR?"

"Yes, but I took the class six months ago. How many pushes and puffs?" My mind flooded with images of the first murder victim I'd failed to revive. Dixie Honeycutt.

The dispatcher gave the lifesaving information carefully as if speaking to a child, but I still struggled to take it all in. I placed the phone on the table and began. It wasn't perfect technique, but that didn't matter. Did it? My skin crawled with adrenaline, racing up and down my arms like electricity. *Come on! Live this time! Live!*

The EMT workers found me inside the tent still giving Lucky's lifeless body compressions and puffs of useless air.

"We've got it now," a female voice said as I felt a hand

on my shoulder. I yanked my gaze away from Lucky. It was the older EMT worker, a woman I'd seen once before. My mind grasped for the information. A retired principal. Her partner, a male EMS worker, gently moved me to the side, and Uncle Eddie helped me stand.

He placed a strong arm around my shoulders and walked my boneless body toward his truck. "Are you okay, Jo Jo?" His voice was tinny with fear.

I kept marching, onward, refusing to halt, my arms aching from pumping Lucky's chest so many times. Lenny's yips trailed after us, growing more faint by the step. I needed to go back in that tent and get him. He would worry about me. Finally we reached the back of Uncle Eddie's truck.

"It's okay, *mi niña*. It's okay," my uncle crooned. "It's not your fault."

Tears leaked from my eyes and down my chin and onto my shirt. "I couldn't save him."

"Shh."

I could never save them. Never. Senora Mari was mistaken when she said I was strong. What a joke.

Chapter 4

Aftermath

When Detective Lightfoot stepped from his newly issued black-and-white SUV, I could've sworn I'd stepped into an episode of *CSI: West Texas*. Gone was the khaki uniform he'd worn like a second skin for so many years as a deputy in Big Bend County. Instead he wore a navy blazer and white button-down shirt, along with his familiar Stetson. We had developed a loose partnership, for lack of a better description. Basically, he investigated crimes for the Big Bend County Sheriff's Office, and I tagged along as a reporter for the *Bugle*—when I could convince him I wouldn't be in his way. In Austin, I never imagined I'd finally find my way to the crime desk when I returned home to Broken Boot.

"You okay, Josie?" Lightfoot's black eyes filled with concern.

I flushed with embarrassment, sniffing and wiping away any remaining tears of shock with my knuckle. I'm not much of a crier, and when I do it's not pretty—unless pretty ugly counts.

"She's fine, just tired." Uncle Eddie handed me his handkerchief. "Jo Jo gave CPR until the ambulance got here."

With a grimace, Lightfoot fished a bottle of water from his jacket pocket. "Rinse your mouth out with that until you find something stronger."

I obeyed by spitting into a nearby cactus.

"That's my girl." Uncle Eddie laughed.

I checked out the new detective's polished boots and turquoise bolo tie. "Didn't realize you went to church on Fridays," I said, shielding myself with sarcasm. "Or are you on your way to an interview?" Tiny butterflies of attraction danced in my stomach, and I wanted them dead. Love had done me wrong, big-time. And love could go play in someone else's sandbox.

He popped his cuffs. "Detective duds. I may get used to them . . . in three or four years."

"Congrats." Uncle Eddie reached out his hand. "Looks good on you, man."

"Can you talk?"

I sniffed. "Yeah."

"Let's walk." He withdrew a small notepad and golf pencil from his pocket. If Lightfoot ever decided to join the modern age and take notes on his phone, the Chihuahuan Desert would instantly transform into a fjord.

A small, delicate head peeped out of the window of Lucky's tent. "Yip, yip, yip."

"Lenny!"

"I'll get him." He placed a hand on my arm. "You stay here."

He stepped into the tent, exchanged a word with the officers inside, and untied Lenny's leash from the tent spike. "Boy, is he excited to see you."

I held Lenny's trembling body in my arms. "Yes, I

know." I blinked away a few more stupid tears. "But you're fine now."

"Yip." Lenny wriggled in my arms and licked my chin. I laughed with relief.

"Don't worry." Lightfoot patted Lenny's head. "He's made of tougher stuff. Isn't that right?" He scratched the long-haired Chi under the chin.

Deputies Pleasant and Barnes had come as well and finished setting the perimeter with stakes and crime scene tape. Two more cruisers from a neighboring county pulled up. Unfortunately, two trucks and a minivan parked in the lot right alongside them. Folks piled out and immediately started unloading their chili-making equipment. I was torn. Didn't Uncle Eddie need me to greet the contestants? Or was the whole event a wash?

Before I could return to my uncle's side, I observed him calmly taking people's names, handing them numbers, and explaining that the rules were posted on the electricity hookups. His voice wafted above the chatter of the hopeful newcomers unloading their gear. "If you have any other questions, come and find me. It's going to be a contest to remember!"

My stomach filled with lead. My uncle, bless his heart, was determined to remain positive even if a dead body lay in a tent only a hundred feet or so from where he greeted his first chili cook-off contestants.

"Right." I turned back to Lightfoot. "What exactly do you need?"

Studying me closely, he began. "When did you find the body?" I froze, looked at my watch. My mind was as blank as a whiteboard. "Uh, twenty minutes ago, thirty."

He nodded slowly. "You need to sit down?"

"Heck no." I smoothed my hair and straightened my shoulders. "I've seen worse. I'm just exhausted."

"In shock, more likely." He gave me a quick once-over, his black eyes filled with concern. "You're not going to faint, are you?"

Who did he think he was talking to? "Cactus flowers don't wilt, Detective," I said with a corny Texas twang and a smile that made my cheeks ache. Suddenly gooseflesh raced along my skin. I crossed my arms over my chest to fight off the cold.

"Exhausted?" He didn't seem to be buying my futile attempt at keeping it together.

Keeping my arms in close to my body, I began to rub my icy hands together. "I had to close Milagro last night, and then get up at the crack of dawn for this shindig. Nothing extraordinary."

For a moment, he merely studied my face. Then he reached out and touched my hands. "Your hands are like blocks of ice."

"It's a nervous thing. They'll warm up soon."

"Stick your hands in your armpits."

I made a face. "Thanks? I think."

"Don't be such a girl." His expression remained stoic, but there was a glint in his eye.

With an eye roll, I did what he suggested, crossing my arms and then sticking my hands in my armpits. My hands began to warm almost immediately.

"Come on." He led me across the grass to where he'd parked his SUV, far enough away from Lucky's tent that I couldn't hear what was going on inside, but not so far that he couldn't watch the comings and goings of the other officers.

"Take a load off." He gestured to the hood. "What'd you see when you arrived? Was Eddie with you?"

Gratefully, I leaned back against the SUV, allowing the Suburban to take my weight. "I was alone when I arrived . . .

except for Lenny. Uncle Eddie came later, but I'm not sure when."

"That's okay, I'll talk to him soon."

I shivered.

"You need a blanket? I have one in the trunk."

"Who do you think you're dealing with? Kim Kardashian?" This new touchy-feely side of Lightfoot was freaking me out. Did he think I was going into shock?

"Who?" He frowned. "Never mind. Go on." He bent his head, and I caught the ghost of a smile.

"Contestants aren't supposed to prepare anything ahead of time, so it was my job to inspect the tents for contraband. I found a half-dozen tents with coolers and supplies stored in them—chili preparations, I guess you'd call them—but I wasn't about to police the contents, if you know what I mean. Actually, Uncle Eddie had asked me to inspect the tents to make sure the water and electricity were working because we didn't want any hiccups this first time out. You know what I mean?"

With his mouth open to respond, I had another thought. "You see, it's like this: if we didn't have everything working exactly right, the town council would come down on Uncle Eddie like a brick. And—"

"I get the picture." He leveled me with his best stoic expression. "You finished?"

I nodded slowly.

He waited a moment to make sure my chatter had run down. "You didn't see anyone?"

"No." I filled my lungs slowly. Trying to relax, I thought back, hoping something worth remembering would float to the surface of my overwhelmed brain. "A couple of RVs and trucks had pulled behind their cooking sites and camped overnight . . . I said that already, didn't I?"

He reread the notes he had taken. "Did you enter Lucky's tent as soon as you arrived?"

Closing my eyes, I thought back to those first moments out of the Prius. "No. We started on the other end of the fairgrounds."

With a nod, he made a note and underlined it. "You willing to take a second look at the body?" His eyes held neither sympathy nor frustration.

If he could function in the face of death, then so could I. Didn't I have experience? Hadn't I proved my ability to handle a crime scene without losing my objectivity?

"I got this," I said, pushing myself up to a standing position.

"He stays out here."

"Yip." Lenny gave me a look of disbelief.

"Don't hate me. It's just for a bit." I unlocked the Prius, cracked the windows, and placed him on the passenger seat.

We returned to Lucky's tent as more cars and trucks fought to find parking spots, indifferent to the deputy cruisers and unaware of the officers' gruesome tasks.

"Detective." From the entrance, Pleasant gave me a sympathetic smile as she stepped aside to allow us room to enter around her statuesque frame.

I forced myself to turn away from the chaos inside the tent for a minute more. Over the fairgrounds, golden beams of morning light embraced the distant hills and awakening desert, etching their beauty into my very soul. It was perfect weather, exactly what we prayed for. Would that we had prayed for a perfect *day* instead.

From inside the tent, I heard Lightfoot's voice. "What's the story?"

"Heart attack if I had to guess . . . which I don't." The quiet tenor belonged to Ellis, the JP. In Texas, a justice of the peace could issue warrants, conduct preliminary hearings, administer oaths, conduct inquests, and perform the usual weddings. He could also serve as medical examiner in counties without a coroner. If he and Lightfoot saw an indication of foul play, Ellis would be sending the body to El Paso for an autopsy. Strangled by budget cuts, the autopsy could take weeks, even in a case of murder.

"Do you have your camera equipment?" Lightfoot asked.

"Keep it in the car. Why, you not up to it?"

Lightfoot chuckled low. "Not up to speed on all the lenses and gadgets you insisted on buying."

"By gadget, you mean a tripod and a video camera?"

"If you say so."

Ellis continued nonchalantly. "You lucked out this time." Silence. "What'd you say this guy's name was?"

"Lucky Straw."

"Geez."

"Get your camera, Ellis."

He was around thirty, with glasses, jeans, and a plaid shirt. My eyes followed him to his black minivan and watched as with graceful movements he unloaded a black camera bag and tripod. "Ms. Martinez." He gave me a smile on his return.

"Callahan. Same as last time," I murmured. Ellis wasn't the first person to assume my last name was Martinez, like the rest of my family. But I was Aunt Linda's niece, plain and simple. Why some folks couldn't keep it straight was beyond me.

He stepped into the tent opening, wearing a slight scowl of concentration. "It's a bit cramped in there, what with all Lucky's things." Outside the tent, he assembled his camera, added batteries, set up the tripod, and began to take pictures of the body through the opening.

"You knew Lucky?" I asked.

"Knew *of* him. He's Lucky's Naked Chili. He's been on the chili cook-off circuit for years," Ellis said.

"I guess I should feel relieved that he was wearing his pants."

Ellis rolled his eyes. "You're not kidding."

"How'd you get here so fast?" Many times, the officers at the scene would certify a body was officially dead because of the pure size of Big Bend County, exactly 6,192 square miles.

"My wife's warming our vegetarian chili in booth number ten."

I froze in disbelief. "How come I didn't know you entered?" Uncle Eddie and I had pored over each entry a dozen times, checking for errors or blanks left open.

"She's not an Ellis." He waggled his eyebrows and laughed. "Said she didn't want to marry down."

"What's her last name?"

"Starr." He cleared his throat. "Her name is Brenda Starr."

I chuckled. "Come on." The famous comic strip about a buxom, glamorous reporter was popular way before my time, but every woman I'd worked with in the news business had been ribbed with comparisons to Brenda Starr.

"You think I would make something like that up?"

"Yes."

"You're right. Her name is Brenda Smith."

A weight lifted off my chest. "Thanks."

"For what? Brenda Ellis would have been a fine name."

"For helping me forget for a split second why we're here."

When he was finished, he placed the camera on the tripod and pointed it toward the body, fiddling with the zoom until satisfied. He stood in front of the camera. "This is JP Howard Ellis, Big Bend County. The date is May 4, 2018. Body found is a Caucasian male, approximately fifty to fifty-six years old. Identification found on the body belongs to Lucky Straw of Odessa, Texas."

My gooseflesh vanished as my journalistic side oohed and aahed over the shiny video camera. How easy was that? Instead of writing all these notes that I might or might not be able to read after spilling my coffee on them in the Prius on the way home, I could video my impressions along with actual images of the scene and the cadaver. "Can I take a look through the lens?"

"No, ma'am." He made an adjustment to the height of the tripod, and then slowly swiveled it from the left side of the tent to the right.

Inside, the deputies went about the methodical task of collecting evidence. All three officers, including Detective Lightfoot, wore gloves. Lightfoot, as the highest-ranking officer, observed as Pleasant took photos of the body and Barnes collected small items of interest from the ground and the nearby surfaces. Barnes, the redheaded, fair-skinned deputy, wore purple gloves as he used tweezers to collect the detritus of Lucky's life that might or might not provide a clue to how he died.

"Turn him over." Lightfoot's deep voice vibrated with quiet authority.

"Wait," Ellis said. "Let me adjust the zoom."

By this time he and I stood side by side. I'd snuck close for a better look—close enough for me to catch a whiff of onions—but he didn't seem to mind.

"Go ahead."

With care and a specific hold, Barnes flipped Lucky's body over onto a blue plastic tarp. "Burnt grits and gravy!"

"Good call, Deputy Lightfoot." Ellis snapped a few photos with his dual-purpose camera.

"Detective," I murmured.

"What was that?" The JP's expression said he didn't know whether to be salty or sweet.

I shrugged. "Sorry. It's just that Lightfoot's a detective, and, uh, well, I'm a Callahan."

His expression clouded with confusion, and then cleared. "That right?"

"Not the end of the world. Let's get on with it." Lightfoot gestured toward the body. "Your camera's rolling." Once all eyes refocused on Lucky, he shot me a warning look. If I wanted to stay, I'd better zip it.

Ellis double-checked that his video was recording every detail and then knelt down near Lucky's head. Snapping away with the sheriff office's Nikon, Pleasant inched closer until all four surrounded the body, blocking my view.

"What is it?" My question busted out before I could harness it.

"Good. Night," Ellis muttered.

"Someone hit him over the head with a sledgehammer, if you ask me." Deputy Barnes crossed his arms across his chest.

I rose on tiptoe and peered over his shoulder to get a better look.

"What killed him?" Lightfoot asked.

"Can't say . . . not until I give him a thorough going-over, and maybe not even then. We'll have to wait on the state for the official cause of death."

Which would be an excruciatingly long and frustrating wait. The state often took months to perform routine autopsies. If murder was suspected, the time frame shortened to a *mere* three to four weeks.

Finally Barnes moved to one side, giving me a clear

view. "How did I miss all that blood?" I asked, remarkably calm. Lucky's expression was peaceful, as if dreaming of trophies and cook-off titles.

"That's not surprising, Josie." Ellis continued adjusting his camera. "He was on his back and most of the blood soaked into the ground."

"Head injuries flow as free as Texas tea." Barnes cleared his throat. "Uh, at least that's what my mother always said."

"In my years of experience, I can tell you I've never seen a hammer shaped like this one. Whatever did this was round, flat, and heavy."

"Sounds like an iron skillet." I clapped a hand over my mouth. You could have heard the proverbial pin hit the floor. I cringed, expecting to be booted from the proceedings.

Lightfoot gave me a warning glance. "Pleasant. You and Barnes search his things. Don't leave a fork or a side of beef unturned."

A large metal pot sat on the cooktop, surrounded by bottles of cumin, chili powder, salt, and pepper. On the wooden cutting board lay a paring knife, plus onion peels, bits of bell pepper, and tomato stems.

Slowly Barnes removed a wooden spoon, dripping with chili, from the pot. "Looks like Lucky got a bit of a jump on the competition."

"The big cheat," Pleasant said with a look of disgust.

"What do ya want me to do with this?" Barnes held the spoon at arm's length as if it might be tainted with the dead man's blood.

"Give it here," Pleasant muttered. "Wouldn't want you to get your uniform dirty." With a disgusted shake of her head, she took the utensil from his outstretched hand.

"Hey, this is a new shirt." Barnes puffed out his chest.

"Fine." She dropped the spoon back in the pot. "I'll bag the chili fixings. You bag the dead guy's hands."

"Give them room to work, Lois Lane." Lightfoot held open the tent flap, and we stepped outside.

"Does that mean you're Superman?"

He cocked an eyebrow. "It means I'm the boss." Flipping a page in his notebook, his gaze turned to the job at hand. "Where's Eddie?"

"Holy guacamole!" Pleasant cried.

Before I could react, Lightfoot was inside. I followed, but it was impossible to see around the shoulder-to-shoulder lineup of Ellis, Lightfoot, and Barnes. Standing on tiptoe, I could just make out Pleasant as she balanced a strange object on the wooden spoon. Carefully she grasped the thing with her other gloved hand, and lifted it away from the table. It was small and rectangular, and it dripped chili onto the floor in big sloppy glops of meat and sauce.

" Appetizing." Ellis grimaced.

"What in tarnation is it?" Barnes made sure to keep his uniform out of harm's way.

"Hand it over." Lightfoot picked up a checkered napkin from a nearby basket and took possession of the unidentified chili-covered object. He studied it for a minute and then wiped it clean with the napkin. "Stun gun."

"Huh." Barnes chuckled. "Somebody must've beat me with a stupid stick. I thought it was a television remote."

I could see the headline in my mind's eye: "Chili Cook Stunned into Silence." Or better yet, "KO'd in the Kitchen." The alliteration was tempting.

"What if he fell when the killer used the stun gun on him?" Pleasant wiped her hands on another checked napkin.

"And hit his head on a skillet?" I asked.

Lightfoot took my arm and led me outside. "That's enough interfering for now."

I yanked free. "Hey, what gives? You've valued my input in the past."

"Not on the scene, mixing it up with officers and the JP."
Nearby, small pockets of chili cooks and their supporters
stood in front of their tents, watching us with open curiosity.
"What about your cook-off?" He lowered his voice. "Looks
like folks need some answers." With a nod, he returned to
the crime scene.

From the road came a squeal of brakes. A brand-
spanking-new Dodge Ram truck revved its engine as an
older couple rolled their cooler across the road and into the
parking lot. I held my breath as the truck lumbered closer.

It was P.J. Pratt, town council member and Uncle Eddie's nemesis. If I didn't come up with a backup plan—and
now—he'd try to blame today's tragic event on my uncle.
He'd start throwing his weight around, questioning our
ability to keep the event on track.

I could see it now. He'd insist we cancel the whole kit
and caboodle, and at the next council meeting, he'd demand
Uncle Eddie's resignation.

Chapter 5

❧❧❧❧❧❧❧❧❧❧❧❧❧❧❧❧❧❧❧❧❧❧❧❧❧❧❧

Where There's a Will . . .

When female screams filled the air a minute later, clue-less contestants, vendors, tourists, and assorted townsfolk hurried over for a better look. The two women stood in front of their RV, wearing robes and pajamas, hair tangled and mussed. "Lucky's dead," cried one on the shoulder of the other. "Now I'll never beat him. He got to heaven as a champion." Huge crocodile tears rolled down her cheeks.

"I know, sister." With the end of her belt, the terry-clad woman wiped the eyes of her grieving friend and then helped her climb back into their RV. "You were going to pulverize that two-faced braggart."

I understood their pain. I would feel the same way if Hillary Sloan-Rawlings were to die before I proved I was a far better reporter. It's not every day one awakes to find their competition stiff *and* dead.

As the crowd continued to drink their coffee, gossip, and watch the officials from the sheriff's office go about their grisly business, P.J. Pratt and Hillary Sloan-Rawlings made their grand entrance.

"What in tarnation thunder is going on, Eddie?" Apparently, P.J. Pratt thought owning your own ranch gave him the right to boss everyone around, same as his cowhands and Herefords.

"I don't know what you've done now, Josie, but I've had more laughs at a funeral parlor." Hillary's throaty laugh made me think of the sound you might get if you crossed an aging Hollywood actress with a braying donkey.

Lord, forgive me.

Just as I opened my mouth to say something socially unacceptable, Lightfoot stuck his head out of the tent, took in the situation at a glance, and quickly headed our way. "P.J." He tipped his hat. "Hillary."

Uncle Eddie removed his hat. "Show some respect, ma'am. One of the chili contestants is dead."

"Oh, my." Hillary slapped a hand over her mouth. "I was only kidding. I'm so sorry."

"What'd you do, Martinez? Was it some kind of accident?"

My uncle paled. "No. He died of, uh, what did he die of?" He turned to Lightfoot.

"We don't know."

"So this could reflect poorly on the town?" P.J. insisted.

"Take it down a notch." Lightfoot held up a hand. "Folks are riled up as it is. We've finally got everyone calmed down enough to go forward with the cook-off."

"Go forward?" Hillary slanted me a look. "Was that your bright idea?" she murmured with a sly smile.

Uncle Eddie placed a hand on my arm. "It was mine. We're going to bring this cook-off off without a hitch."

"Except for someone getting killed." P.J. puffed out his chest like a banty rooster. "I hope you know I'm demanding

Cogburn call a special council meeting to discuss your part in this, Eddie."

Lightfoot glared at P.J. and took a warning step into the rancher's space. "Are you cooking chili?" Lightfoot gestured at P.J.'s dolly laden with fixings.

"No."

"That's good," I said. "As one of the organizers, you can't. It's against the rules." I was trying my best not to smirk.

"Well, I can if I want to . . . just to share with my friends. And you can't say otherwise."

"Why don't you two go on and set up? The sooner we break this up, the sooner folks will get back to cooking." Lightfoot waited until Hillary and P.J. wandered off toward the back of the fairgrounds before returning to Lucky's tent.

From a distance, I spotted the O'Neal woman from the night before, sporting her red-framed glasses. She made a beeline for me, her gaze angry enough to singe my eyelashes. "Don't tell me you intend to cancel? I asked for three vacation days and pulled the kids out of school to enter. And you know why?" Her arms beat the air in frustration. "Because I thought I'd have a better chance of winning the prize money at your pint-sized event."

I swallowed. "And we're glad you entered." A plan began to take hold. I raised my voice for all to hear. "Don't anyone pack up, throw out, or give up on your chili-cooking dreams. We're going to proceed as scheduled. And may the best man, woman, or chilihead win!"

"When do we start cooking?" Dani O'Neal wore a flowered robe over a lace nightgown. She'd washed her hair and ponytailed it wet.

"Whatcha worrying about, girl?" I didn't recognize the wizened old man. "I reckon your cooking skills amount to opening cans from your neighborhood Fiesta." His tattered terry cloth robe didn't quite hide his T-shirt and striped boxers.

"I'll have you know that I like to use fresh ingredients." Her cheeks flushed to a rosy hue. "I'm in the medical field. You can't tell me half of you aren't growing salmonella in your chili pots right this minute."

The reverent hush evaporated as angry remarks flew through the crowd.

In spite of the tension in the air, the sight of the old geezer's white knobby knees was burning a hole in my retinas, and I wanted to scream at him to get some clothes on. But what really chapped my hide was neither he nor the O'Neal woman had expressed fear or sympathy for Lucky, or even curiosity about the hive of activity at the far end of the fairgrounds. Their lack of emotion made me angry and suspicious. I studied them more closely, my Spidey sense springing to life.

A familiar short, middle-aged man, wearing a fringed leather vest led the crowd to the officials' tent. "What in tarnation is going on? Don't tell me someone broke in and stole Lucky's knives again." Whip's face flamed with anger, then immediately fell. Mouth open, he surveyed the crowd, the sheriff's cruisers, the crime scene tape surrounding the tent of doom, and the eyes that refused to meet his own.

"Lucky?" He spun in the direction of the ill-fated tent.

Lightfoot stepped into his path and raised his hands to block the other man's progress. "When's the last time you saw him?"

"Say what? Where is he?" Whip feinted to one side and then lunged around Lightfoot toward the opening.

Again the detective blocked his route, and Whip collapsed to the ground, his dark hair falling in his face. He swallowed hard. "What's happened to him?" Lightfoot drew breath to speak, but the other man addressed those of us standing around gaping at his pain. "Somebody say something!"

"Lucky Straw is dead." Lightfoot reached down and helped the other man to his feet.

Whip's shoulders caved, his face paled, tears sprang from his eyes. "Nah, he ain't."

"Miss Callahan found him." Lightfoot gave me a nod.

All eyes turned to appraise me. I could see their suspicions stamped on their faces. What had I seen? Why was I in Lucky's tent? Had I killed him?

With another jab at the corner of his eyes, Whip shoved his hair behind his ears and turned to me. "Was it his heart?"

"I'm sorry." Anguish closed my throat and forced me to mumble, "I don't know."

With a hard look, Lightfoot stared down the O'Neal woman, the old man in the robe, and the rest of the contestants and families that had gathered around. "You folks go on about your business. Let me talk to this man alone."

I turned away with the rest. "Josie, you stay."

Once the coast was clear, Lightfoot quietly took the other man's measure. "You friends with the deceased?"

"We were partners." Whip's face flushed all the way to his huge ears. "I mean, we were chili-cooking partners. We traveled around together entering chili cook-offs. It's what we did for fun."

One thing about solving murders that I don't like: everyone appears suspicious. Even then, I found myself observing Whip through Lightfoot's eyes. Who else would have easy access to Lucky's tent? And have known what he was likely to touch and in what order?

"You shared this tent? Or did you have your own?" Lightfoot asked.

Whip pointed to an open-sided tent with a blue canvas

top on the far side of Lucky's. "That one's mine. We competed against each other something fierce, but he allowed me to store my cooker and coolers in his tent."

"Why's that?" I found myself asking.

"Folks are less likely to handle your property in a tent that zips shut."

I glanced at Lightfoot and found him watching us both, his eyes narrowed in thought. "You stay out here last night?"

Whip pointed to a small silver Toyota truck with an Apache trailer still connected. "That's mine."

"Why didn't you keep your things locked in your camper? Looks safer to me than any tent."

Deep lines gouged Whip's forehead. "'Cause I wouldn't have any room to walk around in that thing. That should be obvious as the nose on your face."

Lightfoot pulled out the small notepad and pencil that lived in his breast pocket. "Where were you last night after the reception?"

Whip's eyes grew wide. "Hey, what do you mean by that?"

"Did you go to Pecos Pete's?" Lightfoot's tone never varied. "Stroll down Main Street? Take in the sights?"

I wanted to ask, *What sights?* But I remained mum.

"Nah. We did walk over to Two Boots dance hall for a bit."

"Did you argue?"

"Hey!" He yanked his hat from his head. "Cut that out. We had a drink and listened to the band. Then we drove over here."

Lightfoot made a note. "What time was that?"

"I don't know." Whip shrugged. "Twelve, maybe."

"What'd you think of the band?" I asked before Lightfoot could get in another question. Ty Honeycutt and his compadres had gradually become the house band at Two Boots. I wasn't sure they were all that and a bowl of grits, as my Granny Callahan used to say, but customers seemed to like them. At least after a drink or three.

"Better than cats making whoopee." Whip grimaced.

With a narrow-eyed stare in my direction, Lightfoot cleared his throat. "What'd the two of you do once you got here?"

"Went to bed." The chili cook frowned. "And not together. Got it?"

"Yes, sir." The stoic detective made another note, but I swear I caught a twitch at the side of his mouth.

"Why're you asking me all these questions?" His gaze flew from one suspicious face to another. "It's more than likely he was poisoned at that place her family calls a restaurant." He pointed wildly at me.

"Are you crazy?" I smiled a can-you-believe-this-guy? smile at the dozen or so people who had failed to follow Lightfoot's order to scatter. They stared blankly, failing to see the humor.

"Did you taste what you were serving last night? Nasty enough to give a buffalo food poisoning until Christmas."

Uncle Eddie chose that moment to appear. "We've received high ratings in magazines and newspapers from Broken Boot to Juárez. What are you gabbing on about?"

"Is that a fact?" Whip snorted, thrust his hands on his hips, and rocked back on his bootheels. "That stuff you call gluten- and dairy-free was toxic." He swung his arms wide, preaching to the crowd. "In fact, I could've cleaned my toilet with it, only it would've added to the germs instead of getting rid of 'em."

My uncle's face flushed a deep red. He clamped his mouth shut, his lips straining from the effort to hold back colorful, I-don't-care-if-you're-a-customer-or-not verbiage. He gave me a pitiful look, like a dog who's begging to be let off his leash to chase the neighbors' squirrels—just one time.

I gave him a stern shake of the head and a sympathetic smile, but I was fighting my own need to blast Whip and his random act of culinary libel. "We don't usually serve special dietary items." I lowered the volume and added what I hoped was more congeniality. "When Lucky demanded gluten- and dairy-free items—in the middle of an extremely busy reception—I immediately asked our chef to prepare something especially for him." I didn't flinch, though truthfully I had no idea what Senora Mari and our head cook had thrown together other than refried beans.

"So you say." Whip's lip curled, throwing his glasses off-kilter. "How do I know you didn't serve him rotten meat just for demanding his due?"

"That's a lie," I said in a low voice. When I lose my temper, my voice drops to a whisper.

"Now, now." Uncle Eddie grabbed me by the arm and placed himself between me and Whip. "Detective Lightfoot." He paused to wet his lips. "Does that fella in there look like a man who's died from food poisoning? You got a good like at him, right?"

Lightfoot shook his head. "We don't know what killed him, but it doesn't look like any food poisoning I've ever seen."

"You would say that." Whip thrust his hat on his head with a show of temper, unaware it was on backwards.

"Okay, that's enough. We'll give you more information when we have it."

Whip remained along with me and Uncle Eddie.

"That's all for now." Lightfoot pocketed his notes. "And don't disappear," he said, giving Whip a pointed look. "I'll be talking to you again, real soon."

"We didn't do anything wrong, Lightfoot." My uncle's face had paled beneath his tan.

"I'm not saying you did." With a nod, Lightfoot walked back toward the entrance to Lucky's tent where Barnes and Pleasant waited.

"You know what *Mamá* would say." Uncle Eddie wiped the perspiration from his face with a red bandana.

I gave him a quick hug. "Are you kidding? She's so politically incorrect, she'd say it serves him right for demanding anything but traditional Martinez Tex-Mex."

I squeezed his hand. "Look on the bright side." I plucked his handkerchief from his other hand and wiped a tear of perspiration from his earlobe. "She'll have something to scold us about for the rest of her days."

He chuckled, though it didn't reach his sad, brown eyes.

A little ways away, more onlookers gathered, some confused, others scared, and too many murmuring about the inconvenience of a canceled chili cook-off. My heart sank at the disappointment and shame Uncle Eddie would feel, for he would consider it his own personal failing.

That's when I spotted Bridget Peck and another ICA official pulling up in a blue Volkswagen Jetta—yellow and red ICA flags flying from the back windows.

Taking my uncle aside, I murmured under my breath, "Go tell everyone we're not canceling one single solitary thing." I grimaced. "Not yet anyway." He gave me a one-armed hug, glanced with trepidation at the ICA officials, and hurried over to calm the contestants.

By the time I reached the parking area, where I'd spotted the coyotes only hours before, Bridget and her fellow official had unloaded their gear.

"We have chairs for you, all set up at the officials' table."

"Do they have double cup holders?" Bridget pursed her lips in disapproval.

"They have a cushion."

Her companion laughed and closed the trunk. "Yes, but do they have a footrest?" Short and plump like a raisin, his smile was infectious. Beside the car, they'd unloaded not only chairs, but a rolling cooler and a crate on wheels filled with binders, pens, and Fiji Waters. Another crate, filled with humongous trophies and other awards, rested in the dirt next to the rear passenger door.

"Let me take those," I said.

"Sure thing," the man said with a courtly wave at the metal-and-canvas chairs.

I stuffed one under one arm and then struggled to pick up the other. Even folded, the chair was clunky, refusing to stay closed, poking the tender underside of my arm.

"She's going to drop them. Then what?" Bridget's lips pursed so tightly that deep lines like a freshly plowed field appeared around her mouth.

"Then she'll pick them back up again." The man handed me the second chair so I wouldn't have to bend over and dislodge the first chair from its strategic position. "You sure you wouldn't rather take a crate? Much easier."

I smirked. "No way. You wouldn't rob me of my work-out, would you?"

"Stop your yammering, and let's get on with it." Bridget grabbed the rolling office and trudged out of the weedy parking lot toward the tent that bore a large white OFFI-CIALS' TENT banner.

After only a few steps, they halted to stare at the ambu-lance, the deputy cruisers, and the assembly of officers and EMT workers. "Good Lord." Bridget turned to me, her face pale as flour. "Don't tell me someone's been hurt, already."

"Well—"

At that moment, the EMTs appeared from the tent, carrying a motionless shape draped in a blue blanket between them. Lucky's body. Carefully, they placed it on the gurney and then slowly began to roll it through the grass toward the waiting ambulance.

"No, no." Bridget Peck's voice was a thready whisper. "What's going on? That's Lucky's tent." With a thud, her book bag fell from her shoulder and hit the ground.

"Sure looks like it," her fellow official said in a quiet voice.

I swallowed. "Um, yes. He, uh, had an accident."

"What kind of accident?" she demanded.

"Not *exactly* an accident, more like . . . an altercation." And it hit me like a bolt of lightning. If Lucky's death was a murder, maybe they wouldn't have to shut down our event. It wasn't as if we'd provided faulty wiring or tainted water. I swallowed my doubts. "I don't know much, and it's not for me to say." I leaned in. "Could be foul play."

"Foul play?" Bridget tried for scorn, but I didn't miss the solitary tear coursing down her cheek. She drew back her shoulders, like an officer on a sinking ship, determined to hold on to his pride. "We'll get to the bottom of this." She cast a hard eye across the fairgrounds. "We're shutting this event down if I get one whiff of anything that indicates you and your organization had anything to do with his death."

"That's not necessary, is it?" I asked, hurrying along behind—metal chairs banging the undersides of my arms and my hips.

"Of course it is! You trying to discredit the ICA?" Bridget was on the move, shoulders rigid, muttering to herself.

"No ma'am," I countered meekly. "But wouldn't you receive more negative publicity if you shut us down without just cause?"

"*Without just cause*," Bridget grunted. "Says you and

who else?" Unceremoniously, she and the man dumped their bags on a table just inside the officials' tent and rolled their crates of notebooks and trophies to one side. "Where's the sheriff?" They marched from the tent and made a beeline for the first sheriff's deputy in sight.

I had lagged behind, but I saw Barnes shake his red head at their questions and then point a freckled finger to where Lightfoot stood talking to the JP outside Lucky's tent.

"We've a right to the truth." The other ICA official's expression was grim.

"Who are you?" For Lightfoot to be anything other than polite meant he was on edge.

"We're from the ICA." Bridget's proclamation turned several heads.

Lightfoot glanced at me, a question in his eyes.

"International Chili Association. This is—" I began with forced politeness.

"That's Sam, and I'm Bridget Peck." The older woman stuck out her hand with such force that her gray curls bounced. "We're the official judges for this here chili cook-off."

Lightfoot put a hand to his hat and dipped his chin. "Did you know the deceased?"

The two officials glanced nervously at each other. "Course we did," Bridget said. "He's been on the circuit for about ten years."

"The devil he has." Sam gave his partner a sharp look.

"Since he fought the ICA decision in Terlingua. We were both there, Sam." That time the shrill pitch of her voice turned the heads of two deputies several tents away.

Lightfoot's brows lifted.

"International Chili Association." My cheeks ached from an overdose of smiling.

"And we're not going to allow any mishap to taint the

reputation of the ICA. Let's get that clear." Bridget's hands fisted as if looking for a fight.

With a sigh, Lightfoot tipped back the brim of his hat with his thumb. "This so-called *mishap* means that a man is dead." He glanced at me, his gaze conveying a message I couldn't read. "We don't have any reason to believe it's anything other than natural causes."

The two officials stared at each other in silence. "Is that your honest opinion?" Sam asked, hat over his heart.

Lightfoot's gaze narrowed to a knife point. "Mister. Are you accusing me of lying?"

I stepped back. I hadn't heard the quiet detective lose his temper very often, but one day I was convinced it was going to blow. A gusher exploding all over God and everybody.

"Uh, no, sir." Sam worried his hat in his hands. "That's not what I meant at all."

"Good." Lightfoot's threatening expression cleared. "I suggest you and your partner—"

"We ain't—"

The detective raised a hand. "The two of you get back to the judges' tent and figure out an alternate plan."

"Yes, sir." Sam took Bridget Peck by the arm and forced her back the way they had come.

The taciturn newly appointed detective surveyed the crowd before turning a watchful eye on the deputies and JP cataloging the clues within the crime tape. Lightfoot caught my eye and motioned for me to meet him at the far side of Lucky's tent.

"Can't we please go ahead with the cook-off?" I asked sotto voce.

"Unlikely." He turned his head to watch as the ambulance pulled away, lights flashing but no siren.

"Please." I grabbed his forearm. "For Eddie."

He looked away, but didn't remove my hand. Knowing him, he was trying to evaluate the situation from all sides. "We could separate this section of the fairgrounds off and move the contestants at least a hundred feet away."

"Sure . . ." It would mean moving fifteen or so contestants to new digs. After a brief calculation, I realized it just might work, as we hadn't attracted as many entries as we'd planned. It would be cramped, but folks might be willing to share their sites so the contest could continue.

A frown appeared between Lightfoot's eyes as he studied my hand on his arm.

"Thanks! You're a lifesaver."

I turned to go and he tapped me on the shoulder. "Tell me you and your uncle had the wiring checked out by a certified electrician."

"Are you kidding? We weren't taking any chances. The head of the fairgrounds committee hired an expert from West Texas to check all the wiring."

Lightfoot actually appeared to be impressed, for once. "How'd you work that out with the university?"

"Tamales."

He shook his head. "Should've known." He studied the parking lot as a dozen more vehicles of various models and price ranges pulled in, many parking in the field alongside the full parking lot. Again the frown line appeared above his long, straight nose. He glanced at me, stretched out his arm, and pointed to the far side of the lot. "Someone's in distress."

My heart nearly flipped over. No, no, no. This day just couldn't get any worse. "Where?"

"The Prius."

"The . . ." It was then I spotted the injured party.

"Yip, yip, yip," carried faintly on the wind.

"Oh, heavens! Lenster!" How could I have forgotten

him? The air was cool, the window cracked, but he was fit to be tied with a cattleman's rope. I cradled him in my arms and kissed his pointed head. He reciprocated by licking my arm until I longed for a towel. Like a noble friend and partner, he'd waited quietly until he could no longer stand not being by my side or a piece of the action. "You're right, buddy. You can come help me wrangle this mystery, these tents, and dozens of angry, frustrated chili cooks. No problem."

Lightfoot had followed me to the car, where he listened closely to my effusive murmurings with a bemused look on his face.

"I can make it happen," I insisted, trying to convince myself as much as anyone else.

"*Everyone* moves a hundred feet, no less." His sober gaze told me there would be no compromise.

"Aye, aye, sir." I lifted Lenny's paw to help him give Lightfoot a proper salute.

"Yip."

Slowly, Lightfoot shook his head at my attempt at levity. I could tell he wanted to issue me another strict warning, but he merely said, "You need assistance?"

"Maybe. Let me get on the phone and see who I can rustle up."

First, I located Uncle Eddie, then together we convinced the ICA officials we could handle the change, and then we called our CEO.

"We'll be there in twenty minutes." Aunt Linda grabbed the reins. "Hold a meeting with the contestants and explain what's going on. If people insist on leaving it's their prerogative. But if they decide to stay, they have to move their own gear and set up their new locations. Don't you dare offer to do it all. We're on our way."

If I had driven to a strange town only to awaken or arrive

to the news that one of my fellow contestants had been murdered, on site, I'd have hit the road faster than a semi runs down roadkill. Well, not unless I was desperate to win the prize.

By the time my family and the rest of the Milagro and Two Boots staff arrived, Lightfoot, Pleasant, and I had moved only three tents' worth of contestants and their stuff. Jumping out of two white F150s—complete with metallic Milagro and Two Boots business labels, a '72 Impala, a Dodge Charger, and various four-door, seen-better-days vehicles, our drowsy staff went to work.

"Someone help!"

I turned just as Senora Mari came around the back of one of our trucks with two gigantic rolling coolers, a handle in each hand. She was weaving to and fro like a Saturday-night drunk.

"*Abuela,* what are you doing here? Did you come to help Aunt Linda?"

"Humph. I came to show these ICA *gringos* how to make authentic Mexican chili."

I grabbed the handle of one of the coolers. "But you know you can't compete, right? It's a conflict of interest."

She frowned, her lips pursed, and then she beat her chest with one small hand. "I don't care. I will give it away. That will show those know-it-alls."

Aunt Linda set up a table for her mother-in-law and another for her own wares. She immediately began to win fans. "Howdy, folks! The cavalry has arrived. Come on over and enjoy some breakfast tacos and coffee. Even brought some cinnamon rolls. No charge for the coffee and cinnamon rolls. And tacos are only a dollar."

I raised an eyebrow at the fee.

She narrowed her eyes at me. "Can't afford to give away the farm. They don't have to buy them. It's their choice."

You would have thought we were selling ice water in Hades. The line for grub grew exponentially, snaking down the length of the fairgrounds. First ten, then twenty, now forty people, mostly adults with a handful of kids thrown in.

I cringed at how the parents would explain all the cops to their children. As I helped serve, the cooks passed by, looking no worse for wear. Only a few appeared to be overly concerned about the death of one of their own. Poor Lucky wasn't a favorite with this crowd. Or maybe they were just relieved to have one less competitor.

People are strange when it comes to winning five hundred dollars.

After several tents, coolers, baskets, and generators were moved, Uncle Eddie made an announcement. "Folks, we appreciate your patience. What's happened here is a horrible thing."

"Horrible," a boy of maybe three repeated. His grin said he had no idea what the word meant.

"Now I've talked to some of Lucky's friends." Uncle Eddie gestured to Whip and the wizened man from before— now clothed in Bermuda shorts, a tank top, and flip-flops. "They assure me Lucky would've wanted us to proceed, seeing as how much he loved to compete."

"Darn right," Whip said. A quiet exuberance floated throughout the crowd.

Bridget Peck stepped up, clipboard in hand. "The official start time will be in one hour." She held up her official rules and regulations binder. "As most of you know, it is at the discretion of each local organization to decide whether you have three or four hours to cook your chili. Due to all the hoopla this morning, you'll have only three hours."

The crowd murmured.

She held up a red air horn. "When the horn blows, you start. And not a second before."

"My ingredients can't just set by for an hour. They'll turn." It was the O'Neal woman with the red glasses.

"Some of us need more time," yelled a voice from the back.

"That's not my problem." Bridget's stance was more Calamity Jane than Annie Oakley, which had me wondering if she was packing.

"What if we have to share our site?" Whip demanded.

Eddie stuck his fingers in his mouth and whistled, loud and long, finally gaining their attention. "Some share, some don't. Everybody's going to start in one hour. End of story."

The O'Neal woman cleared her throat as if she would spit like a cowboy chewing tobacco. "Rank-amateur event. If this is the last time I lay eyes on this sinkhole, it's one time too many."

My uncle stared her down. "If you don't like it," he drew a breath, "then you can pack up your gear and go home."

Chapter 6

Questions Asked

An hour later, after everyone pulled out their pots, pans, and country music—except for one guy practicing yoga while Mozart wafted through the open window of his expensive sports car—Bridget Peck blasted her air horn.

And they were off. They had a big job ahead of them because the ICA rules were clear. All chili had to be prepared on-site during the competition. I had no idea why any of these would-be pioneers would want to murder Lucky Straw with a blow to the head. And why was a stun gun discovered in Lucky's prize-winning chili? Had he been trying to stun his attacker and dropped it?

A heart attack would have been unlucky enough. But no. Someone decided our humble fairgrounds was the perfect location for a grisly murder. So much for the name Lucky that he'd worn like a badge of honor. How about *Unlucky, Luckless,* or even *Wretched* Straw? I immediately asked for forgiveness for my callous thoughts. The poor man's body wasn't even stone cold. It wasn't his fault being murdered was the epitome of bad luck.

"Come on, Lenny. Let's help where we can." We smoothed the waters by helping folks lug their stuff to a new site, saying a comforting word to those daunted by Lucky's death, and sharing a smile and a howdy with strangers.

We stumbled upon Dani O'Neal's campsite. She stood over her cook pot, studying the concoction inside.

"Mm. That smells like awesome."

She ignored me. "Don't bring that dog any closer." Her eyes remained riveted to her chili. "Don't want him to contaminate my culinary offering."

"I get it. No doggie germs." I kept my voice light, determined to remain positive. I backed up a few steps and then a few more for good measure. The word *offering* made me think of witches, Mayan priests, and Baptist ministers. "Can I help you with anything?"

"Yip." Lenny was always ready to help, though most folks suspected he was in it merely for the spoils.

"That would be illegal." She continued to stir, adding in canned tomatoes, a bag of shredded fat-free cheddar, and diced onions.

I didn't bother to tell her that my only concern was whether or not she had running water and electricity. I was too shocked by the sight of her stirring fat-free shreds and raw onions into her chili. "Uh, right." My gaze fell to a naked Barbie and an abandoned water pistol. "Where're your kids?"

At the mention of her children, her eyes narrowed. "What do you know about them?"

"Well." I took a deep breath. "I was the one who led you and your daughter to the bathroom last night. Remember?" The little hairs along my arms rose. Something about Dani O'Neal was a bit off. Her ponytail, robe, and gown were long gone. In their place, she wore a tight librarian's bun, a

Laura Ashley flowered prairie dress, and black combat boots.

After a long pregnant pause, she slowly nodded. "Okay, then." She stepped out from beneath her canopy and raised a hand to shield her eyes from the bright desert sun. "They're at the taco stand, bringing us back some breakfast."

Though I looked in the same direction, I couldn't make out anyone shorter than five feet.

"The judging will take place at twelve thirty." I looked at Lenny, and he looked at me. I hated to be the bearer of bad news, but adding in those last-minute items, which wouldn't have time to marinate, had killed her chances for a prize.

She etched a smile on her face. "So I heard."

"Well, then, best of luck!" As we walked away toward the next contestant, my canine companion made a run for the back of Dani's canopy, barking as if a herd of cats were hiding inside.

Behind the canopy, an iguana the size of my bathtub lounged inside a huge cage. "Yip, yip, yip." Lenny pulled at his leash, longing for a game of chase.

O'Neal hurried over, metal spoon held high. "Keep that long-haired rat away from Elliot."

"Calm down, Danielle." Whip strutted into view.

I gathered Lenny into my arms and held his trembling body close. "He's only trying to protect me."

"Well, he's ruining Elliot's nerves."

Whip cleaned his frameless glasses with the hem of his shirt and gave me a tired smile. "She's always going on about that reptile's nerves. Personally, I think he's got a brain the size of a gnat."

"I didn't know you two knew each other."

Dani's expression turned stony. "We've met a time or two."

He threw an arm around her shoulder. "You could say I taught her everything she knows about how to make a decent chili."

Cheeks flushed, Dani pushed him away. "She doesn't want to hear you putting on airs. You big blowhard." There was a silent, furtive exchange between them.

"Uh, she's right." Whip tucked a lock of lank hair behind his ear. "We don't know each other half as well as I wish we did." He forced a laugh.

If Whip was still carrying a torch for Lucky's fiancée, what was going on between him and Dani? The possibilities made me long for a hot shower.

I cleared my throat. "Anyone who eats your chili could get salmonella from that thing if you're not careful," I said. "You work in the medical field, right? I would think you'd know."

With a look of disgust, she raised her chin. "My field is medicine, not zoology." She lowered herself to one knee, reached inside the cage, and ran a finger down the iguana's scaly back. "There, there," she murmured as Elliot promptly scurried under a fake branch.

"Plus, iguanas are an invasive species. He has to go."

For a good ten seconds, she tried to stare me down. "But we're miles from home."

"Lock him in your RV. I don't care, but get him out of here. And for God's sake, wash your hands and everything he came in contact with."

"Yip, yip," Lenny said.

I agreed with my long-haired Chi. Dani didn't seem to be much of a cook, and Elliot's slithering tongue had turned my stomach.

"Why don't I put his cage in the minivan?" Whip knelt down beside her. "I'll open the windows for a bit of cross ventilation. All that shade? Why, he'll think he's died and gone to reptile heaven." He found a stray piece of lettuce on the ground and poked it into the cage, waving it slowly before Elliot's fixed gaze.

As I turned to make a getaway, Dani quickly stood and made her way back to her chili. "What did the police find out about Lucky?" she asked in a voice loud enough to turn Whip's head.

"Nothing definite." I frowned as she stirred her chili without first washing her hands. Bridget Peck was going to get a full report.

"Come on. They suspect it was murder, don't they?" She studied me like an owl inspecting a field mouse.

I shrugged. "Why would someone want him dead?" I pitched her a softball, but would she swing?

Biting her bottom lip, she made a sucking sound. "He was a cantankerous, selfish, old coot." She glanced over at Whip, who was attempting to feed Elliot with a piece of lettuce. In a whisper, she continued, "He was a bully, but he didn't deserve to die."

"No? Even though he shoved you and your kids into welfare?"

Spoon frozen in midair, her eyes widened. "How did . . ." She visibly relaxed. "Oh. I can't believe I told you that." She licked her lips. "I didn't deserve what happened to me, but that doesn't mean I'd commit murder. Forget it."

"Didn't you mention something about him sabotaging your chances at another event?"

She pushed her heavy-framed glasses higher on her nose. "He wouldn't share the water hookup with me."

"And?"

"And I had to walk the length of a football field to wash my produce and get the water I needed for my recipe."

I was immediately suspicious. Why hadn't she brought her own water, like many other contestants? "Did you tell the officials?"

Once again, she frowned at Lenny. "I most certainly did, but they merely issued a warning." She threw the spoon onto a folding table covered with chip bags and candy wrappers. "What is taking those kids so blasted long?" Without a backwards glance, she marched off, her flowered skirt billowing behind her.

"The iguana goes!" She didn't halt or slow though she clearly heard me. "Immediately!" Without turning around, she lifted a hand above her head and waved.

"She's not so bad." Whip washed his hands at the water faucet and added some antibacterial soap. "Just a bit desperate."

"If you say so."

Elliot's tongue slithered through a hole in his cage.

"Yip, yip." The Lenster wriggled with excitement.

"By all means, Lenny, say *adios* to the salmonella-spreading dragon." I lowered myself until the reptile and I were eye to eye. "If you're here when we get back, my friend, it's the SPCA or the Taxidermy Brothers for you."

I checked my watch. Another hour and a half left until chili cooks, young and old, ready or not, would bring their thirty-two ounces of chili to the officials' tent for judging. Most folks would compete in the official ICA categories: traditional red chili, chili verde, and salsa. Plus the one we'd added with Bridget Peck's approval: people's choice.

Without delay, we hustled to the Prius, where I recovered my notebook, favorite gel pen, and a protein bar from my book bag. I tossed Lenny into the shotgun seat and slid behind the wheel. I checked my watch again just to be safe and proceeded to make notes on everything that had happened: Lucky's body, tripping over electrical wires, who'd

said what outside of his tent, and the mixed signals I'd received from Dani O'Neal, from her out-of-date outfit to her
obvious lack of chili-cooking skills. A few minutes later,
Lenny and I exited the four-door and continued on our hos-
pitality tour of cooking tents and chili cooks.

A glance at Lucky's tent showed the ME and the sheriff's officers still hard at work collecting evidence. There
would be a singular moment to share my astute observations with Detective Lightfoot. Until then pots needed stirring and cooks needed calming.

After six more tents of rattled but persistent chili cooks,
a growl like that of an angry bear cub sprang to life from
my canine companion. Russell, the huge man with the long
wavy hair from the cook-off reception, was headed our way
with two calico cats on leashes.

"Watch that dog."

"That's inventive." I pulled out my cell. "Mind if I take
a pic for Lenny's blog?"

He placed a cat under each arm and posed. "My mother
always walked her cat, Prissy, every day at four o'clock."

"Smile, please." I snapped away.

He lowered the cats to the ground. "They enjoy explor-
ing, same as dogs, but I don't let them out among the great
unwashed." The cats locked their maleficent tawny eyes on
Lenny, hunting for signs of weakness.

My canine sidekick dropped his behind in the dirt. "It's
okay, Lenster, they won't hurt you." As soon as I spoke,
they raised their backs and began to spit and hiss like furry
teakettles.

Russell gave me a sly grin. "Your dog doesn't like cats."

"He likes *friendly* creatures of all makes and models."

"Yip."

"If you mean me, I'd be a heck of a sight more friendly
if I hadn't had to move my site first thing this morning."

He had a point. "I apologize for all the trouble."

Without taking their eyes off Lenny, the cats perched on their owner's giant feet. "Weren't your fault. Guess Lucky wasn't so lucky after all." The giant guffawed.

"Hardly seems fair to laugh."

Russell came at me faster than a bobcat chasing a chicken. "Fair! That jerk stole Becca away from me when I was laid up in the dad burn hospital."

"The blonde on his phone?"

"When'd *you* see her!" He erupted with anger, and my flight response flared.

"Meowww!" The cats began to wind themselves around Russell's legs.

"Sorry, sorry," he murmured in a baby voice. "Daddy didn't mean to hurt you."

I stepped back. "I thought Lucky stole Becca from Whip." I glanced around for support, but I could see no one out in the open.

"Heck no. Whip dated her back in high school. That was just Lucky's way of making him feel small."

"Did Lucky play dirty?" My mind was spinning. How had Lucky, a middle-aged, dime-store cowboy, won the beautiful Becca from both Whip and this long-haired giant? Maybe Whip's grief over his friend was all an act. And maybe Russell's hatred of Lucky had turned to violence.

I took a deep breath, gathered Lenny into my arms, and prepared to run at the first threat of danger.

Carefully Russell untangled the cats' leashes from around his legs. "What would you call it when the other fella can't defend himself?" His anger fell away, leaving a mask of deep sadness.

"What did he do?" If I wanted him to spill the beans, I had to convince this guy I was harmless. I smiled with both dimples.

Suddenly his jaw clenched and angry fire filled his gaze. He lifted a fist the size of a tether ball above his head and shook it at the fates. "He tricked me." With a sigh, his arm fell to his side. "Took my picture with some chicks in Little Rock at the last chili cook-off."

"Sent one to Becca, huh?" My stretched nerves relaxed a bit.

"Not only that." He sniffed. "He plastered them all over the Internet with crude comments I supposedly wrote." The giant's chin shook. "Don't stare at me like that."

"Like what?" I tried to use the dimples again, but my nerves prevented it. We were standing near the end of the row of shelters and tents. At that moment, not one solitary soul was in view. If his anger roared to life again, he could throttle me in a matter of seconds, long before anyone could rescue me. I took a few steps back.

"Don't worry. I wouldn't hurt a hair on your head, or anyone else's—not even that teeny-weeny dog."

It had been a long, stressful morning. I needed a place to calm down, and now. "Is that Detective Lightfoot coming this way?" I pointed off to the right over his shoulder.

"No, I wouldn't hurt him." He grinned, revealing straight white teeth. "But he is a perfect morsel for a mountain lion." The giant with the cat-shaped heart dared to smirk.

This was too close for comfort. "There were only nine reported mountain lion attacks last year in the United States," I responded sharply.

He gave me a dismissive look. "True, little lady, but bobcats are everywhere."

I wanted to scream. "Just don't contaminate your chili with germs from your feline friends or you'll be . . . d-disqualified."

"Point taken . . . m-ma'am." He gave Lenny a pointed

look, laughed, and marched his cats toward the vendor booths, undaunted by my threat.

Once Lenny and I finished our tour of chili cooks, having answered their questions, calmed their fears, and proclaimed the enticing aroma of their recipes, we made our way to the vendor booths on the far side of the cook-off area. Many of the artisans and craftsmen were familiar, having sold their wares along Main Street during last year's Cinco de Mayo parade and celebration. I made sure to stop by one of my favorites, a tent resplendent with yard animals, fish, and flowers created from recycled and repurposed scrap metal—steel, iron, aluminum, and copper. My heart skipped a beat when I saw the glorious horse head made of pliers, iron gate, and a flowing mane of twisted metal. If I were to win something like a chili cook-off one day—except, of course, the contest could have nothing to do with baking, canning, pickling, or food preparation of any kind—I'd purchase the magnificent horse head.

"One day," I sighed.

"Yip, yip," Lenny barked, making serious eye contact with a weenie dog made of copper springs.

I scooped him into my arms and kissed his pointy head. "I won't forget you when the Wells Fargo wagon comes to town."

At the end of the row of vendors, we found a fireworks booth filled with sparklers, poppers, bottle rockets, giant rockets on long sticks, missiles, and other strange things I failed to recognize. It was manned by none other than Frank Fillmore. "How do you find time to operate your booth and prepare for tonight's spectacular, spectacular?"

He frowned in confusion at my reference to *Moulin Rouge*. "What's the big deal?" He stuck up a thumb and pointed over his shoulder to the distant platform filled with gizmos and rockets. "I only have to check the wind velocity fifteen minutes before showtime and program any last-minute changes to my calibrations before I set the night sky ablaze."

I picked up a box of sparklers and pretended to read the label. I didn't know why, but I felt sorry for the guy.

"Something wrong?" Fillmore asked. "Or do you have a question?"

"Is this a sideline or a full-time gig?"

He grinned. "I'm a hobbyist, but it's my passion."

"You retired?"

A shadow passed over his face. "Technically, no. But at my age, it's difficult to find someone willing to give me the opportunity to prove myself, no matter my years of experience."

"What field are you in?"

He hesitated as if embarrassed.

"I only ask because you must be pretty smart to launch rockets without starting a wildfire or blowing yourself to smithereens." I shrugged. "Unlike me. I'm challenged by my cell phone."

He chuckled. "I've had at least three careers, most recently in human resources."

No wonder his manner seemed at odds with his utilitarian coveralls. I swallowed down my pride. "A layoff brought me home from Austin," I managed a crooked smile. "You know what they say. When God closes a door—"

"Yeah, yeah." As he had the night before, Frank rubbed his forehead. "It's just that the windows keep getting smaller and smaller."

"Hey, I might be able to help out. After the show, I'll make sure to include the name of your business in my Cinco de Mayo article for the *Bugle*. Plus, I'll get the word out on social media that Fillmore's Fireworks are fantastic."

One corner of his mouth kicked up. "Maybe I should add *fantastic* to the name."

I laughed. "Wouldn't hurt none." I dug in the pocket of my jeans, praying I'd find a wad of ones. "I'll take, uh, four boxes of sparklers. Is it difficult to program your shows?"

"My *displays* are a bit sophisticated for their size." He paused in order to take a handful of bottle rockets from a young couple, place them in a brown paper sack, and make change. "Anyone with basic computer knowledge could program most fireworks displays. This one doesn't challenge me as much as I'd like, but it keeps my creative juices flowing . . . so to speak."

He'd parked his white cargo van behind his booth. A sudden swish of a cat's tail in the front window caught my eye. "Who's that?" She was a fat orange tabby with a sweet face.

"Yip, yip," Lenny complained.

"That's Tabitha."

"Ah."

He chuckled. "I know what you're thinking. What a boring, overused name for a cat. Right?"

"No." I smiled. "If her name is overused, which I have no idea whether or not that's true, I would have a better chance of calling her by the correct name."

"Huh. So your dog wants to introduce himself to my Tabitha? Or does he want to test her claws?" Laughter erupted from deep in his belly. I couldn't tell if he was being sarcastic or not. He straightened a tower of sparklers and added more bottle rockets to his red, white, and green display.

His laugh was too contagious for me not to join in. "Oh, he wants to introduce himself and then lay down the law of the land. He's bossy that way. But he'd never hurt her. Engage her in a game of tag? Most definitely." I rubbed him behind the ears.

"Yip."

I laughed at the innocent expression Lenny wore. "I wouldn't want to place a wager on his ability to resist. Don't think too harshly of him. I believe he's jealous of cats and their independent natures."

"May I?" He reached out a hand toward Lenny.

"Of course." My long-haired Chi was a good sport as long as strangers refrained from petting him more than twice. Three times on Thursdays.

"I admire your freedom, my little friend. My Tabitha and I live in that van you see. She doesn't get out as much as you do, I bet."

"Oh, I like it. It looks very comfortable." I was trying to make him feel better about his circumstances and failing miserably.

He frowned and shook his head, a disgusted look on his face. "I got it for a steal."

"That's great."

"No, literally, they cheated me out of my money. The power locks and windows don't always work."

"That's not cool." The poor cat.

"Most of the time, I merely have to replace some fuses, but there's always an occasion arises when I'm far from home that I have to take it into the shop." With a twist of his wrist, he snapped open a paper bag and shoved the sparklers inside. "What's the word on the dead guy?"

His abrupt change of topic threw me for a second. "I don't know." I shrugged.

"Sure you do. I saw you hanging around his tent, talking to that detective."

"You think they'd tell me?" I crossed my fingers. If I wanted more inside information from Lightfoot, I had to prove I could keep facts and theories to myself. "Last I heard, they thought he might have fallen and hit his head."

Lenny and I exited his canopy, and Frank placed an OUT

TO LUNCH sign with a movable second hand on one of the tables. Suddenly he smiled. "Come on. I'll show you the setup. What'll it hurt?"

"What if other customers stop by? I wouldn't want you to miss any sales."

"Nah," he said with a shrug. "It's good for them to wait, builds excitement."

The smile had transformed his face. I could see how proud he was of his work—how he needed and wanted to share what he'd created.

Lenny whined and I scooped him into my arms.

"Shh. It's okay." He licked my face over and over.

I didn't think this guy Frank was blessed with a family and friends like I was. His was probably living the life of a loner, driving to remote locations, setting up fireworks shows for hours and days on end without any backup.

I followed him, leaving a fair amount of space between us for good measure. "Do you always work alone?"

"No." He marched through the scrub and rocks like a man with a mission until we arrived at the display platform. "These gears and whistles all have Chinese names I can't pronounce." He chuckled. "I could try if you want me to."

I shrugged. "No, that's okay. How do you read the instructions?"

"Trial and error."

"No. Way. That sounds like the perfect way to lose a thumb or your hearing." I'd had a small bottle rocket explode in my hand. Things had sounded out of kilter for several hours afterwards.

"You're right. That's not exactly true. They come with both Chinese, English, Spanish, French, and Korean instructions. They even have languages you'd think they made up just to confuse the rest of us."

I smiled. He looked as if he needed some encouragement. I didn't know an awful lot about fireworks, but at second glance the platform he'd built as a launching pad for his show wasn't that large, and the amount of fireworks—gears, rockets, fuses, and whatnot—didn't look as if they'd give a show that lasted longer than ten or fifteen minutes. But what did I know?

"This looks like quite a setup. How long do you expect the show will last?"

He thrust his hands on his hips and cocked his head to one side. "How many minutes do you suppose Mr. Mayor Cogburn requested?"

I bit my lip to keep myself from checking my watch. "Twenty minutes?"

"No." He chuckled again, but it sounded as if his vocal cords were grinding the words through a meat grinder. "That would have been too reasonable for the amount of money he agreed to pay."

Frank's bitterness was leaking out in spite of his attempt at civility.

"Mayor Cogburn can drive a hard bargain." Lenny and I continued our way around the platform. "I hope you stood up for yourself."

"Of course."

"So how long of a show did he request?"

"Thirty minutes."

"Lord, have mercy." Now ten extra minutes didn't sound like a lot to me. Still, if he was paid by the minute and he'd underbid to get the job . . . and he didn't have any cash flow to speak of . . . well, it could seem like an eternity to the poor guy. "Please forgive him, but he thinks it makes him a strong leader to drive a hard bargain."

His belly laugh filled the air. "Oh, I forgave him, all right, once he'd agreed to an adjustment to my original invoice."

After getting the tour, Lenny and I cruised back over to the officials' tent and found an empty chair. There was no sign of either one of the officials, which was just as well. I needed to process all I'd seen and heard over the past four hours. Almost everyone seemed to have a reason to dislike Lucky Straw. I could imagine any one of them punching him in the face, but killing the guy was a stretch.

"Maybe he did fall and hit his head." I glanced at Lenny. "It's possible."

"Yip."

Lenny was right. Hadn't I learned my lesson? Sometimes people kill other people the same way I might kill a fly with a fly swatter. It wasn't the fly's fault he was born to aggravate people to distraction. But it didn't make him any less dead.

Chapter 7

Lucky's Heart Needed a Bit of Help

Lenny and I approached the officials' tent, dragging our tails behind us. Bridget Peck was flipping through the entry forms in a file folder while her friend Sam played solitaire.

"Can I get you guys anything?"

"Why is it people always say *guys* when what they actually want to say is *y'all*?" She turned to Sam. "Haven't you noticed that tendency, especially in young people?"

Sam glanced up and gave me a vacant smile. "Sure."

"Do you have everything you need?" We'd provided sandwiches, snacks, cold drinks, and water for the officials. Aunt Linda had even provided chocolate brownies with pecans and gooey centers.

"I would love a fan." Bridget Peck was dressed in her bright yellow T-shirt and visor. It was about seventy degrees and windy.

"What kind of fan did you have in mind?" If I drove about three miles down the road, I'd pass the chapel where they still passed out paper fans on hot summer days, emblazoned with *Juárez Funeral Home* on one side and the Mother Mary on the other.

"I don't rightly care, child. Y'all just bring me a fan, 'cause I'm about to pass out."

Sam gave me a nod and went back to his solitaire. I checked my watch. "We only have a few minutes until it's time to start the judging. How about something cold?"

Without waiting for an answer, I tied Lenny's leash to the table leg and dashed for the *paletas* vendor I'd spotted on our tour of the fairgrounds only moments earlier. When I returned with three different flavors—mango, coconut, and strawberry cream—Bridget blanched.

"What kind of Popsicles are those?"

"Mexican. And they're cold. You're going to love them."

With a frown, she unwrapped the coconut one and gave it a small lick. Her countenance cleared and she lunged for a bite. Sam took the mango, and I took charge of the strawberry cream.

"You want a lick?" I asked my long-haired Chi.

Lenny didn't bother to answer. He scooted under the table and lay down, resting his head on his paws.

At Lucky's tent, Lightfoot stood talking to Ellis. The JP had his camera case in one hand and his medical bag in the other.

I hurried over. "You leaving without saying good-bye?"

"The rest will take place at the morgue, and then it's off to the state lab." Ellis checked his watch.

"What do you think killed him?" I asked a bit too innocently.

He fought a smile. "Why bother asking? Weren't we in his tent together?" Something in his expression made me doubt my powers of observation.

"Did he fall or was he clobbered with a skillet like I thought?"

"We're still collecting evidence." Lightfoot gave me a stern look.

"Please tell me something." I leaned closer, lowering my voice. "Come on. I've been collecting evidence myself all morning."

A silent message went back and forth between the two men. Ellis blanked his expression. "We discovered Lucky has a pacemaker."

"Whoa." That added another layer to the cake. "Was it working when he died?"

"Hard to tell, but most likely."

"What about the stun gun? Could he have been playing around with that, shocked himself, and then fallen and hit his head?" It would be a relief to not have another murder on our hands. One small town can take only so much mayhem.

He exchanged another quick glance with Lightfoot. "It's possible." Ellis shifted his feet. "Look, the detective can share more with you if he's so inclined, but I've got to get going." He headed for the row of chili contestant tents and shelters.

"Where's he off to?"

"Checking in with the wife to make sure their chili hasn't suffered in his absence." Lightfoot removed his hat and wiped a hand across his brow.

With a twinge of impatience, I watched the JP leave. "How will Ellis know for sure whether it was Lucky's pacemaker that killed him or the iron skillet?"

Rolling back his shoulders, Lightfoot blew out his breath in exasperation. "First, it's highly unlikely that his pacemaker failed. That happens only on TV. Second, you seem to be the only person convinced he was hit with a cook pot."

"If I'm wrong," I interrupted, "then where is Lucky's cast-iron skillet—the one Whip claims he never left home without?"

"Barnes and Pleasant will keep an eye out as they secure the scene." Lightfoot's gaze narrowed. "You can't hurry the process along, Josie. Ellis will contact the victim's doctor, who will provide the information on his pacemaker."

"I can help you there. He was always going on about his ailments." Whip was up close and personal before I saw him coming.

Lightfoot made ready to take notes. "Do you know the name of his doctor?"

"Samantha something or other. It's in the medicine bag around his neck."

Both men stared at me, waiting for a revelation. "I didn't see a medicine bag this morning or anything else around his neck . . . except for his apron."

"Where could it be?" Lightfoot asked.

"Nowhere . . . wait. Last night he lost it at that shindig." Whip pointed at me, too close for comfort. "You were there, weren't you?"

I nodded slowly. "I remember." I held my fingers about six inches apart. "He said it was a leather bag about so big. Like a medicine bag—but not." I shot a glance at Lightfoot to gauge his reaction to my basic knowledge of Native American accessories.

"What did he keep in it?" he asked, ignoring me.

"Let's see." Whip screwed up his face, like someone either drunk or suffering a tremendous hangover. Or like someone who'd lost his best friend. His half-open eyes were red, and he wore a smear of toothpaste across his chin. Beneath a heavy dowsing of chili powder, I could still make out the words on his red T-shirt, *Naked Chili Burns in All the Right Places*.

"What did he carry in the bag around his neck?" Lightfoot asked as he scribbled something down on his notepad.

"A card with his doctor's name on it and something else." Whip grabbed his head. "And something real important, if I could just remember."

"House key?" I offered.

He gave me a look of disgust. "No. That ain't it."

"Was he allergic to medicines, bees, anything you can recall?" Lightfoot studied Whip closely.

The older man began to twist the end of his shirt, as if wringing out a washrag. "Heck, no. He had a cast-iron stomach. Could eat a jar of jalapeños and never flinch."

"Emergency numbers, maybe?" I asked. The poor guy needed an energy drink or a pair of jumper cables to give his brain a jolt.

He slapped the sides of his head. "Numbers! He kept the serial number to his pacemaker and the warranty information in that thing." Reeling, Whip dropped to one knee, as if remembering had sapped his life force.

"Are you okay?" Lightfoot and I exchanged a glance. Was Whip putting on a show for our benefit?

"I'll be all right . . . You got any coffee?"

"Where's your RV?"

"I can't go back in there." He dropped his head and drew a shuddering breath. "Last time I made coffee in that kitchen, Lucky was alive."

Lightfoot caught my eye. "Don't you have coffee in the officials' tent?"

"Could be." Could also be that I didn't want to leave this potential suspect behind, to miss out on any crucial information he would give the detective in my absence.

"I'd be eternally grateful." Whip grabbed my hand and pulled it to his chest, dusting it with chili powder.

"Sure." I withdrew my hand and wiped it on the side seam of my jeans. I'd taken three steps when I spun around.

"Was that the only place he kept the number for his pace-maker? He didn't keep it anywhere else, like a wallet or a safe?"

Whip lowered himself carefully to the ground. "I'll just sit here until you get back." His voice was wafer thin. What a drama queen.

Back at the tent, Lenny was snoring. I filled a paper cup with what I prayed was coffee, though it was so black and slick I could've sworn it was motor oil.

"Only thirty minutes until we get under way." Bridget and Sam appeared to be playing go fish. "I hope you haven't forgotten anything." Entry numbers had been taped to the judges' table, disposable tasting spoons and sample cups placed at each spot, and lined trash cans positioned in reach.

I prayed Uncle Eddie had followed our checklist to the letter. "Why? Is something missing?" I was a bit ticked at their lack of concern. "What else is there to do but wait for the entries?"

"Cheating is under way as we speak." Sam shuffled the deck and then shuffled it again.

Bridget slapped her hands together. "Listen to him." She gestured wide, encompassing the fairgrounds before her. "Right now, some contestants are bending the rules while others are breaking them."

"I have to make an emergency coffee delivery."

"If you want to protect the integrity of this event, then you better join your uncle policing the contestants." Her beady eyes burned with religious fervor.

"Uh, well." For Uncle Eddie, I'd do anything. "I'll get right on it. But what kind of cheating should I be looking for?"

"Tell her, Sam." She folded her hands in her lap, nodding for him to proceed.

He began to deal a hand of ten cards each—gin rummy,

if I had to guess. "Look for folks taking precooked chili out of their coolers or RVs, trying to pass it off as fresh."

"Wouldn't they have already brought it out?"

He shook his head and studied his hand. "Contestants panic near the end, especially the first-timers. That's when they bring out that Tupperware container of chili they made at home, just in case."

"How am I supposed to catch them?"

"Your presence is a reminder for them to do the right thing, follow the rules, not act on their baser instincts." Bridget frowned over her cards.

I sighed. "Anything else?"

"Store-bought meat." With a smile, she moved three cards together in her hand.

"Excuse me?"

Sam studied Bridget as she rearranged her hand once again. "All meat is to be cooked on-site. Some folks cheat by bringing precooked meat."

The coffee was cooling and my patience was wearing thin. "Any tips on finding those prepared meats?"

"Wrappers," they said in unison.

"Got it." I'm afraid I stomped away. Found Whip and gave him his lukewarm cup of coffee, and explained to Lightfoot my new tasks.

"Sounds like that's your priority." Lightfoot tried not to smile.

I watched Whip drink his coffee and toddle back to his tent to finish his chili preparations. "What else did he tell you?"

"Not much."

"What about the pacemaker serial number? Where else did Lucky keep it?"

"He couldn't remember, but he did remember the doctor's name: Samantha Castillo."

"Have you called her yet?"

With a shake of his head, he pocketed his notepad and pencil. "You understand that we're not talking about only one phone call."

"True." He would have to call the doctor's office. That call would be followed by a call to the surgeon who'd implanted the pacemaker, which would be followed by a call to the manufacturer, and on and on.

Uncle Eddie appeared from behind Whip's tent. One look at my face and he swooped in to give me a quick hug. "It's gonna be okay, Jo Jo."

"You bet it is. You still on patrol?"

He grimaced. "Only made one circuit, but apparently I'm supposed to keep this up until it's time for the judging to start."

"I'll take this turn." I glanced at my watch. "You see to Lenny and drink a cup of coffee. You can relieve me in fifteen, twenty minutes."

In the daylight, more of my uncle's gray hairs stood out. "Lightfoot? Uh, Detective Lightfoot, please tell me this was a heart attack." Worry creased Uncle Eddie's dear face.

"I wish I could, but the death looks suspicious."

Uncle Eddie took his cowboy hat in his hands. "I don't care if they demand my resignation." His expression reminded me of a depressed basset hound. "It's the kids at the Big Bend Children's Home who'll suffer. It took us months to plan this fund-raiser so they could buy new playground equipment." With a sniff, he found his handkerchief in his pocket, blew his nose, and turned to go.

"Nonsense." I grabbed him by the arm. "Look around. These chili cooks aren't letting a little thing like death stand in their way, and neither will we."

Lightfoot caught my silent plea. "Everything appears to be in order. Everyone is going about their business."

From the parking lot appeared a familiar figure. Mayor Cogburn in his rhinestone cowboy getup with Mrs. Mayor at his side. Surprisingly, she had ignored her matching outfit for a prairie dress and bonnet. If I wasn't mistaken, she was wearing her costume from our recent Homestead Days Music Festival.

"Detective," the mayor called, still a far piece away. "What in blue blazes is happening in these fairgrounds?"

"Uh, Jo Jo. I'll take this round." Uncle Eddie waved at the mayor and then turned tail and hurried away to hunt for chili-cooking cheaters.

"Where does your uncle think he's going?"

"Howdy, Mayor Cogburn." My smile stretched from ear to ear. "Mrs. Cogburn, that's a beautiful costume."

She straightened her bonnet and checked to make sure both her pearl earrings were still in place. "I bought this at a craft fair in Fredericksburg last weekend."

"Eddie Martinez can't run from me, young lady. He's got some explaining to do."

"How can I be of service, Mayor?" Lightfoot stuck out his hand.

The surprised mayor didn't forget his manners and shook the officer's hand. "You can start with the dead body."

"Is it in there?" Mrs. Cogburn stared at the tent with wide, frightened eyes.

"No, ma'am. The body's been taken to the morgue."

She visibly relaxed. "Who was it? Surely not someone we know." She took the mayor's arm.

"A tourist, from what I hear." Mayor Cogburn patted his wife's hand.

"One of the chili cooks from out of town."

"I heard he had a heart attack."

Lightfoot shot a glance my way. "It's possible, but not confirmed at this time."

"Save your rhetoric for the media." He nodded in my direction. "Let's get it all out in the open."

"But, Mr. Mayor, Josie's writing for the *Bugle* these days." Mrs. Cogburn gave me a warm smile, not realizing she was shooting my chance of gathering inside information in the foot.

"Hmm. That right?"

I assumed a downcast expression. "I do write the occasional article for them, sir."

"Well, let's just consider this a press conference. Let those magpies from Marfa and Fort Davis call the sheriff's office for the nitpicking details."

"Well?" Mayor Cogburn's eyes narrowed.

"The dead man was hit on the back of the head or he fell. It's unclear whether the blow killed him or he was dead before he hit his head," Lightfoot said.

Well, well. Lightfoot hadn't shared the bit about the stun gun in the chili, had he? And why was it there? Had it been dropped or hidden in Lucky's flavorful concoction?

"Could this have been caused by negligence on the part of the cook-off organizers?" The mayoral couple in unison shifted their gaze to me, catching me in their critical net.

I opened my mouth to refute the accusation.

"No sign of negligence on anyone's part, except maybe the deceased's."

"Explain, sir."

"If you could see the inside of the deceased's tent you would immediately note how organized it is. The only thing out of place are several extension cords just inside the tent opening," Lightfoot said.

"Did you or did you not provide extension cords for the contestants?"

"I did not. It's not customary to provide them, and furthermore we don't have the money for a hundred extension cords," I said.

"Why not?"

Was the mayor serious? "This is a charity event."

As if on cue, men and women started filing by where we stood. Each hopeful contestant carried the large thirty-two-ounce cup provided by the judges, the cups filled with their chili. Some carried two, some used trays, and others gripped the cups tightly in their hands. Those that carried them in their hands wore padded gloves or gripped pot holders.

"Watch out," a young boy cried, barely managing to hold on to his tray as two large cups slid first to one side and then the other.

"Oh, let me help, precious." Mrs. Mayor stepped close to the little boy, who quickly stepped back. The cups again slid to the other side of the tray.

"You can't help him, Mrs. Mayor." Cogburn grabbed his wife's arm and pulled her back. "He or one of his parents have to carry it to the judges' table."

"Why, that's ridiculous."

I shrugged. "But it's the rule." The rules were a pain in my backside. "Hey, kid. What if I walk alongside and point out any potholes?"

"Okay."

All four of us traipsed along with him, joining the stream of chili bearers to the ultimate temple of official judging.

Chapter 8

✔✔✔✔✔✔✔✔✔✔✔✔✔✔✔✔✔✔✔✔✔✔✔✔✔

And the Winner Is . . .

Slowly and steadily, like the Little Engine That Could, the boy managed to safely arrive at the judges' table with his precious cups of chili—in spite of being hounded by one officious mayor, his well-meaning wife, an observant detective, and me.

Bridget checked the numbers on the cups and marked her list. "Where are your parents, boy?"

"None of your beeswax." And he promptly ran away.

Guess he'd had enough of unknown-adult supervision for one day. I watched him run toward the edge of the fairgrounds, and my brain clicked his identity into place. He was an O'Neal, not one of the two I'd seen near the bathrooms at Milagro, but the other one. What was his name? Had I heard it before?

For the next twelve minutes, there was a flurry of contestants delivering cups of chili and salsa, entry numbers checked, and nervous questions by the contestants. "Does it matter what temperature it is?"

"No." Sam accepted the cup of chili from the wizened fellow from the morning, now dressed.

"What if it has beans?"

"Don't enter it in the traditional category."

"But I already did." An older woman, who looked vaguely familiar, cried.

"Next," Bridget proclaimed, dramatically drawing a line through the old woman's name on the list.

"Perhaps this once?" I asked.

With a snort, Bridget added the woman's name to the correct category.

"What if my salsa verde isn't green?" a familiar voice asked.

"Stranger things have won in the past." Sam added Russell's cup to a long line of salsa verde entries on a nearby table.

"I am here," cried Senora Mari. She held a large plastic cup carefully in her two hands.

"Mamá!" Uncle Eddie hurried to her side. "You can't compete, we discussed this."

Bridget Peck barred his way. "Mr. Martinez, Senora Mari has my permission to place her chili alongside all these other entries."

Uncle Eddie's mouth fell open. "But—"

"She's not eligible to win, but Sam and I discussed it. We couldn't live with ourselves if we didn't taste Senora Mari's chili." Bridget took the plastic cup from my *abuela* and placed it at the end of the judges' table. "It's not every day we meet a grand prize winner from Guadalajara."

Senora Mari smiled beatifically, carefully avoiding the eyes of her family.

"Thirty seconds, ladies and gentlemen. Thirty seconds until the contest is closed." Bridget stood, stopwatch in hand, determined to break the hearts of anyone too idle to make the deadline.

"Why is it so important to deliver it on time?" Whip said, squeaking in with a handful of seconds to spare. "It's the taste that matters, dang it."

"Organization and time management is the key to an excellent chili, Whip. You should know that by now."

"I'd think with Lucky dead and all, you'd make an exception for a person being unable to see properly to cook because that person might have tears in their eyes."

"Time," Bridget proclaimed with triumph.

The crowd surrounding the judges' tent burst into applause.

"We understand that this has not been an easy day for many of you." Muttering broke out in the crowd. "Still," she said, raising her voice even louder, "you persevered and did your very best to achieve your culinary dreams this day."

Sam elbowed her in the side.

After an answering glare that could have melted his eyeballs into butter, Bridget threw back her shoulders. "May the best chili win!"

Again the crowd roared.

A tap on the shoulder had me turning around. "Oh, my gosh." It was Aunt Linda, looking her usual gorgeous self, only a bit tired and shell-shocked. "Have you been selling tacos this entire time?"

She laughed and five years fell away. "No, Jo Jo. I had most of the staff here to help me, remember?"

"How'd we do?"

I could see the wheels spinning as she ciphered what she'd sold during the hours I'd interviewed and investigated—if you wanted to call it that—the fairgrounds and the suspicious death of Lucky Straw.

"We came out ahead by a mile, even giving away the

coffee and the cinnamon rolls." Aunt Linda wasn't one to talk numbers. She played our successes and struggles close to her chest.

"Who's left?"

"I sent the Milagro staff home a couple of hours ago to open for lunch. Tim and Mitzi are still over there selling what's left of the tacos and sodas." The couple were bartenders at Two Boots dance hall, and fast friends of Uncle Eddie's.

"Are you heading out soon?"

Before she could answer, Uncle Eddie spotted her and crushed her in his arms. "You did it again, hon. Thank you, thank you."

"She's the best," I said. They were the cutest couple.

"And I'm so proud of her." He kissed her, and she brushed her cheek as if wiping it away. Still I couldn't miss her blush.

"I'm out of here." She disengaged gently from his arms. "When will you get the results?"

"Y'all will get the results in about an hour . . . so cool your jets." Bridget Peck delivered her directive to the crowd of contestants through a mini megaphone she'd produced from thin air.

Russell appeared at the edge of the crowd, cats in tow.

"Yip, yip," Lenny's voice rang out.

Bridget turned from the judges' table, spoon at the ready. "Get that dog out of here! You're interfering with the neutrality of the judges' area." Since neither Lenny nor I had entered the cook-off, I wasn't sure what she was talking about. I scampered around the entry submission table and unattached my canine friend from the table leg.

"Yip."

"Ah, geez, Lenster. Potty break?"

"Yip."

"Meow!" From nowhere the two cats appeared, hissing and spitting.

"Get those felines out of here before you contaminate the whole kit and caboodle."

Russell pushed his way through the crowd around the judges' tent. "Donner. Blitzen. Come here." Like good cats everywhere, they ignored him.

I scooped Lenny into my arms, turning my back from the table of chili entries, determined to show the officials I had no wish to contaminate their samples.

"Give him to me." Aunt Linda appeared at my elbow. "I'll take him home."

"Take him for a walk first."

"Don't worry your head about that."

Russell lifted the two cats by the scruffs of their necks and they immediately became neutral sacks of sweet, docile fur.

"Out." Bridget pointed a long, officious finger toward the parking lot.

"We're going, aren't we, girls?" Russell said.

The crowd closed behind Russell as he ignored Bridget's command and headed for his tent.

I said a quick prayer that Elliot the iguana wouldn't be the next pet to make an unseemly appearance. A salmonella outbreak would equal a murder in Bridget's book, any day.

"I thought you had this under control." Mayor Cogburn had pulled Uncle Eddie to one side. "What do you call this?"

Mrs. Cogburn laughed. "Good fun, right, Detective? I've never laughed so hard in my life." She shot a glance over her shoulder to where Bridget and Sam stood tasting the entries, backs stiff with self-importance and outrage.

Lightfoot smiled his first true smile of the day. "Seems to me that cats and dogs would worry her less than a dead body."

"How much longer until they announce the winner?"

Mayor Cogburn had the knack for ignoring his wife's sage advice.

"Still forty minutes, unless certain individuals won't leave us in peace," Bridget muttered, never turning away from tasting and making notes next to each entry.

With a flirtatious smile, Mrs. Mayor drew her husband away from the officials' tent. "Let's check out the vendors. There's a booth over there selling silk shawls. Maybe they have one to match my new dress." Her prairie dress was green and purple gingham, but maybe the stars would align as they usually did when Mrs. Mayor had her mind set on a new fashionable purchase.

"What about you?" I asked.

Lightfoot checked his phone. "Barnes says everything's packed up or closed off. Just as soon as I sample some chili, I'm heading over to the sheriff's office to write a report."

My stomach grumbled. "I'll join you."

"You're going to miss the announcement of the big winners."

"Unlike our cadaver, I'll live."

Before we could skedaddle, Bridget's sidekick, Sam, brought out the trophies and displayed them across the front table. Alongside the Texas-shaped awards, they placed red and white ribbons for second and third place. Uncle Eddie appeared from the depths of the tent, carrying white Milagro envelopes—which held the prize money for the first-place winners and the people's choice award. He spotted the mayor and Mrs. Cogburn now sitting in the front row and flapped the envelopes at them in greeting.

While Lightfoot and I sampled a chili apiece, the judges had put their heads together.

Bridget Peck blew her air horn before I could cover my ears. "Gather round, folks. It's time to announce the big winners."

Rancher P.J. Pratt pushed through the crowd, trailed by Hillary Sloan-Rawlings and his wife, the artistic gallery-owner Melanie.

"Hold up a cotton-pickin' minute." P.J. was as loud as any air horn. "The town council decided that Hillary should give out the prizes." He took the beauty queen's hand and presented her to Bridget Peck as if she were the First Lady and the Queen of England all rolled into one.

Uncle Eddie hurried over. "The rules say the ICA officials have to announce the winners, P.J."

"It benefits our citizens." Melanie crossed her arms in defiance.

"True, but this is Uncle Eddie's event." This trio of troublemakers had better keep their greedy hands off my uncle's hard work.

"What do you say, Mr. Martinez?" Bridget Peck's face had turned to stone.

Uncle Eddie glanced at Mayor Cogburn and his wife. "I say . . ." He threw back his shoulders and tucked his thumbs into his belt. "I say we play by the ICA rules."

The crowd applauded enthusiastically.

The actual announcement of the winners was anticlimactic. The winner of the traditional red chili category was a woman from Waco, who cried, "Don't mess with Texas!" and wiped her tears with her husband's shirttail.

Everyone applauded, if a bit quietly.

After the announcement of the traditional red chili category, the chili verde was next. The wizened old man, white legs now covered, pointed a finger at the crowd as he claimed his trophy and two hundred and fifty dollars. "Doubters, look upon me and weep."

The crowd laughed, which made him even angrier. He

began to spout something about God's judgment on Lucky and death to those who took advantage of others until Sam pulled him aside for a picture.

Finally, Mr. Hailey, from Barnum and Hailey's Emporium, an old family friend, claimed the prize in the salsa category. As he accepted his award, his round belly jiggled with laughter. I'd heard his business was struggling to stay open, and I prayed the prize money would keep his dear establishment open a little longer.

"This year we decided to make an exception to the rules." Bridget Peck waited for the crowd to quiet down. "Since this cook-off is not yet an official ICA-sanctioned event until next year, we have decided to award the people's choice award to Senora Marisol Martinez."

The crowd cheered.

"Mamá?" Uncle Eddie found her at the edge of the crowd and led her forward.

"Didn't I tell you I would show them how to make chili the proper way?"

Mayor Cogburn stepped forward. "Pratt, stop hogging the spotlight and clear out of the way."

Outflanked, Pratt and his women moved aside.

The photographer for the *Bugle* took photos of the winners with their awards along with the officials, and even the proud event organizer—Uncle Eddie.

"I am so proud of you, *Abuela.*" I gave her a quick hug.

With a pat to my cheek, she said, "Of course, you are. But don't worry, it's not too late for you to learn."

The Cogburns and other friends gathered around and I slipped away.

I said good-bye to Bridget and Sam, making sure to thank them for giving us a chance, even after Lucky's death and my *abuela*'s brazen stubbornness. I was too exhausted to care enough to see if we'd passed muster. Uncle Eddie could ask the hard questions: Would we be welcome to hold one of their hallowed ICA events next year? And would they be so kind as to list our event on their website? I gave my uncle a saucy salute, two fingers to my temple. He responded with a wry smile and a shake of his head as I left him to wrap up the loose ends with the rest of the cook-off volunteers.

I was halfway to the Prius when I remembered Lightfoot. He was nowhere in sight. I wanted to discuss my thoughts on the case, with the sole intent that he would share his thoughts on the case with me. I decided to take one last tour of the chili cook tents. I could easily combine my tour with sampling chili and discussing the case with Lightfoot—if I didn't make it too obvious for his taste.

I began with Dani O'Neal's site. "I'm sorry you didn't win."

"Oh, it's you and that dog. Should have known." She looked up briefly from pouring out the contents of her chili pot. She wore giant pot holder gloves on each hand and held her head to one side to avoid the steam from her brew.

"Where're your kids? I bet they were disappointed."

She ignored me and finished emptying the last of her chili concoction into an empty plastic gallon jug. She then threw the plastic jug into the metal garbage barrel to the side of her shelter.

"Where's Elliot?" I tried to make my question sound casual, but I was more than happy to see her destroy the salmonella-infected concoction. Perhaps there was a slight chance her chili was untainted; but I'd seen her return to her cooking without washing her hands after handling him. That was enough for me.

"Does it matter?" She slammed the lid of a large blue ice chest and rolled it onto the grass along the outer perimeter of her site.

"Sure it does. You competed for your . . . kids. That

makes it important." I'd almost let the cat out of the bag. If she wanted to pretend those three tykes were hers, I had to find out why.

With a dramatic sigh, she fell onto the chest. "Not my kids."

"I'm sorry." I was always stepping into it with both moccasins. "I didn't mean any insult."

She waved a hand. "Chill. They're not even mine."

My mouth fell open like a doofus. "Whose kids are they?"

"Janice. My sister. She needed a break from her brats so she sent three of them with me."

"How many did you leave her with?" Would Janice agree that her children were *brats?*

"One. The baby." Dani raised up enough to lift the lid of the ice chest and bring out a wine cooler. Cherry breeze. Then with a quick glance my way, she stuck the unopened bottle under her arm, removed her glasses, and cleaned the lenses on her white tee. "Don't look at me like that. So I *lied* . . . a little. I never actually said they were mine."

"Why in the world would you do that?"

"Sympathy, I guess." She rolled her eyes. "They're not brats—at least not most of the time. I just wish I knew what I'd done wrong."

"Well, let's see." Did she really needed me to spell out how crude it was to temporarily adopt children to win the sympathy vote?

"I just knew those kids would push me right up to the top."

No longer shocked, I was downright disgusted. But I wasn't about to share my true feelings with this possible suspect when an investigation was under way. "What time did you start your preparations?" I asked, treading lightly.

"Is that a trick question? Nine o'clock, like everyone else."

"Sorry. It's our first time hosting a chili cook-off and I need some feedback."

Her gaze narrowed.

"Everyone was supposed to start at eight, but with Lucky's death and all, I figured some folks got distracted."

"Not me. I was glad to see the end of the old coot."

"The arrival of the deputies didn't wake up you and the kids?"

"These guys are up every day at six, rain or shine." She glanced to her left and then her right. "Speaking of kids."

"Did you find any time to yourself this weekend?" Had she woken earlier than her borrowed offspring and wandered out onto the fairgrounds, perhaps in the direction of Lucky's tent?

"I run every morning at five, kids or no kids. That's my me time. Look, I gotta go find them before we end up in the ER on the way out of town."

I watched her go. Then I circled the tent just in case she'd lied about Elliot and his whereabouts. We found his open-air cage, but there was no sign of the green iguana. We moved on.

I tasted two traditional chili samples and one chili verde before I came across Russell and his feline friends.

"Howdy," I called, determined to get to the bottom of this murder, if indeed that's what the tragic event of the day actually was.

"Howdy, yourself." He was sitting outside his tent, the two cats in a large cage behind him. "Name your poison."

I had a bit of room left in a corner of my belly, but with chili one has to be careful. "Salsa and chips, please."

He glanced at Lenny.

"Yip."

"Polite dog, as far as canines go."

"Yip."

"Don't push it," said the tall giant of a man.

"You know my family organized this event?"

"That so?"

"I'm conducting an informal survey on how to improve for next year."

"Go right ahead, but I don't see as how you can improve on a murder."

"Right." Smart aleck.

He piled a plate full of chips and handed me a cup of salsa. "Want something to drink with that?"

"Dr Pepper?" A Texan can never get her fill of the world's best carbonated beverage, especially when paired with spicy Tex-Mex.

"Coming right up."

"Did you see anything suspicious this morning?" I decided to come right out with it.

"No, but I saw that woman with the kids jogging like a javelina with a hangover."

I paused, distracted by the image of a small wild boar weaving through the brush, landing in a bed of cacti, and passing out.

Russell misjudged my silence for disapproval. "I don't mean nothing by it. Want some chili to go with that measly helping of salsa?"

"No, thank you. And if it's so measly why did you serve it to me in a small cup?"

He grinned. "Business is business, as they say in Big D."

"Were you jogging as well?" I avoided staring at his girth.

"Yip."

"Have a chip." He threw a chip at Lenny, but I intercepted it with my foot and ground it into teensy-weensy pieces.

"Choking my dog isn't on the menu."

"Yip." Lenny lapped up the small pieces without incident.

"Jogging?"

Russell patted his stomach. "As you can tell, I don't jog. But I do like to stretch my legs every morning around five thirty."

Which would have given him just enough time to bean Lucky with an iron skillet and drop a stun gun in his chili. That stun gun was a puzzle.

"Industrious," I muttered.

He lowered himself into a camping chair and took a swig of the beer that'd been in the cup holder. "Nah. I can't sleep like I used to, my legs get restless."

"What about your wife?" It was a shot in the dark.

"What wife?" His smile was a bit too familiar.

"You know," I shook my head. "The one that called you *hon* at the reception last night."

Russell's lips thinned. "What about her?"

My shot in the dark had hit the bullseye. "Did she see anything suspicious?"

"Just the inside of her eyelids. She could sleep through a tornado, even if it took the roof off and her bed with it."

I sighed. "Poor Lucky. At least he died doing something he loved."

"Humph. Don't feel sorry for him. He did what he loved every day of his life."

"Yip."

"What was that?"

"Made people's lives miserable."

"That's a bit harsh."

"I'm not going to sugarcoat it. He was a mean son of a biscuit eater. All those years in charge at Texas Power. That man had enemies."

Lucky had to have worked at the utility company at the same time as Bridget's father. It was odd neither one of them mentioned it earlier. "You worked for him?"

He shrugged. "Might have. Heck, yeah, sorry to say, I did."

"Why enter if you suspected he'd be here?"

"That's it, don't you see? Those of us that worked for him and suffered under his petty tyrannical moods, we compete to beat him at the thing he loves most."

I studied the man and his long gray braids. He didn't appear to be overly passionate in his hatred toward Lucky.

"When did you work for him?"

"Ten years ago."

"Did he fire you too?"

"I quit. No matter what he told folks."

I'd reached the far corner of my stomach. It was quit eating or burst. "Want the rest of these?" I asked, offering him my chips.

"Trash can's over there."

I turned to leave and he called me back. "Wait. I did see something suspicious."

With an effort, I kept my face blank. "What's that?"

"Whip coming out of Lucky's tent."

"When was that? Five thirty?"

He scratched his head—quite the performer. "Not my first time around the fairgrounds, but my second. I'd guess that was closer to five forty-five."

"I'll make a note."

"Hey."

I turned around once again. "Yes, sir?"

"Make a note to make the prizes bigger. Plenty of folks are still hurting after Texas Power laid them off a few years back."

"Will do."

I finally decided that Lightfoot had left the premises without telling me. There was no sign of him. I was on the way to the Prius—for sure this time—when I spotted Whip loading supplies into the back of his minivan.

Even though Lightfoot had questioned him, what would it hurt for me to toss a few innocent questions about the contest his way?

"Need any help?"

"Yip."

Whip pasted on a smile, but I hadn't missed the distress in his reaction. "I only have one more load."

"Leaving already? Didn't you win a ribbon?"

"Yeah. Second place in the salsa verde." He had a large black duffel bag in one hand and the trunk lid in the other. With his foot, he was kicking the duffel into the back for all he was worth, but that cargo section was so full he could've set up his own flea market.

"You're not taking any of Lucky's things, are you?"

He gave one last shove with his foot and slammed the trunk closed. "Why would I do that?" he asked, refusing to meet my eye.

"You didn't find Lucky's iron skillet?"

His jaw muscles clenched. "I'll have you know I packed *my* iron skillet, Miss Martinez."

"Callahan."

"Whoever you are. Not Lucky's, but mine."

"Where do you think his iron skillet ran off to? Could he have left it at home?"

Glancing to his right and his left, he stepped closer. "He'd sooner leave his jockey shorts. That skillet was his lucky charm."

"Maybe he loaned it to you, and you just forgot."

He frowned. "Shoot, he'd never let anyone borrow it, not even me."

I tried another tack. "I wanted to ask how we can improve our contest next year."

"As long as you don't have another murder, you should be fine and dandy."

"Funny. Did you see anything or anyone out of place this morning when you first stepped outside your tent?"

"Who said I slept in my tent?" He backed away, his elephantine ears turning red.

"Isn't that what you said to Detective Lightfoot earlier?" I was obviously bluffing, but I was trying to rattle his cage. In fact, I remembered quite well that he'd slept in his Apache camper.

His countenance cleared. "Oh, sure." He tried a smile. "Out of place. Hmm, well, I think I saw a couple of people milling around."

"Who was that? Did you recognize them?"

"A dark-haired woman was jogging, a regular Nosy Nell."

"How's that?"

"Until she noticed me, she was peeking in tents and other people's shelters."

"Sabotage?"

He shrugged and pushed a lank hair out of his face. "Not that I could see, but very curious."

"Was there anyone else?"

"Just Russell stretching his legs."

"Did you talk to him?"

"No. He was too fast for me. Didn't meet my eye."

"Not a Nosy Neil, then?"

"Heck no, minding his own business." He slammed the back door of the minivan and locked it with his remote. "I've got one more load that's not going to carry itself." Without another word, he hurried off toward his tent.

"Oh, Whip?"

He turned, an angry, impatient look on his face. "Did Lightfoot give you permission to leave town?"

Without replying, he stomped off.

Chapter 9

Break-In at Pinyon Pawn

I retreated only as far as the quiet interior of the Prius. It was nearly impossible for me to blow off my family responsibilities when it came down to it—Uncle Eddie being my adopted father, for all intents and purposes. After a few seconds it became clear the sun was too bright, and though exhausted, my mind was too full of murder and mayhem.

I began to write down the last of my observations.

My editor's tool for helping me move up the journalistic ladder, the police scanner, was staring at me. It was perched on the passenger seat, light blinking. I waited for something to happen, but other than a loud crackling sound every few seconds, nada.

"Barnes." The crackle became words. Tense. A female dispatcher.

"Go ahead." He sounded as if he was chewing.

"What's your twenty?"

"Round Robin." That time I heard a distinct swallowing sound.

"There's a 10-15 at 203 Pinyon Street."

"Oh. Sheriff on his way?"

"Negatory, good buddy. Sheriff's taking a stand."

I'd heard a rumor that Wallace was on a hunting trip—which would explain the reference to *taking a stand*. Only it wasn't deer hunting season. Or maybe I was wrong.

"I'm on my way." Barnes was excited, by the sound of his voice, anxious to be first on the scene.

"Roger that." I'd warrant the dispatcher was supposed to stay neutral in case folks—like me—were listening in, but I could hear the laughter in her voice.

I was guessing that a certain detective was listening in, unwilling to reveal his whereabouts especially if he was in close proximity to Pinyon Street. The only two businesses I could recount in that location were Pinyon Pawn and Trail Head Bail Bonds. Either business seemed a likely place for a robbery.

In the blink of a gecko's eyelash, I was driving the Prius, two wheels on the ground every time I took a curve. How could I get access to the scene? Would they toss me out on my proverbial ear? In the back of my mind, I considered the upcoming edition of the *Broken Boot Bugle*. Today was Friday, which meant I'd missed the deadline for Sunday's edition. Wednesday's paper was going to be a real doozy, chock-full of stories on Cinco de Mayo, the chili cook-off, and now a burglary.

At least I wouldn't have to fight the likes of Hillary Sloan-Rawlings for this story. Sumter Major's loan of the police scanner was proof of his intention to groom me for the crime beat. I had to smile. The Broken Boot crime beat was as dangerous as a prairie dog parade, but it was mine.

The block was short. I could see a white and black SUV at the far end of the street. Couldn't see the tag, but the cleanliness of it and the glossy shine made me think it was

Lightfoot's. On my end of the street only one cruiser had pulled across the road. In a high-speed chase, the bad guys would roll up on the sidewalk and easily evade Deputy Barnes's car straddling the middle of the street.

Which meant there were no bad guys on the scene.

I parked at the end of the block. From my car I could now see Barnes standing in the doorway of the establishment, his head turned in my direction. As if I hadn't seen him, I turned away, walked away from him and the corner—which I rounded until I came to the alley that ran behind the street. When I approached the back of the business, I discovered a sign at the back door. PINYON PAWN. ACCEPTING GUNS AND AMMO ONLY ON THURSDAYS. NO ANIMAL CAGES OR KENNELS.

No sign of Barnes from this angle. I approached the door and slowly looked inside.

I didn't step any farther because my way was blocked. If I kicked any of the debris with my foot, I'd be disturbing the crime scene. So I soaked it all up with my eyes. From my shoulder bag, I retrieved my notebook and pen.

There were items scattered on the floor from the back door, throughout the main room, and all the way to the front door, clearly visible, as the place was rather small.

Items that appeared to me to have very little value: record albums, a baby seat, a CD player, a tricycle, and two girls' bikes with baskets. Shelves were turned over, and I realized the item I'd been staring at for the last few seconds was the cash register. I swallowed back a nasty taste. This was someone's livelihood scattered across the floor like so much trash. I blinked back emotion. Was there anything left to sell that wasn't damaged or destroyed?

Suddenly the front door opened, and I jumped back into the alley. I pressed my ear to the outside of the door.

"No sign of forced entry." The voice belonged to Barnes.

He must be on the phone. "I'd say they used a crowbar or a meat cleaver." He broke into delighted laughter at his own wit. "Yes, sir." He spoke with sudden deference and seriousness. Someone on the other end hadn't found his laughter well suited to the situation.

I ventured to peek around the doorway. Barnes's back was to me as he surveyed the room. "A lot of broken merchandise: radios, televisions, baby stuff." There was a pause. "No, sir. I can't tell what's missing. If you were to ask me, which I guess is what you're doing, I'd say it was vandalism—everything appears to be on the floor."

"Don't think about disturbing my crime scene."

"Ahggg." I jumped backwards, thunked into Lightfoot's chest, thwacked his chin with the back of my head, and landed on his boots.

"Huh." The air whooshed from his lungs. "Watch out!" Before I could permanently change his voice from bass to tenor, he grabbed me by the arms, lifted me off his feet, and set me down to one side. "Are you out of your mind, woman?"

My heart was racing. "Only on Fridays." I laughed. "Oops, guess today's Friday, isn't it?"

"Who tipped you off?" He retrieved his hat from the weeds. "And don't give me your Spidey senses bullcrap."

The blood rushed to my cheeks. Lightfoot didn't swear, at least not in front of me. For him to use even a mild expletive meant I'd done some damage. "Sorry about that." I gestured helplessly. "You okay?"

He began to slap his Stetson against the side of his leg. "I might ask you the same thing." A bit of dirt and a bird feather fell to the ground. He frowned, a deep line appearing between his pitch-black eyes. "I'm waiting."

While I considered my answer choices, I straightened my brunette braid so that it lay over my left shoulder and smoothed the bottom of my chili pepper red Milagro golf shirt.

His eyes narrowed, too close to a glare for comfort.

"I heard it in passing." I shrugged. "You know how gossip travels in this town."

Raven brows lifted for a second and then plummeted, giving him the expression of an angry bull.

"I bet she heard it from Maria." Barnes swaggered out the door, thumbs in his belt. He glanced from me to Lightfoot and shook his head in disgust. "You know, the wind?"

"No," I said.

He puffed out his chest, pulled in a lungful of air, and warbled the familiar lyrics in a high tenor that matched his fair coloring.

I grinned. "Yeah, I've heard it—just wanted to see if you'd sing it."

His freckled complexion reddened. "What are you doing here?" He shot a glance at Lightfoot." You ain't supposed to be at our crime scene."

I stared around him. "What crime?" A large hand clamped onto my shoulder.

"Walk behind us, got it? You touch so much as a loose hair on your shirt, you're out on the seat of your Wranglers."

I stepped out of Lightfoot's grasp, chin tucked, trying for cowed and intimidated. "Yes, sir. Not even to swat a scorpion from your hat."

One side of Lightfoot's mouth twitched. "Ten paces behind Barnes. Got it?" He stepped around me and gestured for Barnes to follow.

"Aye, aye, Captain."

"What is it with you and seamen?" Lightfoot murmured.

Pulling his hat down over his eyes, Barnes gave me a steely-eyed glare and turned abruptly away.

Once they'd entered the store, I followed and halted just inside the doorway.

"You call the owner?" On the far side of the room, Lightfoot lowered himself onto his haunches, the better to stare directly into the front door's damaged lock.

Barnes cast me a suspicious look. "Just got off the phone with her."

"Who's *she*?" I resisted the urge to open my notebook.

Lightfoot stood. "Bubba's mama."

Bubba owned the BBQ joint of the same name. His mama, Mrs. McAllen, was a tough old bird. She was sweet as pecan pie around town, but I noticed that her six-foot-four-inch son jumped whenever she looked at him cross-eyed.

Stepping over a toppled copper planter with a plastic rubber plant still inside, I discovered shelves and their contents scattered as if a twister had blown through on its way to Oklahoma.

A white blur caught my eye through the gated front window. A white Lincoln darted into a parking spot followed by a loud, metallic screech as the fender ground into the curb.

"I thought she lost her license when she took out Bubba's picture window." Barnes hurried outside to help the elderly woman from her car.

Lightfoot gave me a stern look. "Who told you about the break-in?"

My neck stiffened at his tone, so I took my time. "Let's see."

"Knock it off or you'll be wailing to that editor of yours about not getting your story." He caught my reaction. "Sumter Majors did this? What'd he do, give you one of his police scanners?" He threw back his head and groaned, then his gaze became hard as flint. "He did, didn't he?"

"Maybe."

Bubba's mama marched through the door on Barnes's arm, hissing and spitting like an alley cat on garbage day. "What in tarnation's going on?" She dropped the deputy's arm and straightened up as far as her rounded back would allow. Behind her glasses, I observed the shine of tears. With a purse of her lips, her head snapped in my direction. "What'd they do? Call for a dinner break?" She might be bent over from osteoporosis, but the bite in her voice demanded she be taken seriously.

"No, ma'am." I inched back toward the wall, hoping to disappear into the woodwork.

Lightfoot removed his hat and stepped between us. "Mrs. McAllen, do you keep an inventory of your goods?"

"I'm waiting on you to answer, girl."

Lightfoot lifted a brow and crossed his arms across his chest. "This ought to be good."

I gave him a look that would have frozen pond water. "Well, I'm an investigator."

Lightfoot's brow lowered, a bull ready to charge.

"Of sorts." I licked suddenly dry lips. "I'm investigating local crime for the *Bugle*."

She stepped closer and gave me a slow look from my boots to my braid. "The *Bugle* could use a good toot of young blood, if I do say so myself." After a glance at the notebook in my hand, she tottered off toward her office.

After Barnes and Lightfoot followed in her wake, I breathed a sigh. I was alone at last. I stood perfectly still, searching the floor and the room for a pattern to the clutter. Wasn't that what they did on television? Looked for clues, a pattern to things that would reveal something about the criminal's psyche? I opened my notebook and began to note the items on the floor, the ones left untouched, and those utterly destroyed. My heart sickened at the hours of work it would take to put Pinyon Pawn back together. How many employees did she have? I caught myself just as I started to kneel down and begin picking up the scattered items. It was a crime scene after all, no touching allowed. I did permit my gaze to land on first one thing and then another, and then I walked back to the open front door to view the place from a slightly different perspective.

"What do you see?"

I jumped *again*. "How do you always do that?"

Lightfoot watched me from the doorway to Mrs. McAllen's office. "Practice." A smile played at his mouth.

"Is that your superpower? Walking on light feet?"

"What do you think?"

"I think it's a Native American thing. Your name *is* Lightfoot." Sometimes I say stupid things.

His eyes narrowed, searching my face for signs of ridicule. He must have decided I was sincere—in my own ditzy way. "Lightfoot is English Welsh."

"Shut. Up." Other times I'm just dumber than a doornail. "You're Native American and . . . you walk lightly."

Glancing around the room, he removed his own notepad from his breast pocket and his usual stub of a pencil. "Look it up. Lightfoots immigrated. No Native blood."

I moved closer, hoping to sneak a peek at his writing. I'd expected a list of items, but instead I spied a list of adjectives. "You can't deny you have Native American blood."

"Are you so sure I'm not Mexican?"

"Yes." I studied his sharp cheekbones and crossed my fingers. "Why else would you permit Senora Mari to call you *Indian*?"

After a pregnant pause, he gave a quick nod. "My father is three-quarters because his father's father was a Lightfoot." He held up a hand to stall my interruption. "And he was three-quarters as well."

Something familiar stirred in my memory. "Your parents live in Albuquerque, right?"

"Yes, but closer to the Mescalero Apache Res."

In the other room, I could hear Bubba's mama giving an account to Deputy Barnes of what was missing and where things should be.

"Crowbar, right?" I pointed to the gouge in the front door.

"Close enough." Pencil poised above his notepad, he turned. "What's missing, to your eyes?"

Little butterflies of happiness started to soar in my belly. Unless I had lost all my senses at the fairgrounds, Detective Lightfoot was asking for my opinion. "There's not a lot of stereo equipment out here." He didn't write that down.

What had I missed?

"Lightfoot." Barnes's voice held urgency.

"Guns and jewelry." The words exploded from my mouth before the freckle-faced deputy could steal my thunder.

"Bingo."

"She says the gun safe is missing."

With a slight nod in my direction, Lightfoot pocketed his notepad and pencil. "What about her jewelry?"

"We're headed that way. Want to come?"

We followed Barnes and Mrs. Bubba to a back room that held a microwave, fridge, and metal cabinet. The older woman grabbed ahold of the small black fridge and started to pull. She was surprisingly strong and had inched the thing across the faux wood linoleum before Lightfoot and Barnes jumped in to help. "No need," she insisted. She pushed Barnes out of the way, walked to the space behind the fridge, and opened a panel in the wall. Made of plywood, the hard outer surface appeared to be the same color as the bisque drywall, but on closer inspection, it was plywood painted the same color. She pried open a small door with her fingernail and removed a metal cashier's box from the recess.

Barnes and Lightfoot exchanged glances above her head.

Slowly she placed the box on a nearby Formica table. From inside the neckline of her blouse, she withdrew a slender gold chain that bore a minuscule key. Inside the unassuming container were pearls, topaz, jade, gold chains, and diamond wedding rings. Before she closed and locked the box once again, I could've sworn I spotted what appeared to be a championship ring, glittering with diamonds.

"Is anything missing?" Lightfoot's voice was firm and steady.

"No." She grabbed the fingers of her other hand. "But you gotta get my weapons back. They're my bread and butter."

Only in Texas.

"What was in the gun safe besides guns?" Barnes placed his hand on his holster.

Her mouth turned down like a horseshoe. "Not just guns. Weapons, son. High-caliber, military-grade, police-issue weapons. Every kind."

"Show me your license to sell firearms."

With a grunt, she removed the support stocking on her right foot and handed Lightfoot a worn and folded bit of paper. "Here you go."

"Why do you keep it in your stocking?" Barnes asked.

"'Cause it falls out of my shoe otherwise."

Gingerly, Lightfoot attempted to unfold the license using only his fingertips.

"Mrs. McAllen?" I chuckled at her dry sense of humor.

"Yes, dear?" Her eyes were filled with mirth.

"You wouldn't happen to be missing a stun gun from your gun safe, would you?"

She knit her brow for a moment. "Why, honey, I think you're right. I knew there was something else missing, but I just couldn't put my finger on it."

"How many stun guns did you own?"

She tilted her head to stare at the ceiling. "I want to say there were three, but I could be wrong." With a frown, she turned to Lightfoot and stared pointedly at his notepad. "Four. I'm missing four stun guns."

"Not any chance you placed them somewhere else?" I asked as Barnes and Lightfoot exchanged a glance.

"No." She raised her chin. "I don't keep those out for the public to see. If someone asks me . . ." She bit her lip. "Uh, well. Someone did ask about a Taser earlier this week, but it wasn't a stun gun."

"Who was it?" I asked softly.

"It didn't register right away because they're not the same—even though most people think so." Mrs. McAllen worried her wedding rings for a spell.

"Who asked?"

"I don't know who it was." She swallowed again. "Someone called and spoke to my son."

"Can't see how he has time to work over here and manage Bubba's BBQ," Barnes said.

"I wasn't feeling too chipper on Monday so I stayed home." She glanced at me for support. "When that happens I forward the phone here over to the BBQ so he can handle it."

"You get many calls, Mrs. McAllen?" Lightfoot asked.

"Once or twice a day, but one is always Bubba, checking in on me."

"Someone called about a stun gun on Monday?" I prompted.

"Yes." She nodded, eager to pick up the thread. "Bubba called to see if I had a Taser in stock. I told him *no*."

Lightfoot tapped his pencil against his notepad. "Man or woman, who called?"

"I'm sorry. You'll have to ask Bubba. He'd remember." She smiled proudly.

"I'll give him a call, Detective." Barnes unclipped his phone from his belt.

"Start dusting for prints. I'll call him."

"Oh, do you really have to get that dust all over everything?" The older woman's lips pursed.

"We had a suspicious death at the fairgrounds today." Lightfoot cleared his phone screen. "What's Bubba's number?"

"Oh no. You would ask me that."

Mrs. McAllen joined the majority of cell phone users by pulling out her cell phone to search for her own son's phone number. After an excruciating number of minutes, trying in vain to find Bubba's number without her glasses, she eventually found the rest of her personal contacts—with the help of her dollar store readers—and rattled off the digits.

With a nod at me, Lightfoot stepped out to place his call.

I found a folding chair and helped her into it. "What is the difference between a Taser and a stun gun, Mrs. McAllen?"

"You know those weapons you see the police using on that reality show?"

I nodded, but I was clueless.

"Those are Tasers. They shoot probes twenty-two feet, and the civilian ones are good for fifteen feet."

"Wow." I suddenly had a vivid image of Lucky being shot by a Taser from the opening of his tent.

"Yes, ma'am." Her eyes grew wide. "Poor criminals flop around like fish."

I could picture the dead chili cook's upper torso. "Do they leave marks?"

She leaned forward, a storyteller sharing a ghastly tale in the night. "They do. Two marks close together like a snake." She held up her fingers. "One to two inches long."

Had Ellis found marks on Lucky at the lab? "And a stun gun?"

"Well, you have to be in close range to use one, for starters. Up close and personal."

"It doesn't shoot these . . . probes?"

"No. You have to hold it against an attacker's body." She reached into the mini fridge and pulled out an orange Fanta. "Would you like a cold beverage, hon?"

I was tempted by the cool, neon orange color, but I was wired enough. "No, thank you. I can't imagine holding a stun gun against a violent attacker. Sounds dicey."

"Right." Attached to the side of the fridge was an antique-looking bottle opener. With a surprisingly strong motion, she whipped the bottle top off and sent it flying. "You would need to be strong and agile." She waved an arm down her body. "Which I am not."

"Does a stun gun leave marks?"

"According to an article in the *Austin Gazette*, a stun gun doesn't always leave marks, and it won't knock someone unconscious."

"No?" I digested her remark slowly. Part of my brain insisted the stun gun was an essential element in the death of Lucky Straw.

"It definitely leaves marks sometimes because I saw a young man with marks on his arm that he said were caused by a stun gun."

"Where was this?"

"On that reality show with the cops and the fugitives."

"Fugitives?"

"Mostly they're drunk folks who are driving under the influence. Those shows are just a ploy to raise money for police pensions, if you ask me."

"More likely the money goes to operating budgets." It wasn't hard to remember Lucky's freckled chest covered with white curly hair. If there had been any marks, I was too rattled to see them.

"If the victim is squirming or trying to get away, it would leave multiple marks."

I studied her sweet, motherly face. "Why are you interested in those cop shows, Mrs. McAllen?"

She glanced at the walls and the floor, searching for an answer. "I sell weapons here, but I don't know anything about them. Makes me curious as to why folks buy them and why they're in such an all-fired hurry to get rid of them."

"There must be all kinds of laws you have to follow." I didn't have any doubt Mrs. McAllen knew more about the weapons she sold than she was letting on. What was interesting was why she didn't want us to know.

"Sure. But if someone tells me they want to buy or sell a gun, they have to deal with Bubba."

"He comes over here just for that?" Then I remembered the sign. "Only on Thursdays."

"Yes, ma'am. Folks have to plan ahead if they expect us to deal with something that could endanger us or our customers."

I wanted to laugh at her phraseology, but it wasn't exactly humorous. The word *endanger* stuck out like lips on a chicken. Someone had stolen the weapons from Pinyon Pawn without her knowledge. Were they still in the area, preparing to wreak havoc on our community? Had they killed Lucky, though his body had shown no sign of struggle? Or moved on to another county to lie in wait for law enforcement or to attack another innocent victim?

I stepped outside and found Lightfoot disconnecting his call. He flicked me a look as he made a note. "Either a man with a high voice or a woman with a low voice on steroids. Bubba's words, not mine."

"How often do you see a break-in like this one?" I asked.

He paused to remove his cowboy hat and smooth his hair back into his ponytail. "Goes in spurts until you catch the perpetrator."

"Once a month? Once a year? Every six months?"

He watched me with amusement. "You need a ride?"

I debated. If I rode with him, I could continue to pick his brain. However, if I drove my own car he might be called away or his usual reserve might slam back into place.

"Sure." Anthony or Uncle Eddie would readily give me a ride back to my car.

"How often do break-ins occur in our county?" I asked as he held open the passenger door of the SUV.

He waited to reply until he sat behind the wheel. "I'd say," with a practiced motion, he started the SUV and threw it in reverse, "every three months on average."

I managed to pull the passenger door shut by throwing my entire body weight into it. "What's the next step when this happens?"

With a wave to Barnes, he continued, "Check the wire for similar robberies, first in the neighboring counties—"

"And then throughout the state?" I asked.

"Yes. We run the prints and the MO. Usually we find a connection."

I studied him while he studied the road. In losing his uniform, he'd lost a good portion of his stodginess. "Almost immediately?" I asked just to keep the conversation going.

He threw me an exasperated look. "What did I tell you about TV detectives?" We were blocks away from Main Street, but the traffic had slowed to a crawl.

"They're more handsome and intelligent than real detectives?" I smiled sweetly.

We turned onto Main Street, driving under a street-wide banner declaring BROKEN BOOT'S CINCO DE MAYO, THE FUN FIESTA!

"So you're basically saying criminals are stupid?" I teased.

His brow furrowed. "*Stupid*'s not the word I would use." With deep consideration, he searched for the perfect word.

"Too harsh?"

We'd stopped at a light. An elderly couple as similar as twins with brown skin and dark hair threaded with silver crossed the street in front of us. Lightfoot's gaze followed them until they made it safely to the other side.

"Do your parents ever come to see you?"

He glanced at the light, but though the light turned green, the traffic was backed up into the intersection. "Here?"

I shook my head in mock frustration. "Where else?"

He hesitated for so long I thought he wasn't going to answer. "Once. I usually go to see them during my vacation."

"When was that?" I asked softly, yearning to coax more information out of him.

"A couple of years ago." Something in his face changed with the admission. He gave me a suspicious look as if I already knew the answer. "When I was serious about someone I was dating."

"Right. You mentioned her to Senora Mari when we rode to the station together that time when Anthony was in jail."

He smiled. "That was the first time the senora called me an Indian."

"I'm still embarrassed when I think about it."

"Lenna. Her name was Lenna."

"What happened?" I asked softly.

"She preferred New Mexico, and her career there." The light changed again, and this time we continued toward the gazebo and the band.

"I'm sorry." And I was. Couldn't anyone stay together? Was it too much to ask for a betrothed to stay the course?

Suddenly he smiled, showing all his teeth, and the effect was amazing. "I'm not. Sometimes life gives you lemons, and other times it gives you tamales."

Chapter 10

~~~~~~

Senora Mari's Dream

I woke with a start, the smell of chili and cheddar wafting through my brain.

Senora Mari placed her child-sized hand over my mouth. "Don't scream. It's me."

My pulse raced until my sleep-fogged brain recognized my *abuela*, who had once again invaded my privacy in my own home. "Too late," I said in a muffled voice.

I sat up against the carved mesquite wood headboard and her hand fell away.

She tossed Lenny lightly to the floor and perched in his place on the edge of the bed. "I have something to tell you."

"Yip, yip, yip."

I groaned. "You said it, Lenster."

"Shh!" She reached down and stroked his head.

In spite of my *abuela*'s proclaimed animosity toward my Chi friend, I'd received reports she was coming around. I reached around her and placed him in my lap. "He doesn't like to be supplanted." I kissed his pointy head.

She gestured toward his doggie bed that both looked and smelled like a week-old crunchy beef taco. "That is his home. Plant him there. I have something important."

I was stalling because I could guess what her big news would turn out to be. "You're a regular dream factory these days, *Abuela*." I softened my sarcasm by adding my version of a Spanish accent to the endearment.

She pursed her lips. "You have been home for a year now and your accent is still *insuficiente*."

"True." My comprehension of Spanish was much better than my ability to speak it. "Tell me your dream. Did you see someone die in this one?" I didn't know how Lucky Straw met his maker, but inquiring minds needed to know.

"Do not make fun." She lifted her chin.

"I'm not. I need a lead and you're the closest thing I've got." Lenny turned around in my lap to face her, and began licking her skirt. She was already dressed for the parade and wore the bright multi-tiered skirt with lace trim. Lenny seemed to think the lace was meant to be a doggie treat—if he could only work it off the skirt with this tongue.

"I was in a field of flowers."

"Yip."

"Shh." Senora Mari gave his nose a tap.

"We want to know what kind of flowers."

"Flowers from the moon." She raised her brows, daring me to contradict.

I bit the inside of my cheek instead.

"Yip."

"Shh, dog. Shh." This time she gave him three quick taps to the nose.

"He's just asking what kind of flowers grow on the moon." I slipped down beneath the covers. If she was going to string us along from detail to detail, I was going to rest while she did it.

With a shake of her head, she continued. "Don't look at me as if I am loco. I know flowers do not grow on the moon. But in my dream, there were bluebonnets."

"What do you think that means?"

Lenny yawned.

"I also saw a lightning bolt."

I bolted upright in bed. "On the surface, on a bluebonnet, where?"

"Yip." Lenny jumped into Senora Mari's lap.

Instead of handing him back, she ran a hand slowly from his head to his tail as she considered her answer. "It was electric blue, and it hung in the sky."

"What do you think *that* means?"

Again she slowly drew her hand down Lenny's back. "He's gained weight."

"*Someone's* feeding him scraps?"

She shrugged. "I feed him nothing."

"Forget I mentioned it." She might pretend he was the biggest nuisance on earth, but Carlos told me he'd caught her on more than one occasion feeding him steak bones. "What do you think the blue flowers and lightning bolt represent?"

Lenny sensed she was in a giving mood and rolled over to expose his white belly.

"I have thought about that very thing all morning while you lay in this bed." She did not deny him his pleasure. As his leg begin to jump in response, the corners of her mouth turned up into a rare smile. "Dead people turn blue, *si*?"

"I guess." I swallowed, envisioning a room full of dead people, lying on metal gurneys, naked and blue.

"I believe this to be true." She lifted her palms to the ceiling. "Blue is death and lightning is power."

"So Lucky experienced death by power . . . electricity?"

Her eyes grew wide. "Perhaps it means a misuse of power, like that of a tyrant or dictator." She patted Lenny's stomach and withdrew her hand.

"No, no. Let's go back to misuse of electrical power."

She stood and heaved a sigh. "I cannot change the signs in my dream to fit your ideas. It is death by dictator." Brushing down her skirt, she moved to the door. "Get up or we'll be late."

"Yip, yip." Lenny jumped lightly to the floor.

"You see, your little friend agrees with me. We will be on time." She raised her index finger into the air dramatically. "The future of ballet *folklórico* in Broken Boot and all of Big Bend County depends on us." She lowered her finger and aimed it at me. "Don't forget his costume."

As she marched for the door, I made up the bed. "She didn't mention Lucky, did she?"

"Yip."

"But if blue is dead, and Lucky's dead, I still think her dream means death." I took my skirt and blouse out of the closet. I rolled my eyes. "Or power?"

"Yip," Lenny said in agreement.

"Right. Lucky's dead to begin with. We can all agree that's true."

With his tail wagging a million times a minute, Lenny ran to the dresser and placed his front paws on the drawer that held his *folklórico* costume.

"Wait a minute, senor." I wriggled out of my pajamas and tossed them into the hamper. "One thing is clear." I stepped into my skirt and buttoned my blouse. "You and I need a home of our own that's harder to get to."

"Yip, yip."

"Or a new lock. How's a girl to have any privacy?"

* * *

Thirty minutes later, we were all up early having our usual cup of coffee and morning chat—only it was two hours earlier, due to the parade. "You're telling me that woman pretended to have three children in order to win, but she didn't win?" Uncle Eddie was reading his paper and gathering only the smallest threads of the conversation.

"No, hon," Aunt Linda said. "Those were actually her kids. She just said that to be ornery."

"How did you ferret that out of her?" My aunt had a way about her that brooked no nonsense.

She gave me a knowing smile. "The little girl told me."

I laughed, which caused Uncle Eddie to look up in bemusement at the two of us.

Senora Mari entered from the kitchen, marched over to her son, and slid a plate of huevos rancheros in front of him. "Three children is a blessing."

I watched my *abuela* carefully, but she didn't glance at my Aunt Linda after her pronouncement. Though often salty, she would never insult my aunt's inability to have children. In my *abuela*'s own life, she had known the sting of having only one child in a culture that applauded big families.

"Yes, *Mamá*." The sunny-side egg smiled at Uncle Eddie from the small cast-iron skillet. The aroma of fresh salsa, leftover refrieds, cheese, and onions woke my sleepy brain and had my taste buds calling, *Me, me, me.*

"And what about your favorite reporter? May I too have some, *Abuela? Por favor?*"

"No." She gave me the onceover. "You must fit in your skirt in one hour. If you eat breakfast, you'll pop out of it."

"She's right." Aunt Linda stole a bit of crumbled bacon from her husband's savory mixture. "The salt in the bacon will make your stomach swell. If you'd lost that fifteen pounds you've been going on about, you wouldn't have to worry about a few eggs and beans this morning."

I paused until Senora Mari had all but disappeared through the swinging kitchen door. "I could eat a smaller and healthier portion, the way you fix them." Aunt Linda enjoyed playing with the healthy side of Tex-Mex: black beans, baked eggs, fresh pico de gallo, and avocado.

"I heard that." Senora Mari swung around like a bull about to charge. "You cannot eat the *healthy* ones either, missy. You don't know when to stop."

My mouth dropped open. "Since when?"

"What I want to know is, why didn't Whip's chili win if he and Lucky were such a dynamic duo?" Uncle Eddie flipped to page two. He always did his best to end the familiar argument between his health-conscious wife and his traditional mother.

"That's the answer, isn't it?" I said. "He couldn't muster the know-how without Lucky. And imagine, he'd suffered a terrible trauma." I hadn't actually tried Whip's entry. Maybe my uncle was right.

The cowbell clanged and Lightfoot and Ryan walked in together. The two men were roughly the same height, with Ryan edging out the older man by a couple of inches. Lightfoot wore his now-familiar detective's uniform of blazer, pressed jeans, button-down shirt, bolo tie, and a tan Stetson over his ebony hair and short ponytail. Ryan, though, had dressed for the football field: khaki shorts, West Texas University coach's golf shirt, and a baseball cap over his short, brown, wavy hair. Both familiar faces wore their typical smile of greeting, Ryan's a wide schoolboy grin and Lightfoot's a small lift at the corners of his mouth.

"Yip." Lenny spun around, showing off his *folklórico*

costume of white satin pants and jacket. The white embroidered sombrero would be added at the last minute.

"Hey, Lenster. Love the costume." Ryan picked up my canine sidekick and rubbed him behind the ears.

"Morning, Detective." Uncle Eddie stood and tossed his paper onto the bar. "What's the news on your investigation?"

Ryan rounded on Senora Mari and gave her a hug. He was the only one who could get away with it outside of our family. "What is that fantastic smell?" Ryan asked with a grin.

"Would you like huevos rancheros, Coach Ryan?" She gave him an inviting smile.

"You betcha."

She eyed the detective's somber face for a moment. "I could make you some Texas Eggs, if you want."

"What's that?" Lightfoot asked politely.

"Don't mind her," I said. "It's sort of the same thing, but more cheese and fewer jalapeños."

He chuckled. "No, thank you, though I'm sure either one would be delicious."

"Can I get you some coffee?" Uncle Eddie asked.

"That's why I'm here," Lightfoot said with a smile.

"How do you take it?"

"Black," Lightfoot and I said in unison.

You could have heard a pin drop in the next room. Everyone was staring at the two of us as if we'd suddenly sprouted corn husks out of our ears.

"We appreciate you stopping by to give us an update." Aunt Linda gave Lightfoot a big smile. "Have you figured out whether or not Lucky Straw was murdered?"

"The JP's sending the body off today to the state lab. He's not ready to say it's a murder, but he did state Lucky died under suspicious circumstances."

With a glance at Lightfoot, Ryan walked over to my barstool. "Just stopped by to wish you good luck on your dancing today. Though you're so talented, you won't need it."

I opened my mouth to deflect the intimacy of his comment with something witty, but he interrupted.

"Uh-uh." He placed a finger on my lips. "Accept a compliment for a change. It won't hurt you." Gooseflesh immediately chased any comeback right out of my head and into the next county. Not to mention, my cheeks flamed with embarrassment. "What's going on this morning besides the big debut at the parade?" He ran a hand down Lenny's back.

"I was just about to ask Eddie if he had heard whether or not the town council was pleased with his chili extravaganza," Aunt Linda said.

Uncle Eddie handed Lightfoot a cup of coffee and climbed back onto his barstool. "Another dead body is all anyone's talking about." With a sigh, he dropped his gaze to his food.

"That may be true of the locals, but I met some folks from Arlington at Two Boots last night." Ryan clapped a hand on his friend's shoulder. "They were extremely pleased with your decision to restart after a short delay. You scored some points, Eddie."

"I hope the town council agrees, my friend."

"These huevos will make you big and strong." Senora Mari delivered Ryan's breakfast to the bar. If anyone could cheer up my uncle, it was his fellow coach.

When I looked up, Lightfoot caught my eye and gave a slight nod of his head in the direction of the front door. I followed him outside.

"You have something."

He nodded with a quick glance over his shoulder to make sure no one else had followed. "Pacemaker data shows an interruption around the time of Lucky's death."

"I hate to burst your bubble, but wouldn't it be interrupted if he died?"

He narrowed his eyes in disapproval. "No. Death is recorded in the data as termination. This was something in the programming of the pacemaker itself."

"No. Way. You're saying someone killed him by hacking his pacemaker?"

"Hold on." He raised a hand. "That would only happen in the movies."

"Is that where the stun gun comes in?"

"Not sure, but the serial number proves it was stolen from Pinyon Pawn."

"Could it have interrupted the pacemaker?"

"There's a one-in-one-thousand chance it could happen. The odd thing is that the data report from the pacemaker shows a programmed interruption."

"As in *planned*?" My heart beat faster.

He nodded. "I need to find another expert at the manufacturer who can tell me without getting all defensive what the report means by a 'programmed interruption' and if the stun gun could have caused the pacemaker to fail."

"What about electrocution?" I asked.

"You lost me."

"Remember the extension cords in his tent?"

He shook his head. "Forget it. There were no signs of electrical shock on his body."

The door opened and Ryan poked his head out.

"Hey, you, taking off?" I pasted on a smile and shot a glance at Lightfoot, who suddenly found the need to check his phone.

"Just enough time to do a couple of miles before the parade starts."

"You better get to it. You don't want to miss Lenny's big debut."

As Lightfoot continued to scroll through his messages, Ryan lifted my braid in his hand and let it fall. "Seems to me it's your big debut as well." Without warning, he gave me a brief hug. "Everyone's gonna shine, you included," he whispered in my ear. He stepped back, closed one eye, and aimed an imaginary pistol at Lightfoot. "Later, Lawman." With a satisfied grin, he took off.

I wanted to kick him. "What about the stun gun?" I asked.

Lightfoot waited until Ryan's Dodge Ram pulled onto Main Street and turned right at the light, headed in the direction of the university. "Ellis says there's no marks on the body consistent with a stun gun."

"Go figure," I muttered. "But Mrs. McAllen claims a stun gun doesn't always leave marks."

He cocked his head to the side. "No. You can't always *see* them if a body has freckles or lots of hair, but it always leaves marks."

"Let's say the perp surprises Lucky and zaps him with the stun gun, knowing in advance that Lucky's pacemaker's kaput."

Lightfoot studied the horizon, which meant he was actually considering my theory. "What about the blow to the head?"

"I haven't figured that part out yet."

He gave me a half smile. "Let me know when you do."

For Lightfoot to welcome my sleuthing, even in a backhanded way, was a bit of a surprise and a boost to my ego. "Sure thing. I'm going to have to scramble to write my article by tomorrow's deadline."

He frowned. "Keep your theories to a minimum. Don't want the killer to get spooked."

"When can I let my investigative journalism flag fly?" I kicked a nearby column and dust flew. "I'm still trying to prove myself to Majors, in case you forgot."

With a shake of his head, he turned to go. "Not sure what to say, Josie. Sheriff Wallace expects me to be an officer of the law first."

I watched him go, wishing I was a different sort—the kind who could walk the tightrope between following rules and bending them just enough to further my own career.

Chapter 11

The Cinco de Mayo Parade

That Saturday morning the sun shone bright as fool's gold on the rooftops along Main Street while Barnum and Hailey's and the other businesses on the east side of the street, remained in shadow. The cool morning air warmed as the glowing orb rose higher in the lavender blue sky. The old-fashioned lamps that the town council had installed, along with the cobbled stones of Main itself, added a homey, relaxing atmosphere. Flooded with tourists and locals from the three surrounding counties, Broken Boot's main drag resembled a Western-themed amusement park with a name like Durango or Winchester.

Dressed from head to toe in traditional *folklórico* costumes, the Martinez women maneuvered through the throng. We were quite a sight with our long braids, bright, colorful skirts, and black leather heels. Several people snapped pictures and a few young men whistled their approval as we snaked our way to the back of the parade lineup.

With five minutes to spare, we passed the Broken Boot Bears marching band—along with their award-winning color guard and drill team—and arrived at the white clapboard gazebo the town council erected each year to house the parade organizers. It sat squarely in the middle of Main, effectively blocking off traffic. Mayor Cogburn descended the gazebo steps, clipboard in hand. "Cutting it a bit fine, aren't we, ladies?"

Mrs. Cogburn pushed her way to the front of our troupe. "There'll be no pawing and snorting from you this morning, Mr. Mayor."

He opened his mouth to speak.

"Who was sawing logs all night because he refused to wear his nasal strips?" She turned to the rest of us. "How am I supposed to sleep, let alone wake up on time, with that ungodly racket giving me fits?"

Mayor Cogburn gave us a sheepish look over his readers and placed a check on his list. Squaring his shoulders, he removed a pocket watch from his leather vest. "Three minutes till showtime. Better get a move on."

"Where do we go exactly?" Aunt Linda moved closer, trying to sneak a look at his list.

"Number twenty-seven. Near the end."

"*¡Ay, Dios!*" Senora Mari muttered.

As one, we did an about-face and strutted off toward the end of the line, our colorful skirts swaying around us like a muster of peacocks.

"Toot." A '50s convertible honked politely for us to get out of the road. On the rear deck rode parade favorites like Miss Broken Boot, Miss Big Bend County, and Miss West Texas. Behind them in a red Corvette rode Hillary Sloan-Rawlings, third runner-up to Miss America and the bane of my existence.

Though we started out as friends at UT, I finally realized

that while I was working on *our* assignments, Hillary was working on only one thing—winning pageants. Years later when I returned home brokenhearted, minus my fiancé *and* my job, it was all a bit much to find she'd not only won a coveted faculty position at West Texas University, but she was dating my college sweetheart, Coach Ryan Prescott.

Hillary wiggled her fingers in my direction, and my bubble of parade-day bliss burst. I gave her a measly nod and a half smile in return. A tourist wearing a pink sombrero interrupted our exchange by asking the former Miss Broken Boot to sign her hat. I wanted to puke. If folks continued to fawn over the former beauty queens, I'd have the excruciating pleasure of watching Hillary ride in our annual parades for the rest of my life.

Next came the town council, sitting on bales of hay on a flatbed trailer in front of a sign that read: BROKEN BOOT'S CINCO DE MAYO, A FIESTA OF FUN!

As usual, children of all ages and their parents had festooned their bikes with green, red, and white ribbons to celebrate the fifth of May.

Senora Mari gestured to a Mexican flag hung above the entrance to Pecos Pete's bar. "In Mexico, no one celebrates the fifth of May. You know this."

"Yes, yes. You've told us three times this morning and four times yesterday." Aunt Linda waved frantically to those of us lagging behind to catch up with the rest.

"And I will say it again until someone explains it to me."

Patti Perez walked on Senora Mari's other side. "It's about Mexican independence." She ran her fingers across her brow, searching for the stud she usually wore there.

The older woman came to an abrupt halt. "Mexicans celebrate independence in September."

"They do?" Patti tugged on her synthetic black braids, checking for the umpteenth time they were hanging evenly.

I gave her a look. She knew darn well that Cinco de Mayo commemorated Mexico's resistance to French debt collectors.

Placing a gentle hand on Senora Mari's arm, I urged her forward, hoping to walk and talk. "What do you want explained, *Abuela*?"

"Why all the fuss?" She gestured to a small group of clowns on unicycles, inching their cycles forward and back to keep from falling to the cobblestones.

If memory served, we'd had the same discussion during last year's festivities. "To honor our Mexican heritage and to celebrate spring."

"Such a fuss over nothing."

We reached our place in the parade lineup, three spots from the end. I could see the antique motorcycle and auto club from Brewster County behind us, and behind them, the Army Reserve color guard.

Quickly taking our places, we tucked in our shirts and began to count out our steps.

"Where is Anthony?" Mrs. Cogburn raised up on her tiptoes, craning her neck to see above the crowd and the Junior Rodeo riders in front of us.

"He said they were on their way fifteen minutes ago." Cindy, his fiancée, didn't sound too confident.

A trumpet blat burst from the alley off to our right along with Anthony, Lily, and their mariachi band. The sight of their white suits, red embroidered ties, and matching sombreros boosted my confidence. Between the ladies' beautiful colors and the band's crisp, white sophistication, our act should be a crowd favorite.

"So sorry we're late." While he held his guitar in his right hand, Anthony removed his sombrero with his left and waved it in front of his perspiring face.

A trumpet blew a dramatic fanfare. "But now we're here

the show can begin." Lily tucked her trumpet under her arm and gave a little bow.

"Come here." I gestured for Lily to come closer, and I straightened her tie. "Where were you?" I kept my voice low. In my peripherals, I could see that Anthony was apologizing and making his excuses to Mrs. Cogburn, Aunt Linda, and Senora Mari.

"Tubas are not easy to carry. Larry ripped his jacket trying to climb in the back of Anthony's truck with that small elephant."

"Who had an extra jacket?"

"Forget that. We found the duct tape in your aunt's office."

I gave Lily a disapproving look. "Won't that show? Tacky like?"

"Huh," she grunted. "We taped it together on the inside."

Farther up the line, the high school drum line fired off their opening cadence.

Senora Mari stood at the front of our V formation, like a star on the top of a Christmas tree. Anthony and his bandmates stretched in a straight line from one side of the street to the other right behind.

Suddenly the riders in front of us lurched forward and my pulse lurched with them. The big moment had arrived.

"Horse hockey!" Aunt Linda let out a loud exclamation.

I glanced to my left to see what had her all stirred up.

"Look down!" Gretchen Cruz, the calm, steady attorney, cried from my other side.

I jumped over a horse patty the size of a flattened melon. The Junior Rodeo riders were above the stinky fray. The rest of, swishing our colorful skirts back and forth, weren't as fortunate.

"Smile, ladies, smile," Mrs. Cogburn called, and then let out a squeal as she nearly landed in a pile of horse dung.

The mariachi band played, the crowd clapped, and we swished our skirts from side to side and played leapfrog with the presents the quarter horses left behind. It was a beautiful morning; the sun warm and bright on the hills that lay just beyond the railroad track. Flowers bloomed in window boxes along the parade route and on balconies above Main Street. Everywhere the Mexican flag blew proudly in the breeze along with bright-colored paper banners. We passed Coach Ryan. Up to this point, Lenny had been tucked in the crook of my left arm, which made it doubly dangerous to jump over the obstacles in our path. Each time I hopped, he yipped.

With a quick glance over my shoulder to make sure Mrs. Cogburn didn't see me, I hurried over to Ryan. "Here, take him. I think he needs to do his doggie duty."

Ryan chuckled and took him in his arms. "When a guy's gotta go—"

"Listen." I pulled Ryan along the route as we went. "He's in the dance. You'll need to catch up with us before we hit the gazebo."

"You got it, boss."

"Yip, yip, yip." Lenny reared up and licked Ryan's chin. "Leash?"

I fished it from my skirt pocket and handed it over. "Hurry. Run, don't walk, or I'm dead meat."

"Are you kidding? If we don't make it back and Senora Mari blames me, I'll have to pay at Milagro's from now on for screwing up this sideshow."

With that, he slipped through the crowd and down the alley, disappearing from view as a family of tourists stepped up. I assumed they were a family—it was hard to make out their faces as they all held their phones and iPads aloft to film the procession.

As we marched, my new black character shoes, or pumps,

as Mrs. Cogburn preferred to call them, began to pinch my feet. I was hopping over fewer obstacles from the Junior Rodeo horses, but just when I thought all that nastiness was behind us, I had to hop again.

I marched. I twirled my skirt. I smiled at friends, tourists, and their kids along the parade route until my cheeks hurt.

Finally the parade ground to a halt as the drum corps exploded into an intricate performance of beats, rim shots, and funky cadences that set the crowd to dancing. There was no sign of Ryan and Lenny, but the crowd on this last stretch of the parade was three- and four-people deep. Vendors had set up their carts and booths along the sidewalk behind the crowd, making it hard to maneuver. Ryan would have no difficulty running a play through these obstacles, seeing as how he was a football coach. But what was the holdup?

I glanced at my fellow dancers and exchanged weary smiles with Aunt Linda and Cindy. Anthony's band took a breather and we continued to dance in time to the faster cadence played by the drum corps. Skirts twitched in time; tired smiles remained pasted in place, just a little lower than before.

"Where's Lenny?" Senora Mari turned from her place of honor at the front, a furrow of worry crossing her forehead. For someone who didn't care for dogs, she was showing every sign of concern for my four-legged pal.

"Potty break," I called back through smiling teeth. "He should be here any second."

"No potty breaks, we're almost there." Mrs. Cogburn's stage whisper carried to two twin girls, seven or eight years old, standing at the edge of the crowd. They stared at each other wide-eyed. "No potty breaks," I saw them mouth to each other in horror. As the parade stopped, I overheard their worried complaints. The smaller one pointed to me. "She says there's no potty breaks."

The mother, dressed in celebratory white, green, and red followed the girl's finger to me. She glared.

"Wasn't me."

The drum corps sprang into another rousing cadence and the little girls forgot the horrors of having no access to a potty. They began to dance, grasping each other's hands and twisting back and forth—à la Chubby Checker. A few of the horses blew through their nostrils and pulled against their reins. The young rider in front of me allowed her charge to take a few steps to the right before she led him back into formation. Two or three others on the other side of the Junior Rodeo group did the same. A large, black quarter horse in the middle stamped and snorted in frustration.

"I've heard enough drumming to last until next Fourth of July," one of the club sponsors called, walking his horse closer.

"Are the horses okay?"

"Fine." He patted the strong neck of his charge. "Bored. Ready to move."

Mrs. Cogburn pranced over without missing a beat, still twitching her skirt in time to the drum line. "Each group is given a strict time limit for their performance." She glanced to her left and right. "At least that's what I was *led* to believe."

Suddenly the drum line stopped, and after a few seconds of silence, they changed to rim shots only, and the parade proceeded.

A middle-aged gent on horseback tipped his hat. "That's our cue."

"Oh!" Mrs. Mayor marched quickly back to her place, careful to keep her feet moving in time to the beat.

We surged forward and my heart fell. Lenny was going to miss his big moment. Cindy had sewn his costume to match the ballet *folklórico* theme. He'd had fittings, which he hated, to make sure nothing would fall off during his performance. I tried to smile, hating the fact my eyes were full of tears. What was that about? It was just an old parade.

"Hey, Josie! Josie Callahan!"

It was Ryan. He pushed carefully through the crowd ten feet in front of me. He walked toward us as we marched forward. "Didn't you hear me hollering your name?" He thrust Lenny into my arms.

"What happened?"

He gave Lenny a frustrated look. "Took his sweet time about it. Geez."

"Where's his hat?" Cindy had worked hard on the silk number, adding elastic that wasn't too tight.

"You're kidding."

"You've got to find it."

The twin girls ran up with the miniature sombrero. "Does this belong to *him*?"

"Score." Ryan gave them each a high five as Lenny and I continued to march slowly toward the gazebo and our big performance.

I cupped his chin and placed the elastic underneath, then I adjusted his hat. A careful look told me there was no need to check for horse hockey—apparently the handsome animals had given it a rest.

When we reached the gazebo, the mayor and the town council stood on a metal portable platform. Hanging from the side of the white planking hung a green, white, and red sign: CINCO DE MAYO CELEBRATION. LET THE FUN BEGIN!

The crowd here was at least six deep, with children sitting on the shoulders of their parents and older brothers.

The businesses nearby had festooned their rooftops and balconies with Mexican flags and streamers.

My new shoes felt like shackles on my swollen feet. Lenny's hair was sticking to my arms in several places. And I was so thirsty I began to envision running into Elaine's Pies, grabbing a pitcher of ice water from the waiter station, and upending it over my head. I longed desperately to move to the back of our formation where no one could see me, but Mrs. Cogburn was already motioning for us to take our positions.

Anthony and his band formed two lines, one along each side of the crowd. Uncle Eddie had preset a large, red, wooden box to one side of the gazebo. Now Ryan carried it over his head like a deckhand on a pirate ship. He set it down on the pavement in front of Senora Mari and the first line of dancers and bowed.

The crowd whistled and cheered. "Great job, Coach!"

Lily blew a single clear note into the air. The crowd silenced. With true swagger, she played the familiar opening phrase of *jarabe tapatío* in perfect pitch. The band joined in and we were off. We danced, we smiled, we twirled, and we danced some more until our teeth hurt.

The crowd clapped along with the music, which was invigorating until they began to clap offbeat. I was counting steps in my head. A glance at my buddy Patti told me she was counting out loud. Then the crowd roared. As I twirled into my original place, I found the source of the crowd's delight. Lenny was standing on his back legs pawing at the air. He lowered his legs, turned to the left and panted, turned to the right and panted, turned to me and panted. For a finale, he turned back to the crowd, stood on his back legs again, pawed the air, and then sat down—the better to show off his white silk suit and sombrero. The musicians played their final notes with a flourish, we hit our final marks, colorful skirts on full display, and the crowd erupted as if we'd scored the game-winning touchdown at a Dallas Cowboys playoff game.

"Lenny, Lenny, Lenny!" Locals began to shout.

When the final notes blew and the guitars strummed a finale, I raced to Lenny's side.

"Dance," I ordered.

Again Lenny raised up on his back legs. I took one of his extended paws and pretended to dance with him. Then ever so slowly I walked behind the wooden block, turning him slowly in a circle while he remained on his back legs.

Lenny might not be a poodle, but he loved an adoring crowd.

As the parade organizers hurried us off the street, Anthony and his mariachi band broke into another song, and Ryan hauled the wooden box out of the way. Now Hillary Sloan Rawlings and the other beauty queens could advance into the spotlight. Except that Lenny had stolen their thunder. Too bad, so sad.

We made our way through the crowd, down a side alley, and into a lot filled with horse trailers, riders, a school bus, and excited drummers.

Senora Mari's eyes danced with merriment. *"¡Ay, caramba!"*

"Yip, yip, yip." Lenny licked my chin.

I hugged his tiny body close and kissed his furry head. "You were fabulously awesome!"

My fellow dancers gathered around, tired smiles replaced with wide grins. "Lenny, you did it!" Mrs. Cogburn sounded surprised, though I don't know why.

Aunt Linda and Patti gave us a hug sandwich.

"Yip."

"Sorry, Lenny." Aunt Linda kissed his nose and in return he graciously licked her chin.

"Lenster." Patti held out a hand. He dutifully gave her his paw and allowed her to give him a knuckle bump.

"Did everyone remember their steps?" Mrs. Cogburn wore a hopeful smile.

"From my point of view, we killed it." Gretchen Cruz's breathing was surprisingly a bit labored, her skin damp with perspiration. Months earlier, Patti had done time in county jail until the lamebrains in the sheriff's office realized they arrested the wrong woman. During Gretchen's stint as Patti's defense attorney, I'd never once seen a hair out of place or an issue she couldn't handle.

"How do you know?" Lily walked up, her trumpet tucked under her arm. "You were in the back.

"I object. The witness is accusing counsel of giving false testimony."

Patti delivered a playful punch to Lily's shoulder. "Watch out, shrimp."

When Anthony gave Cindy a brief kiss, his bandmates broke into "Amor Eterno." Tired feet be hanged, we began to twirl our skirts and prance around the embracing couple.

"Bravo." Ryan appeared at the back of our happy group. *"Estúpido."*

The dancing halted as we shook our heads in bemusement at Ryan's poor attempt to speak Spanish. Immediately, the other dancers broke into smaller groups to revisit each stretch of the parade and their performance.

"What did I say?" Ryan asked.

"If you were going for Spanish that means stupid," I said, breaking into exhausted and satisfied laughter. "Try *estupendo* or *increíble* next time."

"Thanks, Miss Know It All." He gathered Lenny and me into a bear hug. "Way to charm the crowd, Lenster."

"Yip."

"Couldn't have done it without you manhandling that box, Coach."

"Nice try. You'd have made it work without me, senorita." He gave one of my braids a tug.

In return, I knocked his West Texas baseball cap from his head.

"Yip."

"Josie!" Aunt Linda called from the far side of the lot. "We're heading back." Her way of reminding me that Milagro's customers would flood through the door any minute. She and Senora Mari hurried over to where Uncle Eddie's white F150, bearing the familiar Two Boots dance hall logo, waited.

"Duty calls." It was our busiest day of the year, not a day to stand around soaking up the celebration with good friends.

I was holding Lenny, but Ryan gently tapped one of my hands with his forefinger.

"Yip." My Chi responded, licking his finger.

"Let's get together later." Ryan kept his gaze on Lenny's ablutions.

I shot a glance at my family, feeling their impatience for us to leave. "Sure, but we don't close until nine o'clock."

His smile was warm and easy. "The band is playing at the gazebo all afternoon. Milagro closes at two, and if I know you, you can make it to the square by two fifteen if you put that sharp mind of yours to it." He clasped his hands together and laid them over his heart. "If you need inspiration, think of me waiting, spurs on, hair combed, hands clapping."

I laughed, remembering his two left feet. "Can't wait to see you in spurs. Have you been taking lessons?"

"Come along this afternoon and find out." He winked. "Later, Lenster."

"Yip." Lenny raised his paw, and the two friends shook. A familiar horn blared. "Gotta go toss tortillas."

"Two fifteen. And don't bother to change; the costume suits you." If he hadn't laughed, I might have taken his compliment seriously. Ryan was giving me his undivided attention today, but I was leery of the reason behind it. I had the notion it had something to do with Lightfoot stopping by Milagro earlier.

Lenny and I hurried off. When we climbed into Uncle Eddie's truck, we were met with silence. Each of my family members stared at me as if I'd grown another nose. Aunt Linda and Senora Mari didn't hide their concern, while Uncle Eddie watched the scene unfold through his rearview mirror.

"I recognize that look you're wearing." Aunt Linda carefully moved a strand of hair from my face.

"She could do worse." Uncle Eddie pulled out, careful to avoid a female rider leading a gorgeous quarter horse down the alley to a waiting trailer.

Senora Mari's gaze followed Ryan as he disappeared down the alley toward the crowd on Main Street. "You be careful. Don't play with lightning."

"I didn't hear anything about him in your dream this morning. You can't throw him into your pot of forebodings willy-nilly."

"I can do what I please. I'm much older and wiser than you." She reached up and took me by the chin. "You are too easily hurt. Protect yourself." She locked eyes with me.

"Okay." I kept my voice low. "I hear you."

She released me and gave my cheek a pat. "And he's not your type. You are simply bored." Slowly she gave me the once-over and a sorrowful shake of her head. "And when young women are bored, watch out."

"Hold on, folks. Been there, done that, burned the

T-shirt. Just because Ryan and I talk doesn't mean anything's going on."

"She's heard you. Right, hon?" Aunt Linda asked with a wink.

"Yip."

Senora Mari gave Lenny a nod. "I am always right. Wait and see."

Chapter 12

Josie and Patti Do a Bit of Shopping

"Josefina, stop hiding at the bar." A tired *abuela* was a salty *abuela*. "Double-check those tables. Lunch service or no, I am going home for a foot soak." Our staff had everything set up and raring to go when we returned from the parade, which gave me time to relax before we opened our doors.

As Senora Mari made a dramatic exit through the kitchen, I eased off my stool onto my own tired feet. Fortunately for me, I'd changed into my flats once we'd returned from the parade. Lenny would be sure to mention in his next blog that black pumps should be sold as instruments of torture and permanently banned from the traditional *folklórico* costume.

"Hey, Jos!" Patti Perez called as she banged on the front door like a one-woman SWAT team.

"Hold your horses, woman." I let her in and locked the door before any hungry customers could find their way inside.

"Tell me you're not going upstairs to take a nap." She

stepped into the waitress station and helped herself to a red tumbler of iced tea and a lemon.

"Why? You got something better in mind?" From long experience, I knew that since Anthony had set up the dining room, he would expect to get the first two tables. Truth was, he could handle all of the tables in our casita wearing a blindfold with one hand tied behind his back. As long as I didn't leave him alone for more than a half hour, he'd be grateful for the additional tips.

"There's a vendor on the street selling silver jewelry. I want to check him out."

"It's too bad my bike needs a new tire."

"Why's that?" she asked with a frown.

"Because that's the only way you'd get me on these stumps again." I gestured to my aching feet.

"Got any ice cream to go with that pity party of yours?"

I laughed in spite of myself. "Hush. You're the one who wants to check out the jewelry vendor, not me, you hussy." Within the Broken Boot Feed and Supply, Patti sold feed, saddles, Western wear, and home furnishings, as well as beautiful silver and turquoise jewelry. After her parents passed away, she'd added the jewelry as an enhancement to draw not only farmers and ranchers, but their wives too.

She sighed dramatically. "Can I help it if I appreciate the finer things in life?" She ran her fingers through her bottle-black hair.

I threw a Windbreaker over my peasant blouse and found Lenny's spare leash under the register.

"Let's hit it," Patti said, already holding open the door. We eased our way onto Main Street. By that time, the crowd I'd seen along the parade route had long since dispersed into window-shoppers and a steady stream of lollygaggers, handling merchandise at the various vendor booths.

"Let's see what earthly delights wait to be discovered." Even though it was May, I had a plan.

"Don't even try."

"What?" I asked innocently.

"Yip." Lenny's bright eyes shone.

"You. Shopping? I don't know which one fits you less, shopping or curling your hair."

My hair was a tragic tale, best left untouched.

I hated shopping for my family and friends for Christmas. Too much pressure to please. Too much to remember about their likes and dislikes. That sounds selfish, right? But frankly, no matter how much I tried to choose something that would express my sincere affection and set their eyes to sparkling, more than one would end up staring at their gift in confusion.

"I've decided it would be smart to combine the Cinco de Mayo festivities that I love with the shopping that I hate."

"Browsing vendor stalls is totally nonthreatening," she said, holding open Milagro's door and then pulling it closed behind us.

I ignored her sarcasm. "If I happen upon the perfect gift for Aunt Linda or a salty *abuela*, my time-management skills will have increased exponentially."

"*Wie geht's*, Lenny?" Fred Mueller called from his booth across the street. The owner and proprietor of Fredericksburg Antiques was a spare man with a white mustache to match his short, salt-and-pepper hair. His sharp blue eyes and wire-framed glasses announced his keen intelligence and demanding personality. I had hoped to sneak by his enticing booth with its aroma of beef summer sausage and smoked cheese until we made our way back, but Lenny dug in his tiny heels and refused to walk, run, or march past the array of rich, fatty foods.

"You'll pay for this, bucko." I scooped him into my

arms." If I gain so much weight I can't take you for a walk, who suffers?"

"Bring on the bacon." Patti laughed at my expression; she could chug beers, eat a tubful of tamales, or whatever her heart desired without packing on the pounds.

With deft precision, Fred straightened his display of gift baskets and cheese balls into straight rows. "Ah, my best customer." He chucked Lenny under the chin.

"How's business?" I asked.

"Yip, yip." Lenny's straw hat slid down over one ear as he raised up on his back legs to paw the air.

"If only all my customers were as enthusiastic." He opened his palm and presented a morsel of summer sausage, which Lenny politely swallowed in one gulp.

"Store closed today?" I asked.

His incredulous gaze made me squirm. "My sister Ilse is manning the shop this afternoon."

Patti pointed out a small gift basket perfect for Senora Mari. Throughout the year, my *abuela* cooked chorizo, but her guilty pleasure was hickory-smoked delicacies from the German descendants of local Texans.

"Why sausage and cheese?" Goth Girl asked. "Is it a family thing?"

He lowered his wire-rimmed glasses. "Ilse's idea of a . . ." He pursed his lips. "What do you young people call it?" His expression cleared. "A side hustle."

I bit the inside of my cheek. "Uh-huh." I caught Lenny attempting to lick a sealed package of smoked gouda and moved him to my other arm. Ever persistent, he stuck his head under my arm and lunged for a sample of cherry venison jerky.

"No!" Patti assumed the role of alpha dog with the flutter of an eyelash.

"Oh, let him try one—someone's got to." He tossed Lenny a tidbit of jerky.

"Yip."

"You're welcome, canine."

Feeling guilty, I purchased the smoked Gouda gift box. "Too bad your nontraditional chili didn't win first place this year. I thought it was yummy." It was odd that Mueller didn't appear to be in a particularly bad mood. Before this year's ICA-sponsored event, the locals competed against one another mostly for bragging rights, but if Mueller didn't win, I steered clear of his icy manner and accusatory stare for at least a good month, even giving his table at Milagro to Anthony.

He frowned. "Your Uncle Eddie's venison chili may have won last year, but this year I would have ground him into chili powder."

With a smile, Patti tried a sample of brie. "Too bad he couldn't enter this year to prove you wrong."

"Of course not. The organizer of such an event must remain impartial." With a little frown, he took a flowered dish towel and wiped the cutting board to clear off the crumbs Patti had left behind. "And he executed his plan with precision, no matter what members of the town council say."

I studied Mueller's suddenly animated face and bright eyes. "What are they saying?" He was a terrible gossip, and a long-time, dedicated member of Broken Boot's town council.

After a brief hesitation, he withdrew a handkerchief from his pocket and began to clean his glasses. "The usual. Anytime there's new blood on the council there's a lot of *Get rid of them* and *Impeach the no-good varmint*."

Patti's pierced eyebrow rose. "I can't imagine Mayor Cogburn, or anyone else on the council, using that word."

He chuckled. "Nor I. But it was a good excuse to say the word *varmint*."

My heart sank. Uncle Eddie had put in long hours of worry and months of planning to impress that hard-to-please group of naysayers. "It wasn't his fault someone was murdered before the event could even get started."

Mueller replaced his glasses and lowered them to the tip of his nose, the better to give me a hard look. "Holding a charity chili cook-off was a top-notch idea—even if I didn't win. But asking the council to admit the event wasn't ruined by the presence of an ambulance, the deputy cruisers, and officers questioning the contestants . . . *ist eine ganz andere Frage*."

I nodded sagely as if German were my second language and not something I'd heard only in the musical *Cabaret*.

Patti patted me condescendingly. "Let me translate. They're never going to let Eddie forget it."

"Is that really what you said?"

He gave Patti a wink. *"Nein."*

"Will you keep me informed? I don't want Uncle Eddie kicked off the council before he can prove himself to those old . . ."

"Farts." With a flourish of her napkin, Patti wiped a speck of brie from her mouth.

Mueller's gaze narrowed. "Would you like a ribbon for your new gouda?" He held up a large red ribbon that cost five dollars. It was an ordinary bow made of glittery ribbon, but I was willing to cough up the dough for the inside skinny on the town council members and their opinion of my uncle.

I held out five ones. "Have we got ourselves a deal?"

With a practiced hand, he grabbed the money, beribboned the gift box, and handed me my purchase. "More than one council member has sampled the gouda today." He glanced up and down the sidewalk as if expecting them to pop out from the alleys and storefronts like a flash mob, and then he leaned across the table. "One even bragged about derailing the whole event."

My ears started to burn. "The chili cook-off?"

He shrugged. "That is what I understood her to mean."

"Her?"

Again, he zipped his lips, only this time he placed the imaginary key in the breast pocket of his plaid shirt.

When a couple approached wearing matching *How the West Was Won* tees, Patti, Lenny, and I slipped away.

"Some bribe." Patti glanced over her shoulder. "He wouldn't even give you a name."

"How many women do you think there are on the town council?"

She looked at me and I looked at her. "Two," we said in unison.

Farther down the block, in front of Barnum and Hailey's Emporium, we found Dani O'Neal and her kids.

The small girl held out a baby doll to her mother. "Make it go potty," she demanded.

"We're not buying nothing, so forget it." Dani yanked the doll from her daughter's hands and returned it to the display table filled with toys and novelty items.

I turned abruptly, hoping for a fast getaway.

"Too late." Patti took my arm before I could step into oncoming traffic—anything to avoid what was coming. "You're on her radar."

"What's it going to take for me to get my money back?" Dani's voice could've sliced granite.

"Money back?" I gave her my best confused and befuddled expression. "For what?"

"For that fiasco you call a chili cook-off!"

I glanced at Patti in exaggerated confusion. "Didn't she win a prize?"

Goth Girl gave Dani O'Neal a dead-eyed stare that would've frightened a water buffalo. "Is that the one that tasted like ant p—"

"Your piddly prizes don't make up for the torment and emotional stress placed upon my children." Her other two children, young boys in shorts and scuffed cowboy boots, had donned UT cowboy hats from the table and were glee-fully throwing an A&M football back and forth from one end of the display table to the other.

"Clearly ravaged by the experience." Patti caught the football midair and tossed it to Mr. Hailey.

"You can shut up, whoever you are."

I stepped between Dani and Patti, intent on preventing my best friend from socking the other woman in the kisser.

"Your faulty electricity killed Lucky. I'm going to bring you up on charges."

"Who died and made you sheriff?" Patti quipped.

Dani feigned left and then lunged to my right, but I raised my arms to keep her out of Patti's reach and a broken nose. "You ever heard of citizen's arrest?"

I glared at Goth Girl, and we locked eyes. Finally she took Lenny from my arms and stalked away. "Come on, Lenster. If I stand here any longer, I'm going to need a shovel to breathe."

"Yip." Lenny made sure to lick Patti's hand when she scratched him under the chin.

"Uh, hem." Mr. Hailey handed each O'Neal child a swirly bright-colored lollipop. "It's a beautiful day to enjoy all the sights and tastes of Main Street. Wouldn't want you to miss the free samples at Elaine's Pies."

"I don't like pie," the little girl wailed.

He chuckled as if she'd paid him a compliment. "A little birdie told me they might be giving away samples of their homemade ice cream."

"Let's go!" the boys shouted in unison.

"Don't think you're getting away with murder. I'll post so many negative reviews online you'll have to move to Minnesota." Dani O'Neal grabbed her little girl's hand and hurried after the boys.

If this O'Neal woman did indeed spread atrocious rumors about Milagro all over social media, how could we ever live down such a catastrophic fiasco?

"Some folks suck all the fun out of life." Mr. Hailey sighed.

"I don't get it. She wasn't upset yesterday." I watched the O'Neal family plow through the tourists on their way to more free sweets.

"She didn't win the prize money, did she?" Mr. Hailey asked.

"Definitely not."

"There you go." He picked up the cowboy hats from where the boys had thrown them to the sidewalk. "She's about the fifth contestant who stopped by today, spouting bile and hard feelings."

"Nuts!"

"Every last one of 'em."

I laughed. "Didn't I see you accepting an award for your salsa?" I was secretly pleased the honor had gone to a local, someone with a vested interest in our success.

"Top prize." With a grin, he patted the pocket on the bib of his overalls.

I laughed. "You having a good day?" I asked.

"Beautiful," Mr. Hailey said. With his round belly and lengthy gray beard, the emporium owner could have passed for Kris Kringle's redneck cousin.

"Do you have a flea circus?" I asked with a smile.

"What, you don't get enough fleas from that shrimp of a dog?"

"Yes, but they refuse to perform in a right-to-work state."

He laughed, causing both his belly and his beard to jiggle. "For you, Miss Callahan, the world." Mr. Hailey lifted a crate from beneath the table and withdrew a purple matchbox with a miniature circus painted on the side. "What happened to the first one I gave you?"

"Oh, Aunt Linda keeps it in my old room on the nightstand." As an adolescent of twelve, full of grief over the sudden death of my parents, overwhelmed by moving in with Aunt Linda and Uncle Eddie, the flea circus had distracted me from my heartache.

I shrugged.

"Don't tell me, the performers moved on?" He cocked his head to the side.

"Exactly." His kindness on that wretched day so long ago still shone brightly in my memory. "I'll take it and three packs of these playing cards with Looney Tunes characters on the back."

A round, plastic-encased item caught my eye. The packaging showed a drawing of lightning bolts zapping a human hand.

"Can't these hurt people?" I studied the warning on the side. *Not recommended for children under three years of age.*

He chuckled. "Not at this voltage." From the crate, he removed a similar device, placed it in his palm, and stuck out his hand.

I jumped as tiny volts raced through my arm. That cheap piece of plastic had my attention. "I'm sold. I'll take three." Who knew who would end up with them, but my heart filled with pride. I was giving my Christmas list a mighty wallop.

Chapter 13

▰▰▰▰▰▰▰▰▰▰▰▰▰▰▰▰▰▰▰▰▰▰▰▰▰▰▰▰▰

Josie Meets Ryan for a Dance

After Patti and I returned from our tour of the best artisans Main Street could offer, I stepped cautiously into Milagro's dining room, expecting to find Anthony drowning in crowded tables and impatient customers. But for some reason the majority of our guests had apparently come and gone by two o'clock. Even though the sign outside said we closed at two o'clock, a large party of old friends still lingered to reminisce about their days at West Texas—their boisterous conversation filling our casita with warmth and goodwill.

Lily left their table carrying a round tray loaded with margarita glasses and red tumblers, empty chip baskets and half-eaten orders of queso. "I have everything under control, Miss Josie," she said as she drew near. And she did. The tough, defiant teen she'd been was no longer in sight.

I gave her a grateful nod and ran upstairs to unbraid my hair and reposition the flower behind my ear. It was Cinco de Mayo, after all. I was nervous, and that was giving me fits. I had no reason to be the least bit excited, concerned, or edgy about meeting Coach Ryan Prescott for a dance in the middle of Main Street in front of God and everybody. In spite of his playful compliment about my *folklórico* costume, I pulled on a simple sleeveless flowered dress that hugged my curves in all the right places. Finally I took a close look at my brown, straight hair, even and ordinary features, and stuck out my tongue. Who was I kidding?

I knew Ryan and Ryan knew me . . . too well. We'd dated in college and been sweethearts joined at the hip. There weren't any secrets between us, just a whole lot of mistakes. Since then we'd both grown up and both been engaged to other people. Geez. It was one dance in front of the whole town and a trainful of tourists. No sweat.

I calmed my nerves to appear normal, and then I was at the door with a wave to Aunt Linda and Anthony.

"Josefina!"

I froze, recognizing the imperial tone that belonged to none other than my strict *abuela*, Senora Mari. *"Sí?"* I didn't turn around, but glanced over my shoulder.

"You are going to meet friends?"

I shrugged. "Of course. Who would I be meeting, enemies?"

She marched over to me and stood within inches of my chin—being a good five inches shorter than me. "Do not act so smart with me, young lady."

I suddenly felt all of thirteen, trying to sneak out to meet Peter Sanders at the football game. For some reason, at that age I thought it would be no big deal to walk five miles of highway in my Sunday dress and best shoes.

I lowered my head. "I'm sorry. Yes, I'm going to meet friends. We're going to listen to the band."

With her gnarled fingers, she gently grasped my chin. "I understand the insecurity you feel." She stared into my eyes, her own burning with intensity. "I was young once."

I tried to laugh it off. "So you keep telling me."

She frowned at the return of my flippancy. "Love between a man and a woman is complicated."

"You're telling me?"

"Yes. That's what I am doing. Telling you, so you will remember the truth."

Sometimes the best way to get through these conversations with my *abuela* was to say nothing at all.

She waited for a response. Not getting one, she said, "Love between a man and a woman is not the best kind of love." She removed her hand from my chin, lifted my own hand with hers, and placed them both over her heart. "This." She tapped our hands against her chest. "Family. This is the best love has to offer. We won't ever let you down."

Through my engagement and through my fiancé's desertion, not a single member of my family had ever said *I told you so.* I blinked. Hard. "If this cheap mascara runs, I'm going to blame you." I sniffed. "Do you understand?"

She kissed my cheek and then slapped it, lightly, as was her custom. "You tell that Ryan if he acts like a boy instead of a man . . . if he treats you like he treats those other women with their short skirts up to their—you know what I mean—and their shirts open to their navels, I will find him, rip his eyes out, and feed them to the chickens."

I laughed. "Don't worry about Ryan. I only see him as a friend. Promise." I wiped my eyes. "And all of our hens died three months ago. Where will you find these eye-hungry chickens?"

She fought not to smile. "Chickens may be hard for *you* to find. Me? I have a nose for bloodthirsty poultry. Tell him not to test me in this."

"It's just a dance." I gave her a quick hug and backed away. "You'll see."

"You tell him," she called as I waved one last time. "Don't forget."

As I hurried away toward the gazebo and the band playing a popular country tune, I called out, "*Buenas tardes, Abuela*."

The farther I walked, the more confident I became until I had to constantly remind my hips not to sway to the music. Every few feet or so, I'd greet a friend or a neighbor. It seemed as if the whole town of Broken Boot was on Main. Later that evening, the street would empty as folks loaded up their minivans and trucks and headed out to the fairgrounds for the fireworks display.

As I drew closer to the gazebo, a cool breeze brought gooseflesh to my arms and neck. Though the days were warm in May, the high desert winds reminded us that our elevation was above four thousand feet. Chairs and tables had been set up around the gazebo. A local country band had crowded into the gazebo and was using it as a bandstand. On either side of the steps leading up to the platform were powerful speakers on poles. The tables cascaded around a makeshift dance floor of cobblestones and wood planking. To each side were stands selling food, drinks, and sparklers. Children jumped up and down as their parents and grandparents talked, ate, and laughed together. On the dance floor, the young and the very old boot-scooted under the bright blue sky with its giant cumulus clouds. The wooden floor was crowded, but I expected Ryan to stand out at six feet and change. Of course, if he was wearing his cowboy hat instead of his baseball cap, he was blending into a sea of brims.

"*Hola, chica*." The voice was low and shady, and I whipped around, ready to shove the stranger away.

"Whoa." Ryan threw up a hand to block my fist. "It's me."

I squeezed out a laugh, realizing I was wound a bit too tight.

"Senora Mari sends her regards." I grinned.

"And she told you to hit me?"

"Don't be . . ." I'd almost said *stupid*, but caught myself, remembering it was an insult he hated from our college days. "How's the band?"

He shrugged. "They're not bad, but this cow manure they call 'new country' is melting my eardrums."

We both eyed the crowd, watching as couples danced within feet of us. A few members of the town council gave me a nod, but to Ryan Prescott, head coach of the West Texas Tornadoes, they gave a wave—especially the wives.

I tapped my foot to the music, hoping he'd get the hint. Now or never. If I stood here like a lump on somebody's head, I was going to go stir-crazy, which would lead to me saying *Adios, amigo* to my newfound confidence.

"Coach Ryan," Mrs. Cogburn called as the song ended. She wore her rhinestone cowboy getup: cowboy boots, denim skirt, and Western shirt, all trimmed in turquoise rhinestones and fringe. Her husband wore the same costume as his wife only with jeans and chaps instead of the flouncy skirt. As they approached, I could see it playing out before me. Mrs. Mayor would dance with Ryan while I would dance with the mayor. Cogburn was harmless, but ever since I'd discovered the mayor and his wife making out in the alley behind Milagro, I'd never quite looked him in the eye.

"Won't you ask me to dance?" She smiled coquettishly.

Ryan shot an apologetic look my way. "Mrs. Cogburn," he began as he took her hand, "would you do me the honor of this dance?"

At that moment, a miracle happened. Patti Perez, like a Goth angel of mercy, appeared at the edge of the crowd.

She waved, and it was enough to help me hatch an escape plan.

"Oh, heavens, I forgot to give Patti Senora Mari's order this afternoon." I gave all three an apologetic shrug. "I'll be right back."

Ryan's gaze narrowed. "What was her order, Josie? Can't wait to hear it."

I glared right back, but kept my smile on tight. "Chickens. In fact, she wanted me to tell you that she wanted to order some new hatchlings as all her chickens are *dead*."

"Chickens, huh?" Ryan game me a knowing glance. "Fits, wouldn't you say?" He had me dead to rights.

"I'll be back soon." I smiled sweetly. "Promise."

Mayor Cogburn didn't appear to be too disappointed. "Josie," the mayor called as I turned away.

"Yes, sir." I had my excuse all prepared.

"It's too bad your uncle's big day was tarnished by another senseless death."

With the blood rushing to my face, I was never so glad for the glare of the bright desert sun. "Even so, he brought the whole thing off without a hitch, sir."

"Except for the death of that chili cook." Mrs. Mayor searched our faces. "What was his name?"

"Caused quite a stir, from what I heard," said the mayor, watching me closely.

"No one could have bounced back after a slam like that except Eddie," Ryan interjected. He and my uncle worked together recruiting players for his team. Eddie had played ball for West Texas in his younger days, a real football hero.

Ryan met the mayor's eye without flinching "Eddie's got grit. He'll give you and the council everything he's got and never complain."

I smiled my thanks, and Ryan answered with a slight nod.

Patti had started moving in our direction, which wouldn't do at all.

"Be right back, folks."

I caught my best friend by the arm at the opposite side of the dance floor and pulled her aside. "Save my bacon."

"Hello to you too." My Goth best friend wore her usual black, but she'd joined in the fiesta spirit by wearing bright pink lipstick and a matching fuchsia choker.

"Keep walking so I don't have to dance with old Cogburn."

"Why not? You like kissing up to important people."

"Do not. I try to promote our business in the community by being decent and kind to folks, which is what we should do anyway." I can sound preachy without too much effort.

"Come on, I've got something to show you."

"Okay." I stole a glance at Ryan, slow-dancing on the other side of the dance floor with Mrs. Cogburn. Perhaps sensing my gaze, he lifted his eyes to mine and mouthed, "You owe me."

I placed my hands over my heart and responded, "I'll be back." I turned to Patti. "But if anyone asks, I'm ordering chickens from you for Senora Mari."

"They come in dozens." She raised a pierced brow in challenge.

"Fine, Simon Legree, let me think on it some more."

"Don't wait, I'd hate to escort you back over to the mayor's table."

"Show me what?" We had walked away from the dance floor, through the crowd, and close to the gazebo.

"What do you think?" She nodded at the bass player—a tattooed young man with ripped jeans, a tee that read *Finger Lickin' Good*, and a black felt cowboy hat like that villain in *The Good, the Bad, and the Ugly*, starring Clint Eastwood.

"Dangerous."

"Yeah, that's what I thought." She smiled at him in a dreamy way.

"No. More. Musicians. Remember?" Her last encounter with a musician had ended up with the country singer dead and her sleeping on the best cot the county jail had to offer until I'd proven her innocent.

She sighed. "Hmm. Did I say that? I don't remember."

A sheriff's department SUV came into view at the end of the block. It slowly parted the tourists and came to a halt on the opposite side of the street.

"I think someone wants to talk to you."

Chapter 14

Another Break-In

Detective Lightfoot lowered his window and waited.

"Maybe he has an update on the murder," I said for her ears only. "If that's the case, I'm moving up the need-to-know ladder, Goth Girl."

She chuckled. "You go for it, Jos. Hate to tell you, but there's not a whole heck of a lot of difference in the view from the bottom to the top in this flea-bitten town." Patti sauntered over to Lightfoot's SUV and leaned in the window. "Nice wheels, Detective."

"What's up?" I asked, yanking her backwards.

He hesitated. "Ms. Perez." Lightfoot and Patti had dated once or twice, but it fizzled after their first attempt at small talk. Not his specialty.

"I get the picture." Patti stepped back. "You want to discuss the Lucky Straw murder, another irksome case for the crime-solving partners, in private. Hmm?"

He frowned. "Something like that."

"Do you mind?" I asked Patti. Though she understood I

was keen to solve the murder and to stake my claim on the crime beat at the *Bugle*, she couldn't help but tease. After all, she was the only Goth princess in Broken Boot.

"Heck no. I've got bigger fish to fry."

"See you later?"

"Depends on how tasty the fish is." She gave Lightfoot a playful wave and began whistling Bon Jovi's "Wanted Dead or Alive" as she headed toward the gazebo and the band.

Lightfoot frowned. "You coming or what?"

I glanced around to see who might have heard this strange request. "Sure. Uh, but how are you going to explain this to your peers?" I didn't have the sheriff's office's procedures memorized or anything close to it, but it didn't take an Einstein to figure out that was a big *no*.

He stared at me for a spell. "Let's just say that I'm investigating the possibility of starting a community police academy and you're my focus group."

My smile must have lit my face from ear to ear, 'cause he managed to smile back. I gave a fist pump, but that made the familiar deep furrows on either side of his mouth reappear and his mouth actually turned down like a sad clown.

"Don't push it."

Immediately, I wiped the smile from my face. Or at least I tried. "Where are we off to?"

"Gold Rush Lighting."

The police scanner buzzed. "You on your way, chief?"

I opened the passenger door. "Front or back?"

He glanced at the radio and nodded toward the backseat. "Don't make me wish I'd left you behind to do . . . whatever it is you do."

I jumped in the back. "All right, chief. Let's go."

Slowly he turned and caught me in his narrow-eyed stare. "Don't call me chief."

"But—"

"No one calls me that, except Barnes. And he and I are going to have a few words about his terminology as soon as this case is over." He put the cruiser in drive and began to weave his way around the pedestrians wandering down the middle of Main Street.

"Isn't that a compliment? Making note of your status?" I watched his reaction in the rearview mirror as the stones in his necklace and tribal bracelet glimmered in the afternoon sun.

"Oh, gee." Sometimes I'm clueless and other times I'm just stupid. "I get it."

"'Bout time," he said under his breath.

"Yeah, I'm sorry. That kind of thing must drive you nuts."

"Nah. It rarely happens."

I smiled at him in the rearview mirror, but he kept his eyes fixed firmly on the road. For a few minutes we traveled in silence. Gold Rush Lighting was north of town, on the way to Fort Davis. "The ME called me," he said finally.

I leaned forward, caught up short by my vigilant seat belt. "It was murder, right?"

This time he scowled into the rearview mirror. "Lucky had a medical record card in his pocket with his doctor's information on it."

"What could the doctor say? I still think he died of electrocution."

With a clench of his jaw and a slight shake of his head, he made a right turn onto Agave Road. "I don't understand why you keep saying that. You have no evidence."

True—but my gut was telling me I was right. "Okay, so what'd he say?"

"*She* told me he wears a pacemaker—"

"Which we already know."

He met my gaze in the rearview mirror. "Well, now it's confirmed."

I sighed. "All that buildup over nothing."

With a jerk, he braked and took the next corner. "That's not the good part. Hold your proverbial horses."

"Consider them held."

"He had a weak heart. It wouldn't have taken much for him to have keeled over on a good day."

"Of course he had a dotty heart. The guy wore a pacemaker."

"Doesn't mean you're about to keel over just because you wear one."

I couldn't remember Lucky wheezing or being short of breath. He certainly had plenty of hot air when he complained about his missing gluten-free foods at the reception. "So he wasn't long for this world?"

He shrugged. "Can't say."

"Well, say something."

"Forget it."

"No, no. I apologize." I undid the seat belt and leaned forward between the front seats. "You need someone to talk things over with. I get that. Someone who thinks outside the box."

"On another plane, more like it."

My wheels started to turn. "Lucky Straw was murdered. Admit it."

He nodded slowly. "I could tell that's where you were headed."

"Don't you think so?"

"No. But you do and I'm curious enough to want to know why."

"One. Burn marks from a stun gun could've been hidden by his chest hair or all those freckles." I counted on my fingers. "Two. There were enough extension cords in that place to choke him to death even if he wasn't electrocuted."

"You're saying someone entered his tent and jimmied the electricity so that he'd be killed if he turned anything on." Lightfoot's brow furrowed.

"That or they created a short so that there would be a power surge and he'd be electrocuted, or fried like a fritter."

"Hah," Lightfoot chuckled. Then he immediately made a face as if surprised he'd laughed at one of my silly colloquialisms.

My wheels slowed. "Hmm. I don't know. That's an awful lot of trouble to only *maybe* kill someone. The killer could've easily been seen."

"In the middle of the fairgrounds?" He shook his head. "With everyone still in bed? Not if they were an experienced electrician."

"You're telling me we need to beat the bushes for anyone with electrical experience?" We turned the corner and Gold Rush Lighting appeared at the end of the block. "Good thing God created the Internet."

As we stepped onto the pavement, Lightfoot gave me a bemused smile. "How could we live without learning how to electrocute someone and sell their brain for medical research in New Guinea?"

"Look at you." I grinned. "You made a joke."

He hitched his belt. "Let's go. And remember to keep your comments to yourself."

I mimed locking my lips and throwing away the key.

Pleasant and Barnes had parked near the front door. Closer to the corner, the owner had parked a black luxury sedan across two spaces. Who else would buy a vanity plate that read 2BRIGHT?

"No sign of any intruders, boss." Deputy Pleasant tipped her hat in my direction.

Inside the store, it was brighter than a desert sky laced with diamonds. I nodded as if I belonged there without question.

Barnes and an elderly woman in luxury loungewear and an expensive mink coat met us inside. The redheaded deputy tipped his hat. "Miss Callahan?"

"Community police academy," I said without a flinch.

He shot Lightfoot a sideways glance. "Didn't know we had one."

"Trial run," Lightfoot said.

The elderly woman with Barnes was wound tight as a two-day watch. She thrust a bejeweled hand at Lightfoot. "Melissa Gold. And it's about time." The rings almost camouflaged her painfully swollen knuckles.

He took her hand gently. "Ma'am, it's a pleasure. I was sorry to hear of your loss. Mr. Gold was a fine man."

The *Bugle* had run an expansive obituary back in January. Mr. Gold and his wife had retired to far West Texas from New York. At first, citizens had scoffed at the idea of anyone making a go out of a stand-alone lighting store, but it hadn't taken long for the successful businessman and his wife to prove their business acumen.

"He wasn't *fine*, young man. He was brilliant." She cocked her head like a wary bird, her eyes bright and shrewd. "If Albert were still alive, God rest his soul, no thief would dare to break into our place." She shook a finger at Lightfoot. "My husband had a way with people. They respected him too much to harm us or our business." Her sad gaze swept the room. "I am grateful he did not live to see this day."

She took Lightfoot's arm and led us, like ducklings, into a store overflowing with desks, tables, and shelves. "Why is everyone here?" I murmured to Pleasant. It was unusual for both deputies and Lightfoot to make an appearance at what appeared to be a simple burglary.

"She claims to be afraid that someone is still on the premises," Pleasant whispered. "If you ask me, she called the sheriff and reminded him of her many donations to the officers' retirement fund." We passed lamps of various shapes and sizes, including a children's section with garish clowns, a Spider-Man knockoff, and a cowboy with a lasso-shaped lampshade.

Mrs. Gold caught me, my forehead wrinkled in bewilderment, as I tried to make heads or tails out of a lampstand that looked impossibly like a bowl of spaghetti.

"Isn't it a beauty? I found that one on the Internet and had to have it." She touched it tenderly. "Reminds me of my late Albert."

I bit the inside of my cheek, vowing to keep quiet as Lightfoot had demanded. But I was dying to ask how a spaghetti art lampshade could possibly resemble her husband. Perhaps he loved a plate of pasta more than life itself?

"Mrs. Gold, would you take a closer look and double-check nothing is missing from the premises?" Lightfoot reached inside his jacket and removed his ever-present notebook. He flipped it open and waited expectantly.

She raised her chin and studied his raised pencil. "I will do what you ask after this deputy searches every nook and cranny where a criminal could be hiding." She patted Barnes on the arm.

The detective nodded his agreement, and Barnes walked across the store and into a back room. "Why don't we look around while he's gone?" asked Lightfoot calmly.

Barnes stepped out. "All clear. I'll check the bathroom." Though he didn't roll his eyes, his tone revealed his skepticism.

"I don't know. Everything looks the same." Her expression clouded. "Oy! Albert's office!" We followed her into a small room with a desk, rolling chair, four tall filing cabinets, dusty wooden bookcases, and a hanging Tiffany lamp. Her gaze passed over each shelf, her arms reaching toward each item. "Let's see." She tried the filing cabinets, but they remained locked and untouched. "Such a relief." She placed a hand over her heart. "If anyone disturbed Albert's files, I'd never get our taxes completed." On a pristine desk sat a new laptop. She ran her fingers along the desk. "Something doesn't feel right, but I can't quite place my finger on it." Pursing her lips, she stepped back a few paces, placed her chin in her hand, and stared. "Do you see anything out of place, young lady?" Along the edge of the leather desk blotter, she'd lined up a brass pencil holder and matching letter opener.

Underneath the desk was a power strip with cords leading to the lamp and an electronic pencil sharpener. "No, sorry." I shook my head in frustration. "If this were my office, which obviously it's not, I'd have my laptop on a charger, but that's because I always forget to charge mine."

"Oh, my dear." She placed a soft hand on my arm. "So do I. Yet, where *is* my charger?"

"Are you sure it was here? Not at home or in a drawer?" Lightfoot glanced at the desk drawers she'd yet to open.

"I never keep it there, but if it convinces you I'm not a forgetful old loon, then by all means, I'll check the drawers." After she and Lightfoot—at her insistence—had checked all the way to the back of both drawers, I crawled underneath the desk to make sure it wasn't hidden from sight.

"Nothing there, ma'am." I wiped a cobweb from the end of my braid.

"Is it possible you left it at home or in a briefcase?" His gaze took in the room again, lingering on the corners and the open closet.

With quiet dignity she said, "I don't take it home and I don't use a briefcase . . . not anymore."

He made a note, but I had a feeling we both were asking the same question. Who would bother stealing someone's laptop charger? What would be the likelihood that the brand would be the same as your own? And why leave the laptop?

"Let's continue." Lightfoot led the way back into the main room.

Cruising slowly around the showroom, Mrs. Gold's eyes grazed the shelves and end tables, the lamps and lampshades, the bulbs and fixtures.

"See anything out of place?" Barnes's brow was low, like a bull. Not an attractive look on a red, freckled, baby face. Made me wonder why he was in such a snit. Did he have plans? A romantic liaison? Wrestling on the DVR and beer in the fridge?

Mrs. Gold ignored him as she continued her perambulation. "Nothing here . . ." She raised her two knotted index fingers and began to point at each item on each shelf.

I shot a glance at Lightfoot, who was making notes while Mrs. Gold did her counting thing. Pleasant caught my eye and wiggled her eyebrows as if to say, *Ain't she a piece of work?*

"Ma'am." Barnes did a lousy job of sounding neutral. "You don't have to count every item on every shelf at this very moment. You can check what's here against your inventory records at your leisure and give us a call. See?"

Worry settled across her brow. "Tomorrow?" She glanced at the shelves and swallowed hard.

Barnes straightened, his expression lightening. "Yes, ma'am." He turned toward the door.

"Tomorrow's Sunday. You're going to take my call on a *Sunday*?"

"We could return your call on Monday?" Lightfoot

made his way to her side from across the room. "But if you prefer to give us your report this afternoon, I'll stay with you." He gave Barnes a meaningful glance.

Straightening her narrow shoulders, Mrs. Gold declared, "I would prefer it."

"You two go back into town," he said to Barnes and Pleasant. "Make sure everyone's minding their manners."

"Yes, sir." Barnes was out the door, faster than a jackrabbit running the hundred-yard dash.

"I'll have my radio handy, if you need me." Pleasant touched her hat and gave Mrs. Gold a big smile. At the door, she took one last glance around the store and shook her head in bemusement.

Mrs. Gold moved into another back room. Lightfoot and I dragged behind. "You think someone actually broke in?" I didn't see anything out of place other than the amount of time we were spending following the old woman around her store.

Lightfoot looked thoughtful. "Doubtful. Though I figure someone or something did make the alarm go off." We entered the windowless storeroom, which was lit by a large bank of fluorescents, and observed as Mrs. Gold made her way through the stacks of unopened boxes. Shelf to shelf, item to item.

"The perpetrator might be closer than you think."

Maybe she wasn't truly afraid. Perhaps the call to the sheriff's department had more to do with being alone since the death of her husband. My throat tightened. I understood loneliness that would make someone act that way. In the darkness of my apartment with Lenny curled up beside me, I sometimes thought of how close I'd come to being married, someone's other half. And though those times were rare, those memories still caused me to shed a tear or two if I'd had a glass of wine with my tamales.

Lightfoot shadowed Mrs. Gold while I took the opposite side of the room. On my half, the shelves were filled with boxes, and inside the boxes were odd bits and pieces. One held filaments, another cords. Then there were the paper bags filled with nails, screws, magnets, and clamps. My nose began to itch and I sneezed. If anything or anyone had disturbed this junk, it was most likely a spider.

"Here's where it should be."

I shook my head to clear my hearing. "What?"

Lightfoot raised a hand to quiet my chatter. "Are you positive? Do you remember when you last noticed it there?"

She held her hands in the air as if holding an imaginary box. "So wide. About eighteen inches by twelve inches. Impossible for it simply to evaporate into thin air, Detective."

"What was inside?"

I inched closer.

Rubbing her chin, she closed her eyes briefly. "It wasn't bulbs or knobs."

"Yes?"

Was that Lightfoot allowing his voice to exude impatience?

"They were yellow, red, black, and green for Christmas and the holidays."

"Hmm." Lightfoot was making notes.

"The green ones are for use in one's garden or greenhouse. That kind of thing." She smiled at me kindly.

"What are we talking about?" I asked.

Brow furrowed in disapproval, Lightfoot gave me a narrow-eyed glare. "Continue, Mrs. Gold."

"Dear girl, we are discussing extension cords. High quality, long lasting, durable, made in the U.S. of A."

"Extension cords like you pick up in the hardware store or Brookshire's."

Her mouth tightened as she placed her hands on her

hips. "I just explained that these were not *those*. *These* were highest grade, premium—"

"Extension cords." Lightfoot thrust his notebook and pencil in his jacket's outer pocket. "That's it? You're sure."

"I didn't say that was all. I said that box and its contents are missing for sure."

I glanced at my watch. We didn't have all day, not if I was to make it back for dinner service, which was strictly nonnegotiable. Unless I wanted my name whited out of the family Bible. I pulled out my phone to do an online search of high-grade, premium extension cords.

"Make your call in the other room." Lightfoot's scowl reminded me of my favorite English professor at UT, who had no patience with phones in his classroom, often belittling the guilty party in front of the entire lecture hall.

I gave him a look that I hoped conveyed I was up to something far more serious than a missed text message. I returned to the main room and found a strong signal. Could these better-made cords electrocute someone? And in what circumstances?

My phone was taking forever to load. As I stood cursing modern technology, Lightfoot and Mrs. Gold joined me. Mrs. Gold was stifling a yawn behind her hand. She tightened her fur coat and flipped the collar up around her neck.

"You can call me tomorrow, if you like." Lightfoot locked the back door.

"You're too kind. Of course I won't call you tomorrow. Monday morning is early enough, dear boy."

I wanted to laugh at her "dear boy" comment and Lightfoot's expression of embarrassment. I contented myself with a grin.

"Mrs. Gold?"

"Yes, dear?" She took a tissue from her clutch purse,

delicately wiped her nose, returned the tissue to her bag, and snapped it closed.

"How would someone go about deliberately electrocuting someone with an extension cord?"

Lightfoot's eyes narrowed. "That's enough excitement for one day." He took her arm and led her slowly to the front door. "Why don't you head on home while we dust for prints and take some photos."

She halted in the open doorway. "It's easier to shock someone with a faulty wire at the base of an old lamp. We repair lamps for that reason time and time again."

"Yes, but if you wanted to do it with an extension cord, how would you go about it?"

A smile spread across her wrinkled face. "Oh, I see. You're tagging along today because you're a crime writer like Castle."

Lightfoot chuckled. It was a running joke between us, the fact that he watched *Castle* and had previously refused to let me tag along on his investigations.

She clapped her hands. "Oh, I'm right, aren't I?"

"No, but I write for the *Bugle*."

Shaking a finger at me, her smile turned sly. "Are you sure? I won't tell anyone. Promise."

I felt a flush of pride. "Well, I do cover violent crimes from time to time."

Lightfoot pushed his cowboy hat back with a thumb. "That's putting it mildly." Once again, he led her towards her sedan.

I shot him a look. "Mrs. Gold, I need your expert opinion. Have you ever heard of anyone ever being electrocuted by an extension cord?"

"Oh, young lady, I have heard of far worse. Stories that would curl your hair."

"How does it work? Is water usually involved?"

"Now, I'm not the CEO of General Electric, mind you. But in my humble opinion, any liquid helps." She shrugged. "And, yes, water is a part of most incidents." Lightfoot opened the door to her car and helped her into the front seat.

It was hard to determine if she was as wise as she made out. "If you plugged an electrical device into an extension cord, and the cord became wet somehow, wouldn't that shock the snot out of you?" I asked.

"Yes, and no." Her eyes widened with excitement. "It's not like some story about some poor schmuck who grabs an electric fence while standing in a puddle of water. A person would have to grab onto a frayed cord with exposed live wires and not let go." She wavered and drew a shaky breath.

"That's enough, Nancy Drew," Lightfoot said under his breath.

"I forgot." Mrs. Gold put a hand to her throat. "I did hear a story years ago about an electrician who was electrocuted when he grabbed a metal doorknob."

"Yes?" I stepped closer.

"He was holding a large reel of extension cord by the metal handle. The extension cord was plugged in at the other end. When he grabbed the door handle it completed the circuit." Her laugh was deep and throaty. "The story goes, he was stuck to that doorknob for fifteen seconds."

"Did he die?"

She shook her head and stuck her keys in the ignition. "Nope. Someone found him in a heap, but he recovered." With a sigh, she reached for the door handle.

"Why don't I drive you home, Mrs. Gold?" I asked.

"I don't know." She worried her bottom lip, her gaze flitting back and forth between Lightfoot's face and my own.

"Detective Lightfoot will follow behind."

She drew a deep breath and flung back her shoulders. "If you think it best."

After seeing Mrs. Gold safely inside her sprawling ranch-style home, we headed toward Main Street. Traffic was such a fright on the way back, I strongly considered lighting my hair on fire so we could drive down the shoulder, sirens wailing, with good reason.

The problem was the tourists in front of us. They kept pulling onto the shoulder to take photos of the desert in bloom, dramatic claret cups and bright firewheel blanket-flowers, with the rugged Chisos Mountains in the background.

"Can't you turn your lights on, or something?"

"Nah. We'll be there soon enough." He waved out the window to a little cowboy riding in an extended-cab F250 in the next lane. "Thanks for helping Mrs. Gold."

"I'm a real Girl Scout." My mind was on the dance floor. Would Ryan still be there when we returned? And would I really care if had lost my chance to exercise my newfound confidence?

"Woolgathering, my mother used to call it."

"Sorry. Thanks for letting me tag along."

He checked his rearview mirror. "Extension cords. Spill it."

"I tripped over a pile of them in Lucky's tent. A pace-maker interruption, for whatever reason, and a surplus of extension cords, are *connected* by the fact they both are . . . electrical in some way. Excuse the pun."

"That's quite a *stretch* there, girl detective." He pulled to a stop in front of Milagro. In the distance near the gazebo, couples still scooted and swayed. From our position, I couldn't tell if Ryan was still around.

"Watch it or I might have to start calling you Shaggy. Or would you prefer Scooby?"

After my attempt at humor, there was a moment of silence. I could see him mentally preparing his response. "After I have that talk with Barnes, I can make time for a talk with you as well. Is that what's needed, Miss Callahan?"

"No," I answered without cracking a smile. Inside, I was chortling with surprise. For a split second, a person like me might think a person like him was flirting.

"You have more dancing planned for this afternoon?" He cast a quick glance at my dress before studying the crowd at the gazebo.

I shrugged and checked the time. Three thirty. "Maybe. Though I should go home and work on my stories for tomorrow's deadline."

"Sounds like a practical idea. How long will that take?"

"Let's see." I began to count off on my fingers. "Pinyon Pawn burglary, break-in at Gold Rush Lighting, and, oh yeah, a murdered chili cook."

He studied my expression. "Seems to me, you could fit in a dance or two and still make it home to write at least one story before Milagro's doors open for dinner."

I hopped out and waltzed around the SUV to his window. "Thanks for letting me tag along."

With a touch of his hat and a nod of his chin his only good-bye, he began to drive slowly down the street until I could no longer see him for the vendor booths, tourists, and other vehicles.

I smiled in spite of myself, enjoying the afterglow of his acceptance, wondering how many people he trusted with that surprisingly playful side of his personality.

A few staff members from Milagro were clearing the warmers, tablecloths, plates, and cutlery from the folding tables we'd set up on the sidewalk. During the day's festivities we'd sold tamales, tacos, pecan praline candies, sodas, and Jarritos, a popular Mexican soda, to the passing foot traffic. Anthony and another waiter folded the tables and started carrying them around to the parking lot, where Uncle Eddie's truck waited with the tailgate open.

"You need any help?" I called to Anthony.

"No, Miss Josie. We're almost finished here."

I waved and turned toward the gazebo and possibly a dance or two with a familiar partner.

"Don't stay late," Anthony called. "We still have dinner service to prep."

"Don't worry. I have a feeling my date may have hit the road for greener pastures."

With a shake of his head, Anthony drew closer. "You're too hard on yourself, just like my Lucinda. And she is *muy* beautiful."

"Watch it." I laughed and turned toward the gazebo and a dance. "I'm not giving you my tables, bucko." Behind me in the distance, I heard him laugh.

Though it was May, the cool night air from the mountains would make for good sleeping weather as it blew through the screen in my open bedroom window.

"*Muy* beautiful, my Aunt Fanny," I muttered. Anthony had a huge heart, so he probably meant it. It didn't hurt that I had helped get the sheriff off his case when Dixie Honeycutt was killed.

I thought of Lightfoot and smiled. Who would have thought a serious-minded Native American detective from New Mexico would appreciate the sophisticated investigative skills of Nancy Drew? But the real question was this: Was he attracted to Nancy's intelligence and simple girl-next-door beauty?

Chapter 15

Ryan Dances with
Another Woman

I had left the dance floor and town square with a flight of butterflies in my stomach, but the Gold Rush break-in had driven them away. Something about the crime was off. Why would someone want to steal a computer charger? And, more importantly, who? This who might know something that would lead us to Lucky's killer. This someone might *be* Lucky's killer.

I sighed as I approached the center of Main Street and the makeshift stage. The butterflies came back with their cousins. Ryan hadn't done more than ask me to dance. I needed to get a serious grip because I'd known him for all of my adult life. We'd been much more than friends in college, but now we got on each other's nerves like siblings.

Thing was, this adult Ryan might have forgotten that I only act tough. He might have forgotten how lonely I could get—so lonely, in fact, that I might take his casual invitation to twirl on a crowded dance floor in front of God,

Mayor Cogburn, and the entire town of Broken Boot the wrong way.

I ran my fingers through my hair, and wiped under my eyes just in case mascara had smeared underneath. I bit my lips and pinched my cheeks. Wait. Since when was I so Scarlett O'Hara? I'd obviously lost my mind.

I gave myself a mental slap.

Flashback to the skating rink in sixth grade. The in-house DJ was playing "Sugar, Sugar" by the Archies—an oldie, but always appropriate to the skating rink vibe. Girls were on one side and the boys were on the other. "Boys pick."

And someone had picked me. In the half dark of the concrete-block skating rink, the disco lights, and the sonorous music, I held that boy's sweaty palm and felt those butterflies come a-calling. Of course, he had a wart on the back of his hand, and of course I never spoke to him. Or skated with him again. But that feeling. That feeling was always welcome.

Not all the serious stuff that could follow, but those butterflies were welcome.

I stepped into the square and slowly picked my way through the crowd that stood along the dance floor, gabbing about their day and a few about Lucky's untimely death.

The band played "Desperados Waiting for a Train," couples slow-danced, Anthony and Lily's younger brother and sister slow-danced hand in hand, half skipping, half lunging, adding the occasional twirl for dramatic flair. And I tried to look cool.

"Hey, Josie, who you looking for?" The mayor and his wife danced closer. So much for avoiding the unavoidable.

"Want to cut in?" Mr. Mayor asked as the two of them continued to move in perfect rhythm.

"Hah." I laughed just in case he was serious.

"Eat your heart out, youngster." They whirled into the flow of a circle of dancers two-stepping around the edge of the dance floor, twirling every eight counts.

Convinced that meeting up with Ryan was beyond stupid, I glanced around for a final time. Then I saw Ryan's cowboy hat in the very center of the dance floor. I couldn't see whom he was talking to because of the press all around him. I took a deep breath. Here goes nothing.

The song changed to "Whisper," the music more sultry and heartbroken.

Mr. and Mrs. Cho from the dry cleaners danced with her head upon his shoulder. As I passed, she raised her head and gave me a nod. P.J. Pratt, who had tried to bully Uncle Eddie from the town council over a few head of Herefords, and his artist wife, Melanie, passed me in a boot-scootin' promenade. Who knew so many prominent citizens of Broken Boot could cut a decent rug?

It was then that I saw him. With his back to me, I had no trouble picking him out by his height, his brown wavy hair, his faded denim jeans, the length of his torso, and the cut of his tight Western shirt.

Why was I worried? This was going to be fun. I tapped him on the shoulder. "Hey, handsome, want to dance?"

He swung toward me, and with him a familiar blonde. Now I saw what I'd missed in the crush of dancers: Ryan was partnering his ex, and my nemesis, Hillary Sloan-Rawlings. And he didn't appear to consider it a hardship. Her hands were clasped around his neck, drawing the two of them close together and leaving no room for the Holy Spirit between them, as they used to tell us at First Baptist.

The butterflies evaporated and in their place appeared green-eyed devils. Which made me feel all kinds of ridiculous. I'd never been a beauty queen like Hillary, and she'd never been as gutsy and courageous as me.

"Hey, Jos." Ryan made as if to remove Hillary's hand from around his neck, but the beauty queen kept swaying back and forth. I couldn't help but notice she'd forgotten to button one of her shirt buttons—the one right over her cleavage. "What happened? I thought I'd lost you." He kept dancing though he was talking to me, mindlessly following where she was leading. They looked so good together, swaying as one, completely in sync with each other.

"Did you catch the bad guys?" Hillary asked. She'd added just the right inflection at the end of her question so I had no doubt that she was being sarcastic and witchy.

"Do I look like the sheriff?" I met Ryan's questioning gaze, but I refused to soften. Tough. I wasn't about to share my investigative secrets with this Miss America wannabe. Okay, I had to admit she wasn't a wannabe. She had placed third in the final round of the big beauty bonanza, in front of a television audience and everything. She just got my goat, without even trying.

"Hey, come on, Ryan. Let's finish the dance, then you two can catch up."

He gave her an irritated look and disentangled himself from her grasp. "We've danced a few dances, Hillary. Ending in the middle of this one won't kill us."

She leaned against his chest and tousled his hair and then smoothed it down slowly, snaring him with her gimlet eyes.

And he wasn't complaining. They'd dated on and off about a year ago. But on again was in their immediate future if she had her way.

"Let's talk later," I said.

He grabbed my arm. "Let's talk now." He led me to a cluster of tables, seating us at one near the back. Hillary followed close behind, taking the seat on his other side.

"I'm not saying a word with her here," I whispered under my breath.

"You don't mean that, Josie." Hillary smiled a toothy smile. She had obviously been listening "We're old friends. Let bygones float away." In college, we'd started out as friends in the journalism department, but she always received the accolades while I stayed in the background doing the grunt work—no matter that I often stayed up late to help her write her late assignments.

I tried. "Where did you come from? I thought you left after the parade."

"Oh, the town council—that's whose car I rode in—took all the local beauties out to lunch."

"I didn't see you."

She laughed and then paused. "Oh, you thought we'd go to Milagro. Oh no. We went to Riata in Alpine. Fillet, salad, baked potato, and blackened salmon."

I loved fillet, salmon, and Riata's expensive vibe, but I didn't need her rubbing them in my face.

"What do you know about the burglary at Gold Rush Lighting, or did Majors send someone else?" Hillary asked matter-of-factly.

"That's all there is to tell." I didn't trust her motives. She had a way of convincing our editor to give her the juicier stories, though technically her job was writing the occasional celebrity feature.

She smirked. "You know who did it, don't you?" She batted her eyelashes like a lovesick calf. "You can tell me. Majors is going to be thrilled you got the inside scoop from that overbearing Lightfoot character, no matter who turns in the story."

"It's my story, Hillary."

She raised her hands in mock surrender. "No argument

here, but just so you know, he did ask me to cover the story as well." She adopted a sad expression. "In case you couldn't deliver the goods."

"What? He wouldn't do that, not after—"

"Please. No need to have a panic attack over it." She smiled a cat-with-the-cream smile. "As it is, he'll want to fire me when I tell him that Ryan and I are going to Austin next weekend."

The bottom of my stomach turned into a block of cement. Back in September, Ryan had invited *me* to join him for a trip to Austin to visit our old college hangouts, like *The White Horse* honky tonk. That answered any nagging doubts I had about making the trip. If he invited her, then he didn't understand me very well or the deep-seated dislike, not to mention, disrespect, she held for me. Why couldn't he have left it at two old friends revisiting their college days? Getting out of town for a much-needed break?

He saw Hillary and me in the same light. What the heck?

"Jos—"

I ignored the appeal in his eyes. "No big deal." I even managed to smile, with teeth and everything. "It's a free country."

Ryan frowned. "Give me a sec—"

With a shake of my head, I placed a hand on his arm. "We're good." I included Hillary in my largesse. "No worries."

He leaned toward me and whispered in my ear, "We'll talk later."

I kept my focus on Hillary. She wasn't going to find any trace of disappointment on my face. "So, you've finished your stories for the *Bugle*?"

Delicately she shook her wrists until her diamond tennis bracelet and matching watch floated down her toned arms and onto her slender wrists. "I was supposed to interview the celebrities this weekend." She wiped the corner of her mouth with one finger and rubbed at her lipstick. "Too bad no celebrities bothered to show up."

I could feel the blood rush to my cheeks. In all the hubbub of helping Uncle Eddie follow the ICA rules for the chili cook-off, attending the dance rehearsals for our parade performance, and writing Lenny's blog, I'd completely forgotten to reach out to my friends in Austin—friends who knew popular musicians and actors who might be willing to make the drive down for the weekend. "Uh, yeah, about that . . ."

With his long arm, Ryan reached over and gave my shoulders a squeeze. "Celebrities don't always follow through. You should know that."

A deep furrow marred Hillary's perfect forehead, and her eyes narrowed.

Ryan added his million-dollar smile. "Not you, Porcupine. The people you rub noses with. You're acquainted with celebrities, aren't you?" He shrugged. "Or at least I thought you were."

She tossed her head. "Of course I am."

I began to make a list in my head of the minimum number of celebrities she could count: the judges at the Miss America contest—five or so—the master of ceremonies, the director, producer, the television bigwigs—did they count? There was always someone performing with a name to draw more viewers. So one more. A dozen. It was more than I knew, but not so many as to elevate her status above mine or anyone else's in Broken Boot.

She drew a deep breath and assumed a thoughtful pose. "True celebrities do move to their own beat." She waved a hand in the air. "Blow wherever the wind takes them."

"No stories for the paper, I guess." I tried to look sympathetic, but I was having a hard time feeling anything but irritated. I didn't want her here.

"I have one about the murder." She lifted one brow and a corner of her mouth.

"Hands off. You know I'm the crime reporter."

She placed a hand on Ryan's shoulder. "She wants to be *the* crime reporter, but it's my understanding that Majors hasn't given her that title."

"Sumter Majors gave you my story?"

With a tilt of her head, she considered for a moment. "Let's see. I told him that I was working on a story about the chili cook-off killing."

"And he told you that it was my story, right?"

"I believe his exact words were: *'Go ahead, and may the best story win.'*"

"Why pay us both for the same story?"

She lifted a shoulder. "Why, hon, the best story makes the front page and the second best makes the next edition . . . after it's been edited down to say, two inches. Maybe even an inch if it turns out that Lucky Shaw—"

"Straw."

"Straw—what a peculiar name—died from natural causes, like a little old everyday heart attack."

Ryan brushed her arm away and stood. "Come on, let's dance." He reached out a hand.

"Nah," I said, standing and pushing in my chair. "I'm not much for two-stepping." The band was playing "All About Tonight," which was causing nondancers to flee the dance floor and others to rush it like a sale on spiral-cut ham at Thanksgiving.

He grabbed my hand and yanked. "None of your excuses, Callahan." He sidestepped a couple whirling by, took my other hand, and twirled me into promenading two-step position. "And don't step on my feet."

I couldn't respond with anything snarky as I was doing my best not to cripple him with the heel of my boots or trip any of the other dancers.

"Relax," he said into my ear, which caused goose bumps to rise on my neck and down my spine.

I drew a deep breath and let the music flow over me, and then something magical happened. My feet took over, and my worries withdrew. Guess ballet *folklórico* was giving me confidence and allaying my fear of making a complete fool of myself.

"Watch out." He pulled us out of the way of a couple doing what could be described only as a '60s pony—only the ponies were running wild and stampeding the other dancers. If I had to guess, I'd say too many beers at the Shiner Bock stand.

I'm not thin, but Ryan did a good job of making me feel light on my feet. As we continued, it became obvious we were making it around the circle of dancers without incident, because he had a gift for leading me out of the path of oncoming disaster.

The music segued into something slower, which failed to be romantic as the lyrics had something to do with beer and the singer's photo album filled with his lady and her truck. Before I could hightail it off the dance floor, Ryan pulled me to him.

I refused to put my arms around his neck like Hillary had done. Who could compare with the third runner-up to Miss America, even on her bad days? I grabbed him by the upper arms.

"About Hillary—"

"I don't care. To answer your question, Gold Rush Lighting was broken into by a thief that needed a spare part."

"What?" He drew back in confusion. "Wait." He stepped

close again. "Let me say my piece without you being so accommodating."

"Be my guest."

"I didn't ask Hillary to dance, she asked me."

I shrugged, and returned the wave of Anthony and his fiancée. "No explanations necessary."

He searched my face. "Okay, uh, good."

"When were you two thinking of going to Austin?" My voice was even and friendly.

"Did you check the White Pony's concert schedule?" Ryan was assuming that I was still going. I had checked, but I wasn't going. No way was I going to be the proverbial third wheel.

"Not yet."

He didn't answer as we continued to sway across the dance floor, not quite middle school Sadie Hawkins dance, but close. "Tell me what's going on with you tonight."

My heart started to thump in my chest until I realized he meant the robbery.

"I can't give you all the details, but I don't think it's a coincidence the robbery and the death of Lucky Straw both had something to do with electricity."

"Doesn't sound right, Jos."

"It does if you consider that Lucky was found dead from a heart attack when he wore a pacemaker."

He guffawed. "I'd bet you my lucky cleats tons of guys die while wearing a pacemaker. Check your facts, kiddo."

"There were all kinds of electrical cords tangled up all over his tent."

"Which proves my point." Gently, he lifted my hair from in front of my eyes and moved it aside. "The guy got himself electrocuted. End of story."

"What about the lighting store?" I asked.

"What about it? Coincidence."

"Which, according to Sheriff Longmire and Sherlock Holmes, I'll have you know, there's no such thing."

"Hah. Tell it to the Pope."

Suddenly, the weekend was way too long. What with the parade, and the chili cook-off, and the murder. I yawned, and it wasn't pretty.

"Sorry if I'm boring you."

"No—" I yawned again.

"Shh." He pressed my head to his chest. "Take a load off, Jos."

For the next few minutes, I closed my eyes and let the music and Ryan's sure guidance take me away. Through my mind floated images of Lucky dead on the floor of his tent, Senora Mari's bright *folklórico* costume, the coyotes in the fairground parking lot, and Lenny in his white *folklórico* jacket and sombrero.

Ryan began to hum in the way he had that was more enthusiastic than on key. I kept my eyes closed and allowed myself to enjoy his closeness. It was really too bad we weren't meant to be a couple. But we'd had our time back in college, hadn't we? Best to move on instead of always looking back. Expecting someone to change wasn't healthy. I sighed.

He patted me on the back. "All better?"

I lifted my head and stepped away. "Yeah, thanks." I rubbed my eyes. "I needed that."

He tipped his worn cowboy hat. "You're welcome."

"How's recruiting for next year going?"

He placed a hand on my lower back, helping me steer through the crowd. "Let's not talk football. I get that you hate it."

I shot a glance at him and caught a whiff of disappointment in his face. "I don't hate it. Just don't want to talk about it twenty-four/seven."

Hillary remained at the table, but she'd found a salad and a Coors Light.

Steps away from reaching my nemesis, Ryan turned me toward him. "I'm not going to Austin without you."

"Then you shouldn't have invited her."

He slapped his thigh with his hat. "Hoowee! You're jealous."

Pulling away, I threw back my shoulders and lowered my chin. "Am not. And don't even pretend that you're interested in either Hillary or me in that way. Don't forget about that student who needed your tutoring skills."

With a glance over my shoulder, he lowered his voice. "Please. Don't leave me alone with her. I'll lose my mind."

I studied his can't-do-no-wrong expression. "Haven't you already lost all your marbles? You invite both your exes on a road trip."

"I didn't invite her, she invited herself."

"Well, you can un-invite her." A few butterflies were flying softly inside my stomach. He said he preferred me to Hillary. If I cared, that would be something to crow about.

"Thought you two had started your own dance-a-thon," Hillary said as we took our seats.

Ryan nabbed a baby carrot from her bowl. "Let's have one next year. We'll have it on Presidents' Day."

I laughed. "That's practically the only day not taken for a community event."

"We could always cancel the tamale-eating contest."

"What?" Ryan shot a glance at me. "And lose a dozen free tamales?"

I started to grind my teeth. "I didn't hear any complaints."

Hillary shrugged a delicate shoulder. "You'd be the last to hear."

Ryan's retort floated through the suddenly quiet night.

"Don't work too hard. Wouldn't want Lenny to miss his blog post tomorrow." Several heads turned.

I was going to wring his neck. Though everyone with a brain had figured out that I wrote Lenny's gossipy—and sometimes snarky—blog, I preferred to keep the illusion sacred. "I'm headed home to make sure he gets a good night's sleep. He likes to write every morning at six o'clock sharp." Which was indeed the time he woke me for his morning constitutional.

As folks started talking, Hillary had the last word. "Always helping out where help is needed, Josie. The town council should give you the key to the city."

I ignored her and threaded my way through the crowd, waving to friends and determined to keep my head up. I left the crowd around the gazebo behind and continued down Main Street, back to Milagro and the preparations for dinner service. Tonight should be a great night for the restaurant, helping us pay our bills from the lean winter months when tourists preferred cruises out of Galveston to Mexico or the Caribbean.

By the time I reached the front door of our casita, I'd brushed aside all thoughts of Ryan, Hillary, the trip to Austin, and the butterflies that had swirled in my stomach for the silliest of reasons. Senora Mari was right. Again. I whispered a prayer of thanks for the constant love of my kooky family, and then entered our restaurant ready to serve not only our hungry customers, but my family and their needs, with an open heart.

Chapter 16

Questions and Answers
on the Rocks

"The cows have come home to roost."

"*Olé.*" I gave a salute to the staff and Uncle Eddie, choosing to ignore the fact that his favorite witticism made entirely no sense.

Senora Mari removed my waitress apron from its hook and handed it to me at the cash register. "So, you danced with the coach?" Her lips pursed and she nodded, convinced that she already knew the answer.

"No, I had better things to do."

She studied my face. "Well, now you have tables to set."

"What could be better than that, right Jo Jo?" Uncle Eddie laughed at my expression. "Oh, we're going to have a great night. Did you smell the money in the air?" He gestured to the crowd on Main Street.

"Don't say that." Aunt Linda stepped out of her office. She wore her usual pencil behind one ear and her bright flower behind the other. "You'll jinx us." Her gaze surveyed the entire restaurant, taking in the state of the dining room, entryway, bar, and finally the staff and their uniforms.

"Oh, hon. Be happy. We're going to make money tonight." Uncle Eddie danced across the floor, reaching for his wife to join him.

She laughed and allowed him to lead her in a few steps and a twirl. "Okay, okay." She pushed him away with a hand at his chest. "We have five minutes until we open." She gave me a pointed look. "Double-check your stations."

We made quick work of it, which was a good thing. When we opened the front door, three parties of four walked in. Groups and couples kept coming over the next thirty minutes and we had a waiting list by five thirty.

I was on my way to the bar to drop off an order for a sangria swirl, with a sugar rim—if you please—when I spotted a familiar brunette with red glasses. Dani O'Neal. I'd had about as much as I could take of the woman the day before, so I was praying she wouldn't see me at the end of the bar. Of course I shot a glance her way from behind my order pad to find her staring straight at me.

"I didn't realize you were a waitress." She studied my outfit. "I'm not hating. I had to wait plenty of tables after I was laid off from Texas Power."

"Oh?" This woman made me uneasy. Even though she said she desperately needed the prize money, she was all kinds of crazy. That led me to suspect she had other motives for entering our inaugural event, like keeping tabs on Lucky Straw, plotting his demise, or hitting him over the head with a skillet.

A couple was seated farther down the bar, but their gazes were locked on the Mexican soccer game on the television screen. When the Chivas made a goal, the man slammed his hand on the antique oak bar. "Pay up."

The woman shot a glance at Dani O'Neal, and then at me and Anthony, who was filling in as bartender until our new employee arrived.

After their attention returned to the screen, Dani patted the barstool next to her.

"Sorry." I shrugged. "No can do. I've got three tables that just ordered their drinks."

"Later, maybe?" With an air of desolation, she sighed and took another sip of her frozen daiquiri.

"Depends. Who's with your niece and nephews?"

She gave me a level stare. "What? You think I'd leave them in a strange hotel on their own?"

I flushed. "Not exactly."

"My sister arrived an hour ago. When I left them, they were watching Dora."

"Ah, that's awesome." I hated to see anyone so depressed and bearing such a heavy air of loneliness. As I returned to the dining room, I still caught myself glancing around the room for those kids, just in case she'd lied about having a sister as well.

About twenty minutes later, I had a lull. Four tables had received their entrées: steaks, pecan-encrusted tilapia, the usual fajitas, and chile rellenos. I retreated to the bar area for a soda water with lime.

"Hey, can you watch the bar for a minute?" The new bartender, one of Ryan's over-twenty-one defensive ends, glanced in the direction of the little *niños'* room.

"Sure, but make it quick."

He winked and hurried off, remembering just in time to not go through the dining room. "See? I remembered." He gave me a confident nod and left through the kitchen.

Before her, Dani had three empty Shiner bottles. No way was I about to ask her if she wanted something else to drink. "I'm surprised you're still in town."

"I already asked for the days off, and the kids like it here."

"Speaking of . . . where are they?"

"They're with their mother." She lifted one of the bottles to her mouth and tipped it to her lips. Only a drop came out.

"Ha." I nodded at Anthony, who dropped off an order for three whiskey sours and a Dr Pepper. "Remember, you already pulled that on me, and then you came clean."

"I did?" Her expression said she was utterly lost. "Oh, yesterday. I was just messing with you." She smiled. "They belong to my sister."

"Why should I believe you this time out of the gate?" I made the drinks with care, not wanting to be too stingy or too liberal with the whiskey. "If that's the case, then where are they now?" The woman was obviously either a terrible liar or a pathological one.

Anthony was making sure not to miss a word, fascinated by our conversation.

Dani gave him a sweet smile. "Hi. What's your name?"

"Anth—"

"He's engaged to a girl who used to wrestle on Telemundo."

He laughed. "She's a real tiger." He picked up his drinks and laughed again. "You better watch out for her, she'll rip out your liver."

I bit the inside of my cheek. His fiancée was the sweetest, most timid creature I had ever met. Who else would have sewn Lenny's *folklórico* costume by hand?

Dani sighed. "They're at the Cogburn Hotel watching *Home Alone*."

"By themselves?"

She frowned. "No. With their mother."

Argh. This woman was on my last nerve. And where was that fill-in bartender? He should've been back by now. I walked from behind the bar and took a peek at my tables. So far, they were fine. In fact, too fine. They needed to move along down the road and make room for another group. A couple sat on a wooden bench just inside the door while a family of four waited outside for their name to be called.

"I was a waitress my freshman year of college."

"That so?"

"Yeah." She took a sip of her drink. "I was a cocktail waitress at the Atlantis Beach Club."

"In the Bahamas?"

She rolled her eyes. "Come on. I meant the one on Padre Island."

"Sounds like fun."

"Yeah, the guys were hot, the money was awesome . . . at least on Friday and Saturday nights." She sighed. "More fun than the *medical profession*, that's for dang sure."

My ears pricked. "What part? Are you a nurse or what?"

"Guess again." Her voice was petulant, which I blamed on too many daiquiris.

"Let's see. You're an X-ray technician?"

"No." She gave me a sly smile. "But I am on the technical side."

"You're a radiologist."

"Close, but you won't guess." I turned around to respond, and she was standing right behind me, peering over my shoulder at the dining room. Great. All we needed was for her to cause a scene. Slowly I walked back to the bar and, thankfully, she followed.

I patted the barstool that she'd abandoned, hoping she'd take the hint. "You like to cook, so you must be a dietitian."

She mimicked my actions by patting the barstool in front of her. "No. I work with pacemakers."

The bartender waltzed right through the dining room, passing me on his way back to the bar. "*Gracias*, Jo Jo."

"You're welcome, but that's *Josie* to you."

He winked again and stepped behind the bar. Within a matter of seconds, he'd brought another round for the couple at the end of the bar, cleared Dani's empty glass, made her another strawberry daiquiri, and settled in to watch the game.

"You're a surgeon?"

"The look on your face is priceless." Dani O'Neal climbed back on her barstool and slammed her hand down on the bar. "No, of course not. I work for a pacemaker manufacturer."

Like the woman in front of me, I suddenly felt a bit off-kilter, as if the room had tipped a little to the right, and as if I too were slightly inebriated. What was the likelihood that Dani would have worked with Lucky Straw at Texas Power, competed against him in our chili cook-off, *and* worked with pacemakers? The odds were astronomical.

"Lucky wore a pacemaker," I managed.

She screwed up her face. "That so?"

"Let's get some food in you. You like jalapeños?"

"Ooh."

I marched into the kitchen. "I need an order of jalapeño poppers."

Carlos, our head cook, ignored me.

"What did I do now?" Though bad tempered on a regular basis, he usually acknowledged me when I called out food items needed for my tables.

"My sister says you didn't invite her to dance *folklórico* with you."

"Since when do you have a sister?"

He gave me a dark look. "Last year her father married my mother."

How old is she? Did he mean a child? Did it matter? I could picture young girls and boys dancing with our troupe just as soon as I had a lobotomy. That was the only way for me to gain the patience needed to work with a large group consisting of women, men, boys, and girls. Once we added little girls, the rest would insist on joining as well.

"What if I give you Patti's number instead?" I asked. Carlos had been itching to ask Patti out for a year now. And I could wheedle with the best of them.

His expression changed immediately from surly to surprised. "Oh yeah?"

"But be cool, don't come on too strong. She'll carve out your gizzard with her nails."

"Come to Papa."

"Ew."

"Take the ones under the warmer."

"I'll give you the number tomorrow when I'm not so busy."

"Put those back where you got them from."

"Just kidding." I pulled out my phone and read him the digits, which he scribbled on his arm with a felt-tip marker. I'd have to text Patti later to give her a warning.

I found Dani with her head propped on her arm, eyes closed. "Here." I gave her shoulder a shake. "Eat these."

With a big smile, I checked on my tables, handed them their checks, and helped Lily bus their dishes in preparation for those waiting.

While Senora Mari handed the next group of customers their menus and took their drink orders, I hurried back to Dani.

Eating the poppers gave her the semblance of being all there. "If you're not a surgeon, what is your position? Do you work with the manufacturers?"

With great relish, she dipped one of the fried delicacies in ranch dressing. "Pacemaker and EKG tech at Vista Heart Institute."

"And what does that mean?" I had to take care of those tables or lose their goodwill for the rest of their meal. "Hold that thought."

With practiced alacrity, I recited the specials—Steak Ranchero, marinated skirt steak with shrimp and our creamy diablo sauce; and the Three Amigos, three four-ounce grilled chicken breasts with bacon, poblano peppers, Senora Mari's special sauce, and jack cheese—both with rice and beans. Everyone was in the mood for the Three Amigos special, which made taking their orders a breeze.

I found Dani much more alert than when I left her. "How many brands of pacemakers are there?" While in the dining room, I'd thought of the perfect question to test her knowledge.

She shrugged. "I work with eight different manufacturers, but I can never remember all their names."

I called my food order into the kitchen and prayed she'd let something slip that would prove her guilt. "What does a pacemaker EKG tech do?"

She wiped her mouth and managed to wipe her lipstick onto her chin. Dani O'Neal was feeling no pain. "I check in with patients . . . make sure they aren't having any problems with their pacemakers after their surgery."

I moved her plate with the last popper on it out of reach. "Yeah?"

She frowned. "I remind patients over the phone about their remote device checks." She began to count off on her fingers. "I document data records to their electronic record—"

"Electronic records. Who has access to those?"

She pouted and pointed to her plate until I returned it. "Well, there's the patient, me, the surgeon, my supervisor, the other pacemaker techs."

"Uh-huh."

"I don't have access to the electronic records of every pacemaker in the world, only the ones implanted by doctors at my hospital. And then, only the patient records assigned to me."

The rest of the night was a whirl of activity. When I returned to the bar, Dani was gone. I was tempted to call the Cogburn Hotel to make sure she got back okay, but I knew from previous experience they wouldn't connect me to her room. Instead I called Lightfoot and left a message to spread the word that a woman with dark hair, red glasses, and jalapeño breath might get lost on her way back to the hotel and to keep a close eye out.

I needn't have bothered. Not twenty minutes later, the Big Bend County JP, Ellis, and Lightfoot walked in looking like two sides of the same coin. Both wore pressed jeans with a crease down the front, a button-down shirt, and a blazer. Only difference was that Lightfoot wore his sheriff's-issue Stetson and Ellis wore its straw cousin.

Senora Mari greeted them at the door. *"Hola, ¿muy bien?"*

"Okay," they answered in unison. She seemed entranced by their blazers, or maybe it was their bolo ties. Lightfoot wore the turquoise and silver one I'd seen over the past few days while Ellis wore twisted black leather with silver tips.

"You two brothers?" she said with a straight face.

I gently removed the menus from her hands and gave her a look.

"Don't give me the stink eye. I know they are not brothers." She pointed to Lightfoot. "He has a ponytail, and the other one, I can see his ears and no little-girl ponytail."

The whole business with Dani O'Neal had me a bit

wigged out. "If you two aren't just what the doctor ordered."

As they took their seats, Ellis observed the overflowing room. "You always do this much business?"

"Cinco de Mayo weekend. It's always this way."

"Yet you don't look tuckered out."

I guffawed. "Don't let my bright eyes fool you. I'm tired, but I'm excited for the business."

"This is good." Senora Mari smiled one of her rare smiles, all teeth and crinkling at the corners of her eyes. "Order the specials, you will be very satisfied."

"Yes, ma'am." Lightfoot's gaze traveled to the blackboard and the specials written there.

"Good. Josefina, write these down. Which one do you want?"

"They might want to look at a menu." I tried to communicate with my tone of voice that it was time for her to go back to her wooden stool at her hostess station, but she ignored me—a special talent of hers.

"Three Amigos is very good." She tapped her chest. "I created that name. Do you like it?"

Without moving a muscle, I did a mental eye roll. In this part of the country, almost everyone knew that *Three Amigos* was the name of a Steve Martin movie, an album title by a popular Tejano band, and a menu item in restaurants from Broken Boot to Brenham.

Lightfoot gave the blackboard his somber consideration. "Three Amigos, *por favor.*"

"I'll take the Steak Ranchero." With a smile, Ellis handed back his menu.

Senora Mari gave him a quick once-over. "This does not surprise me." She handed me the menus. "But you will enjoy it, and that's what counts."

I stepped close to the table and lowered my voice. "Did you hear back from Lucky's surgeon?"

Ellis glared as if I'd stepped into his house with horse hockey on my boots. "That's not something you need to worry about."

"Doesn't matter." Lightfoot skewered salsa onto his tortilla chip from the green woven basket in the center of the oak table.

"You crazy?" Ellis asked.

"Doesn't matter because she's going to ask anyway. And she's going to keep on asking until you tell her."

His brow knitted and he glanced at me and then back at Lightfoot. "I have rules to follow, confidentiality policies."

I wasn't about to point out that he'd been open about the details of Lucky's death at the chili cook-off. "I understand." I gave him a smile, took their drink orders, and hurried off to refill a coffee and two iced teas on my other three tables.

I wasn't too worried by Ellis's proclamation. I might be a waitress on the outside, but I was an investigative-reporter-in-training on the inside. And my insides were stronger than any rare and expensive telescope at the McDonald Observatory in Fort Davis.

Unfortunately, when I returned to their table, Ellis stopped his conversation until I'd delivered their drinks: Dr Pepper for Ellis and black coffee, per usual, for Lightfoot. Still, I wasn't discouraged. We're a smallish restaurant and my tables were close together. I refilled drinks and checked on my customers until they certainly must have thought I'd lost all my friends.

"Take these." Senora Mari tapped me on the shoulder and handed me a tray of two bowls of drunken beans and a large Queso Martinez filled with ground beef, pico de gallo, guacamole, and sour cream.

I must have looked doubtful.

"You drop them off." She mimed carrying out the tray. "You wait until they have been talking a good minute, and then you slip up slowly behind that one with the ears showing. He will not know you are there until you have overheard part of their conversation."

"What if I don't hear the important part?"

She shrugged. "Why ask me, Miss Investigative Reporter?"

I grinned. "I try it again with the entrées, the refills, and the desserts."

She studied the two men in earnest conversation. "They do not look like the dessert type."

"Then I give them each one on the house."

Her eyes narrowed and she pointed a finger to my nose. "If you have to give something away, you give them an order of sopapillas to share."

"*Sí, Abuela.*"

"You give them more than one order and it's Senora Mari to you." Her words could be cross, but her heart was big—if hidden behind leathered skin and a tight gray bun.

I managed to sneak up on Ellis as Lightfoot was asking him about Lucky's head injury. "Was it a skillet?" Lightfoot's eyes flicked with the effort not to look at me, where I stood a foot or so behind Ellis.

"Josie was right." There was a pause as he turned his head toward the waitress station. "I was able to find flecks of iron consistent with an old cast-iron skillet. Did the deputies find one in Lucky's tent?"

Lightfoot dipped into the salsa. "No. Checked twice, but no sign of the skillet or any other pan, not even a boiler."

When Ellis paused to check his phone, I caught Lightfoot's eye. "Ask about the pacemaker," I mouthed silently.

He shook his head in unbelief, grinned—which was unexpected—and ratted me out. "Is that for us?"

"From Senora Mari, Our Lady of Tamales."

Ellis perked up immediately. "Is that a good thing?"

"Oh yes. It's a very generous thing for her to do as well." I placed the beans and queso on the table. "She is also known as Our Tightfisted Lady of Tamales to her family and friends."

At Ellis's look of confusion, Lightfoot chimed in. "Senora Marisol Martinez started this restaurant out of a tamale truck."

"And her recipes are featured on the menu, no one else's—and she won't let you forget it."

The JP chuckled. "I noticed." He flicked his napkin over his lap. "Tell her thanks for us."

"Did you ever hear back from the surgeon who implanted Lucky Straw's pacemaker?" Lightfoot asked.

"Yes. We should have the electronic detail of the pacemaker data by tomorrow morning." Ellis glanced my way as he chewed a spoonful of drunken beans. "Don't you have somewhere else to be?"

I shot a quick look-see at my tables.

"Nope," Lightfoot said.

I ignored his quip and locked eyes with Lightfoot. "I sure do. Thanks for reminding me," I replied, careful to keep the sarcasm out of my voice.

"Detective Lightfoot?" I needed to convey information to Lightfoot without Ellis picking up on its importance.

"Yes?"

"I left you a voice mail a few minutes ago about a certain problem we were having with one of our customers."

His eyes narrowed ever so slightly. "Did you get it settled?"

"Yes, yes, I did." I was thinking so fast, my brain was

skidding from one gear to the other. "I don't want to disturb your dinner," I said, widening my eyes, "but I sure would appreciate it if you would give it a listen when you have a minute." Ellis was watching our exchange with unwarranted interest. "It's a pressing issue that needs to be discussed." I couldn't be certain, but I thought I saw in his gaze that he understood the importance of my message.

I pasted on a bright smile. "Okeydokey, then. Your entrées should be out in a few minutes."

I wanted to slap myself upside the head. If I'd only kept Dani O'Neal at the bar a bit longer, she would've sobered up and Lightfoot could've questioned her. For that matter, had Lightfoot already questioned her? As Senora Mari wasn't at her post, I darted outside and looked toward the Cogburn Hotel. Truth was, my conscience was bothering me. I should've never let Dani leave without help or at least a few cups of coffee inside her.

Suddenly I heard a voice behind me. "What was so important?" Lightfoot's deep voice nearly made me jump out of my apron.

"I can't believe the lab didn't find anything else on Lucky's pacemaker."

"Calm down." He lowered his voice. "After you walked away, Ellis said the guy at the lab told him unofficially over the phone that it appeared as if the pacemaker had been interrupted—"

"That's old news."

He raised a hand, crossing-guard style. "The pacemaker interruption was caused by a programming error. The coding suggested the device had been configured incorrectly in the factory."

"This guy on the phone was one hundred percent sure?"

With a sigh, he lowered his hand. "He didn't use those exact words, but that's the idea."

"But what if the error occurred after Lucky's pacemaker left the factory? What if the programming glitch happened after it was implanted in his chest?"

I could see his gears turning. "After, huh?"

"Watch out." My heart started two-stepping inside my chest. Maybe I was finally on the right path. "I'm about to start whistling 'The Yellow Rose of Texas.'"

With a frown, he said, "Spit it out. What's going on inside that head of yours?"

"That chili cook, Dani O'Neal?"

Slowly he shook his head. "Go on."

"Well, she had an ax to grind with Lucky Straw."

"I remember; he laid her off from Texas Power."

"But did you know she's a pacemaker tech?"

He pushed back the brim of his hat. "You don't say."

"Which means she has access to her patients' pacemaker codes."

"We covered this. Ninety-nine percent of the time, it's not a pacemaker failure."

Aunt Linda appeared at the entrance. "Nelson, party of two. Your table's ready." A young couple dropped their cigarettes into an ashcan as my aunt held the door.

"What if the killer used the stun gun on Lucky and it made his pacemaker go kaput?"

From the darkness, a man approached from the parking lot. It was Whip, lanky dark hair in his face. "Have you seen Dani?"

"She was at the bar inside earlier," I said, refusing to look at Lightfoot. "Bartender said she headed for the hotel, but I can't be sure."

"Why?" Lightfoot asked.

"No reason." Whip's gaze swung from the front door to the Cogburn Hotel. "The hotel, you say?"

"That's what she told the bartender."

He tipped his fancy cowboy hat and hurried off toward the hotel, a worried look on his face.

"Josefina Callahan." Aunt Linda's glare could skin a buffalo. "You're gonna see kaput if you don't get back to your tables." She could scare the bejesus out of me when she set her mind to it.

Lightfoot leaned in close. "I'll ask Ellis to double-check the body for unusual marks that could've been made by a stun gun." He took my arm and escorted me back to the door. "All yours, Mrs. Martinez."

Aunt Linda smiled. "Thank you kindly. Didn't want your food to get cold." She held the door for us and hurried away.

"Do you think that O'Neal woman made it to the hotel?" Lightfoot asked under his breath.

"Beats me, but someone should check on those kids. They shouldn't be on their own."

His brow lowered. "Is that what she said?"

"No." I shrugged. "She said they were with their mother, but at one time or another, she's claimed to be their mother." The woman was crazy.

"I'll have Pleasant check it out."

Senora Mari came flying out of the kitchen. "¡Vámonos! Your food is getting cold. If they send it back, you're paying for it, not me."

Lightfoot and I exchanged amused glances before heading back to our designated roles. Not for the first time, I longed to be free to sit down and share a pleasant dining experience.

After delivering the specials to Ellis and Lightfoot, I returned with another order for the bartender. The flow of customers had started to slow. Two of my tables had paid and no other customers had taken their place.

Our new bartender looked at me with eyes round with

surprise. "I overheard what that cop asked you. Is that lady in some kind of trouble? Is she a wanted criminal?"

"No."

"She asked me for the ladies' room, but she never came back."

"Anything else?"

"She left her purse." From behind the bar, he retrieved one of those African-looking shoulder bags.

"Let me see that." I took it from him. "I need one frozen with salt and a top-shelf margarita on the rocks with a sugar rim." The restaurant was closing at nine o'clock. From previous experience, we knew that our customers would all be out at the fairgrounds for the fireworks by then. "I'll take it to the hotel and leave it at the front desk."

He shrugged. "Okay." He proceeded to fix my drinks with one eye on the soccer game. And even though I watched him closely for slipups, he made no mistakes.

When he placed the drinks on my tray a minute later, I had to admire his skills. "Thanks," I said loudly to his back as he stood mesmerized by the game.

Startled, he turned to me. "You are very welcome, Miss Josie." He smiled a truly dazzling smile before giving me his back once again.

Keeping a skilled bartender in a town our size was difficult. Who was I to demand his undivided attention? What I should be concerned about was the location of Dani O'Neal. She'd told one too many lies. If she was at the Cogburn Hotel, then I was the next Miss Agave Queen.

Chapter 17

Fireworks

After dropping Dani's bag at the hotel, I hurried out to the fairgrounds. The breeze was cool and the stars were bright as planets. Hanging close to the Earth like ruby red Texas grapefruits. Fort Davis to our north and Big Bend National Park to our south were official dark-sky preserves, which meant their tourists got the most stars for their buck. However, the night sky beyond the city limits of Broken Boot was no slouch. Very little spillover from Alpine and Marfa affected the blanket of celestial beauty that hung perpetually in our desert sky. The only disturbance to this peaceful backdrop was a parking lot full of cars, trucks, motorcycles, folding chairs, Igloo coolers, cooking grills, and an ice cream pushcart full of sparklers and other small-time fireworks.

In the distance, Frank Fillmore had built a platform and filled it with row upon row of rockets and missiles along with more complicated pieces of equipment, which hopefully meant his show was going to be a real doozy—one that I could honestly brag about on the town's web page.

Out in the field of scrub just beyond the parking area and a far distance from Fillmore's launching platform, folks had set up folding chairs and camp stools, all pointed toward the focal point of the evening's entertainment, the thirty-minute fireworks display. This was around the rocks and cacti and in spite of the pebbles, mesquite, and tumbleweed.

Young and old, humble and rich, they'd come one and all to celebrate Cinco de Mayo.

"Happy Cinco de Mayo, *Abuela*."

With an aggravated shake of her head, Senora Mari lifted her chin. "Not a celebration in Mexico, this Cinco whatever. *Loco Americanos*."

"True, but we're a ton of fun. *Sí?*"

She cast her eyes toward the sky. "If you say so." She waggled her hand back and forth.

"Yip," Lenny said.

Three dogs from across the field answered with opinions of their own.

"What about dancing in the parade?" I asked. "You know you enjoyed that."

Shrugging in her usual way, she said, "Perhaps, but the chili cooking. No joy."

"I have your chair, *Mamá*." Uncle Eddie passed us, loaded down with chairs and a cooler. "Jo Jo, you have the flashlight?"

"Got it." I'd brought the largest Maglite we owned, the better to kill snakes and millipedes with while waiting around in the dark.

"Help, the candle's falling." Aunt Linda went by with two citronella tiki torches, a camp torch, and a watermelon.

Lenny retrieved the candle in his mouth, tail wagging, so cute and proud of himself. "Thanks, buddy." Aunt Linda gave him a grateful pat on the head.

I took it from him, laced my arm through Senora Mari's, and lit the path for the three of us.

"Snakes will bite someone tonight, just you wait and see." I was afraid Senora Mari had seen too many old-timey Westerns again. Snakes in the desert at night, sounded like a no-brainer. But snakebites were rare in Texas. A person had a better chance of being struck by lightning than being bitten by a rattler or any other venomous snake. "We couldn't hold the fireworks on Main Street?" Aunt Linda called over her shoulder.

"Just think what happened over in Badger County; two children were bitten by snakes at a picnic last summer." Senora Mari had rattlers on the brain.

"Where were the badgers when they needed them? Why call yourself a badger if you're not going to kill a snake?" I asked with more than a touch of sass.

"Shh." Uncle Eddie hissed. "*Mamá*, someone will hear you. Think of those parents."

I glanced at her. She glanced at me. The corners of her mouth turned down dramatically, like one half of a comedy-tragedy set of masks. "Shoddy parenting."

"Shh," I warned. "There but for the grace of God."

"God didn't make them poor parents."

Finally my uncle found a spot that was flat enough, empty of obstructions, and wide enough for the four of us plus Lenny on his six-foot leash, which would keep him from sticking his delicate nose into the picnics of other feast-strewn blankets.

From the corner of my eye, I spotted Felicia Cogburn, Mrs. Mayor, and her husband, gesticulating energetically, their faces smiling in that way they had of disagreeing before the mayor's constituents. She glanced toward the fireworks and back to the parking lot. The lot was now full to overflowing, trucks and cars alike were plowing into the scrub, creating spaces where none had existed before. Hopefully, one or two of the trucks had their winch attachments 'cause some of these folks were going to be stuck.

We set up our chairs and plunked down into them as if we'd done a month's worth of dishes, or at least Senora Mari and I did. Uncle Eddie, on the other hand, set up the camp stove and went back for the propane. "He knows we're here for only a couple of hours, right?"

"Why ask why?" Aunt Linda said with a laugh, as she made her way back to the F150. I hadn't seen them pack the truck, but I should have known. If anyone could turn a simple outing into a food fiesta, they could. Sure enough, my aunt returned with a card table which she set up, complete with tablecloth, basket of napkins, plastic red, white, and blue plates, and the watermelon. She even produced Dr Peppers and cheese sticks.

"You going to cut that with your teeth?" Senora Mari asked with a grin. She cared for Aunt Linda, her daughter-in-law, deep down, but on the outside she enjoyed giving her the what for.

"Nope." Uncle Eddie produced a long, serrated knife and carefully, without tearing through the paper tablecloth, sliced the snake melon into rings of delicious, cold sweetness.

"Josie!" Mrs. Cogburn was making her way toward me in a hurry, snaking her way through the brush, only once stumbling on a rock. "There you are!"

"Yes, ma'am. What can I do for you?"

A deep frown blazed across the middle-aged beauty's forehead. "You can find out why the fireworks are late."

The mayor arrived only a second behind. "Josie's not on duty, honey bucket."

I'd never heard Cogburn use that endearment, and it was plain as the narrowing of her eyes she didn't care for it one bit. Made me wonder if it was an intentional jab. Made me wonder if he'd had one too many celebratory beers.

"She doesn't mind helping when there's work to be done." She patted my shoulder. "Do you, hon?"

"Yip."

I glared at Lenny, but he merely smiled.

"How can I help?" I stood, trying not to sigh at my short-lived downtime.

"Find that friend of Linda's—Frank what's his name—and ask him when he's going to get this show on the road."

"Why don't you ask him yourself?" Senora Mari asked.

Mrs. Mayor rolled her eyes. "Well, I sent Mr. Mayor, but he came back empty-handed."

"He wasn't there." Mr. Mayor's smile hit the road, leaving behind an ugly slash.

I glanced at Uncle Eddie, who looked at me hopefully. He needed so badly to stay on the good side of the town council and Mayor Cogburn. How could I refuse? "Sure," I said.

"Yip, yip, yip."

"Oh, sweetie puppy likes the idea." Mrs. Cogburn bent down and patted Lenny's head.

"Yip," Lenny complained, not impressed by his new nickname.

"Let's go, Lenny."

"Thanks so much, Josie. Folks are getting restless."

I stole a moment to observe the crowd around me. I couldn't say they were restless. I heard a guitar strumming, kids playing, a baby crying, the sound of savory meat over an open fire, and most of all the sound of laughter and warm conversation.

"Be back in a minute."

Lenny and I made our way, weaving through the crowd, barely avoiding others' vittles. At one picnic blanket,

Lenny rose on his hind legs and begged for a spare rib. At another, he begged for a drumstick. Finally I scooped him into my arms. "Enough. Or I'll have to start calling you Tubby."

It took much longer to walk from the demarcated viewing area for the crowd than it first appeared it would. Instead of one football field, it was more like three. I refused to complain. Couldn't I always use the exercise? Frank must have sweet-talked the fire marshal. How else could he have set up fireworks in a field? But then again, it wasn't a grassy field in the hills of Kentucky. And truth be told, it wasn't a no-burn season either.

After a few mesquite scrapes and a stick from a prickly pear cactus, we made it as far as the Fillmore's Fireworks van. In the distance, the crowd had faded into the haze. The final wisps of sunlight disappeared into the midnight and azure blue of the sky. The stars were no longer grapefruits, but low-hanging friendly spirits. Twinkling, vibrating, watching over us with the strength of the long-departed and the one spirit that set them in place.

The van windows were dark. Lenny pulled me up short and took a whiz on the back tire. "Yip."

"Good boy." What else could I say? My boy knew how to take care of business and mark his territory. Past the van, the Maglite illuminated the platform another fifty feet on. Lights had been mounted to the ground so that the crowd wouldn't focus on the secondary source of light.

I could hear the crickets and locusts whittling away on their hind legs. It was a beautiful night, perfect for the end of our holiday celebration. I didn't know where Frank had gotten himself off to, but I seriously doubted the crowd minded the lateness of the hour. I took Lenny in my arms and cast my light into the scrub on either side. I was wearing my boots, but I wasn't taking any chances. Just because

I couldn't see them didn't mean rattlesnakes weren't on the prowl for mice and rabbits all around us.

"Grr." Lenny's body tensed in my arms.

The hairs on my arms stood to attention. "What is it, Lenster?" I whispered.

First one and then two heads appeared in my peripheral vision, off to my right. I swung the light in that direction. It was the coyote brothers. "Yah, yah, yah." I'd never been on a cattle drive, but I'd seen a movie or two.

Lenny strained against my arms, growling, yapping, and threatening his distant cousins.

"You can forget it. You're not going to wrangle with any coyote. Haven't you heard it's better to pick on somebody your own size so no one gets hurt?" Without giving myself time to reconsider, I spread one arm wide and ran at the remaining coyote. "Git, git, git! Yah!"

They took off at a trot and disappeared into the brush. I waited. I counted to thirty as the night grew darker all around us. The crickets and locusts grew louder, and in the grass I heard the slither and crackle of small creatures below my line of sight.

"Come on," I said to Lenny, "Let's get out of here."

The van was still dark. I flashed my light in the front window. A curtain had been pulled across the breadth of the cargo area behind the front seats, neatly separating the contents from view. It didn't take an Einstein to figure out that Frank slept out here. Despite the hour, I decided to knock just in case he'd taken a nap—unlikely—or got caught up in an extremely long and involved phone call— highly unlikely. I was desperate. Though Uncle Eddie wasn't in charge of the fireworks per se, a magnificent show of lights would put a nice cap on the Cinco de Mayo festivities. And any positive review of the weekend would include a mention of the winners and a favorable nod to his first chili cook-off.

"Frank?" I tapped on the driver's door with a knuckle. "Yo, you in there?" I asked playfully. Best to keep things light and breezy.

I glanced across the wide expanse between the van and the waiting crowd, the darkness deepening to a deeper shade of midnight. Walking softly, I led Lenny to the other side of the cargo van, a better vantage point when it came to seeing if someone, namely Frank, was on his way to or from the launch platform. "Where do you think he made off to?"

A sudden thought had me turning toward the crowd again. Perhaps he was at the porta-potty. When a guy's gotta go, he's gotta go—chemical outhouse or no.

"Yip," Lenny urged quietly.

"You're right. He's probably at that platform with all the fireworks on it." Out of the corner of my eye, I caught a movement. An orange tabby slithered out from behind the curtain into the beam of my flashlight, gifted me with a surly look, and climbed onto the dash and front window of the van. She kept her eyes focused on mine as she bathed first one paw and then the other.

"Yip, yip." Lenny wasn't impressed.

I hoisted him up so he could get a better look at the proud feline.

"Yip."

"Yes, I know, she won't look at you. Don't worry, she's just playing hard to get." Lenny placed his front paws on the window and whined.

"So where's your owner, Tabitha?" She turned her back on us and continued washing. After a few more licks of her tongue, she raised herself languidly from the dash, disappeared behind the curtain, immediately returned to stand on the center console, and then disappeared again.

"What if she's like Lassie? Trying to get our attention? What if Frank's hurt in the back of the van and she wants us to rescue him?" Hadn't I read somewhere that cats could do that kind of thing? "Come on, Lenster." We walked around to the back of the van, where I promptly tripped on a long, round object that turned when I stepped on it, almost causing me to do the splits as my front foot began to roll away from my back one. "Son of a nutcracker!"

"Yip."

"I'm okay," I groaned. "Old Frank needs to be more careful." At first glance, the van's rear doors appeared to be tightly closed, but when I looked again I could make out a slight gap.

I picked up the cylindrical object and started to toss it inside. When I opened the van's rear door, the interior light came on. The object in my hand was a fireworks missile of some type, a familiar cone at one end and three wings at the other. The van itself was far from empty. A bedroll was propped against the cargo door behind the driver's seat. Beside it was an iron skillet filled with a knife, fork, spoon, salt and pepper shakers, and a can opener. Crates of fireworks—rockets, fuses, several boxes with bright labels indicating mine cakes, and a dozen or so extension cords were crammed into every available inch. I gently placed the red missile in a box in the corner, close to the rear door. That's when I noticed the crate beneath it. A yellow hazard tape was attached. WARNING: VOLTAGE MAY CAUSE ACCIDENTAL DEATH.

My curiosity got the better of me. I lifted the first box out of the way and discovered three stun guns in the smaller crate beneath. The air in my lungs evaporated.

"Yip, yip," Lenny said.

"You're right. This whole thing's made me jumpier than a frog in a toaster." I forced my lungs to draw breath.

"What do you think, Lenster? You think he stole these?"

"Yip."

"Me neither . . . but it's mighty suspicious."

If I truly thought that a stun gun had killed Lucky Straw, I'd have danced a jig at the discovery of not one, but three of the weapons in Frank's possession. Tonight's encounter with Dani O'Neal had changed my conclusion.

I no longer had to worry that Uncle Eddie could be blamed for Lucky Straw's death. No faulty wiring, or even a mishap with an extension cord, could've caused his death. And why had the murderer tossed the stun gun into Lucky's chili? Easy. He, or she, wanted the sheriff's department to think the stun gun had interfered with his pacemaker. Once it was proven the stun gun couldn't have killed him, the officers would assume the blow to the head was the cause of his demise. Only Ellis refuted that theory almost immediately. The head injury certainly caused significant blood loss, but not Lucky's death.

Most likely, the killer panicked and then hit the chili cook on the head for good measure. I could sense the answer close at hand, but I was missing the one little piece to the puzzle that would prove to Lightfoot and Ellis that I was correct. No matter what they said, someone tinkered with Lucky's pacemaker. Dani O'Neal.

All I had to do was prove my theory.

Lenny whimpered and wriggled in my arms.

"Shh. It's okay. I won't be but just a minute." I set Lenny down just inside the van.

I wanted to feel the weight of the stun gun in my hand. Sure, I'd seen them on television and in the movies, but never held one. With extreme care, I picked one up. It had weight and heft while still being deceptively light, like a can opener. Part of my brain was saying *Put it back, you're trespassing.* The other part of my brain, the crime reporter side, could've no sooner let it go than I could bypass honey with a warm sopapilla.

What a rush! And then goose bumps began to rise on my arms. "Why does he have these?" I murmured.

Lenny whined again.

"Hm . . . you may be right." What would Frank, a fireworks guy, be doing with stun guns? Fireworks and stun guns—somehow it didn't seem like such a reach for him to have an interest in both. And sleeping out here under the stars, he would need some type of protection.

"Meow." Frank's cat was glaring at us, her head sticking out from the gap in the curtain.

"Whoa, kitty." She took a step forward. "Stop." She stared, back raised, waiting to see what we would do next.

A nagging thought caught hold. These could be the stun guns that had been stolen from Pinyon Pawn. Old Frank could support himself with a bit of burglary on the side. Was it mere coincidence there were three in Fillmore's van? There was only one way to find out.

"Lenny, stay." I pulled his leash through the rear door handle and knotted the end. "This way you and the feline won't get into a tussle, and she won't escape only to be found by the coyotes." I closed the door, careful not to slam it completely shut in case Lenny needed me.

"Watch out, cat. Here I come." With Lenny conveniently outside, I waved my arms like a crazy person until the cat escaped through the curtain and into the front seat. I felt only a twinge of nervousness and guilt at invading Fillmore's private lair. Frank would be preparing to launch his fireworks display, and once the show started, he'd be occupied for at least the next thirty minutes.

Carefully, I shoved boxes and crates to one side, the better to read the stun guns' serial numbers while keeping an eye out for an angry feline. The inside cabin light was off, but the flash from the camera on my cell did the trick. My fingers turned into thumbs as I hurried to forward the images to Lightfoot. Only when I hit send did I notice my cell phone reception was at zero bars.

The photos would be enough unless Fillmore ditched the evidence. I'd changed my clothes for the fireworks. Against my better judgment, I grabbed a stun gun loosely with two fingers, wormed it into the oversized side pocket of my cargo shorts, and covered it with my shirt. It wasn't exactly hidden, but if anyone looked closely, they might think I was carrying a bottle of beer in my pocket. Darkness should mask my covert operation until I could pass the weapon on to Lightfoot.

"Okay, Lenster. Let's go." Gingerly I lifted the box and placed it on top of the crate with the remaining two stun guns inside—exactly the way I'd found them. I pushed against the rear van doors, but they had closed. With my Maglite, it was only the work of a moment to find the handles, but the doors refused to budge. Ugh. Did cargo vans have child locks? Were the cat and I locked inside for our safety?

Great. I'd simply crawl around the boxes and crates, and whatever else was back here stabbing into my knees, and escape out of one of the other doors.

"Lenny, I'll be right out."

Suddenly a fist appeared and began knocking on the rear window. "What are you doing in there?" I couldn't make out the voice, but it definitely belonged to a man. This was going to be extremely embarrassing if Deputy Barnes or, God help me, Lightfoot was on the other side of that door with their gun drawn. I'd be too embarrassed to walk down Main Street for at least a month.

And how was I going to explain myself? I'd start with the truth about finding the missile and then wing the rest. I rose up on my knees so whoever he was could see me through the window.

It was Frank, the fireworks guy. He carried a lamp made to resemble an old-fashioned kerosene lantern. He'd raised it up high, close to his face. No need to guess his reaction to finding me inside his van; I could read his disapproval and outrage in his suspicious glare and clenched jaw. Or maybe it was the way he stood with his legs far apart in a defensive stance.

"Hi, Frank." I gave him a wave and a smile. "Mrs. Mayor, uh, I mean Mrs. Cogburn, sent me out here to see what time you thought, uh, you'd start the fireworks show."

"When it's dark."

"Uh, right. I think she was hoping for a specific time." My knees ached and I felt like a fool yelling through the window.

"I'll decide when it's dark enough. That's my job, not hers."

Taking a deep breath, my lungs working like a bellows, I forced a laugh. "Dark enough. What would that look like?" I made a show of craning my neck to peer at the oily black sky.

"When it's black as pitch," he said.

"I think you've hit it square on the head." I was going for friendly. Anything that would encourage him to forgive my trespassing and open the door, sooner rather than later.

"You think so?" He frowned.

I found myself nodding like a bobblehead. My nerves were stretched tighter than a barbed wire fence, partly because I was in his van—Good Samaritan or no—partly because one of his stun guns was hiding in my pocket.

His brow furrowed and he checked his watch.

I inched my fingers beneath the tail of my shirt. I'd done a fine job of wedging the thing in the pocket of my cargo shorts. Too fine. My hands were icy cold, my fingers refusing to work.

He lifted his lantern high so its bright light shone in my face. I dropped my hand, praying he hadn't seen me reach for my pocket. I wasn't entirely convinced the stun guns in his van had been stolen from Pinyon Pawn. And, honestly, the idea was ludicrous. But someone *had* stolen them and flung one into Lucky's chili. I had to get the evidence to Lightfoot so he could compare the serial numbers and scratch Fillmore from the list of suspects in my brain.

"Hey, Frank, I'm locked in." I tried the handles several times; but his attention was riveted on the night sky.

"Was she complaining about my work?" he asked.

"No. Mrs. Cogburn's excited to see your fireworks. We all are."

Once again lifting his lantern high, he began to inspect the seal on the rear doors, first running his finger along the crack where the doors met and then removing something from the edge of one door—a pebble that he held up to his lantern for a closer look.

"How did you get in my van, Miss Callahan?" He'd dropped his angry mask. Now he appeared to be bewildered by my presence.

For all I knew, Lucky had bought the stun gun on his own—which wouldn't surprise me—and had pulled it out for protection when an intruder entered his tent. Either way, I was as nervous as a calf in a calf roping, watching with dread as the young cowpoke practices swinging his rope.

"I found one of your missiles on the ground."

"My what?"

I grabbed the red plastic firework and held it up in front

of the window for him to see. "Rocket? Missile? I'm not sure. But you must have dropped it on the ground."

"Nah, that's not true. I wouldn't have dropped a missile where someone could trip and break one. Plus, all the missiles I brought with me are included in tonight's fireworks display."

I was getting fed up with raising my voice to be heard. "Hey, Frank, could you please open the door and let me out of here?"

He bent over, his face disappearing for a moment, and my whole body relaxed. The nutjob was finally going to release me. He reappeared just as quickly with a familiar face I adored held next to his own.

"Yip, yip, yip," Lenny said, his body trembling with indignation.

"Hey, Lenster." I smiled, hoping to give him comfort.

"Miss Callahan, go on. You were saying, or should I say, spinning some yarn about my missile."

"Honestly, Frank. I found it on the ground. I wanted to put it back inside your van so no one would get hurt. I didn't break in. The doors were open. I don't think they closed properly."

He nodded and a smile played around his lips. Then Lenny licked his ear, which unfortunately drove the smile away.

"I swear," I muttered under my breath. I was losing my patience. If he didn't open the door immediately, I was going to crawl to the passenger door, knees or no knees.

Again he nodded, but this time he turned the door handle. Nothing happened. "It's locked." He gave Lenny a smile. "Guess I'll have to find the key." He lowered my canine sidekick to the ground and removed a large set of keys from his belt.

"I bet you're wondering how I came to be *inside* your van?"

He was holding his lantern with one hand and sorting through keys with the other. "I figure that you were killing time until I came back."

I smiled in relief. "That's right. Lenny and I were just about to inspect the fireworks setup you've got going over there." I waved at the platform of explosives. "Nah, we were going to check for you over there next."

He lowered the lantern so that the bony planes of his face were highlighted like a ghostly apparition.

I forced a chuckle. "That gives me the creeps."

"I'm a what?" He leaned in closer to the window.

"The way your light is casting shadows over your face is creepy." I enunciated each word very carefully.

"What?"

I raised my voice. "When you hold your lantern that way, you look like a ghost."

He made a silly face. "Is that so?" And then he did that belly laugh thing that was so infectious, and I immediately felt my nervousness lift.

"Now you look like a ghost from the '50s, complete with crew cut."

"Find anything interesting while you were digging around in my personal belongings?" he asked, a key in his hand.

Slowly I lowered my Maglite to the floor of the van. If I ever got out of here I was going to use it to knock another hole in Frank's head. I placed my hands on the window to reinforce the sincerity of my plea. "I didn't dig into anything, I promise. I've only been in here a couple of minutes." I bumped my nose against the window so that he could see my face more clearly. "Frank, please open the door. I'll show you the rockets and mine cakes I found."

He watched me closely, but the key remained in midair. I pressed against the window with my hands. "They have names like Phantom, Black Cat, and Planet. I thought they were magic kits."

He was definitely giving me the willies, standing out there in the dark with his lantern like a character in *The Blair Witch Project*. My eyes were beginning to play tricks on me, seeing all kinds of indefinable, crazy things in my peripheral vision.

Frank lifted Lenny into his arms.

"Please be gentle with him. He doesn't really like it when strangers pick him up." I raised my voice. "He could jump out of your arms or fall and hurt himself."

"I'll put him down when you tell me what you're up to." He held my sweet Lenny in the crook of his arm, his big hand wrapped around his muzzle to keep him from barking. He'd shoved him into the crook of his arm and against his side so tightly that, try as he might, my Lenny's little legs couldn't kick or scratch the nasty man.

"We came to see what you were up to because your fireworks show is late. If you want a good review, punctuality counts. Now give him back." Forget being creeped out by this guy. And forget feeling sorry for the fatheaded, crew cut–wearing dope. His refusal to let me out was on my last nerve.

With a stupid grin on his face, he lifted Lenny higher while bending down to put their faces at the same level. "She's not telling the truth, is she, little poochy?"

With a burst of anger, I grabbed my flashlight, scooted backwards away from the window, scrubbing my knees on the unfinished cargo van's floor, brushing into boxes, and catching my shirt on tools and the points of rockets and the hard corners of heavy launching pads. What an imbecile! Why had I waited so long to get out? I yanked the handle of the van's side door, but it wouldn't budge. Fudge! I launched myself across the van, knocked over two crates, landed with my knee in Frank's skillet, and yanked at the other side door with all my body weight. Nothing. Crudsicles!

My gaze darted from door to door. I hurdled a large ice chest to reach the passenger side, stuck my hand through the curtain divider, and fought to find the lever on the back of the seat to no avail.

I was vaguely aware of the light from his lantern illuminating the interior of the van around me. Finally, I knocked down the curtain with my Maglite and threw the whole flimsy rod, curtain and all, behind me.

"Meow." Frank's cat lifted her head from the driver's seat without further comment.

"Oh, shut up."

I found the lever and flipped the seat forward. With a final burst of energy, I reached for the lock mechanism. "Come on!" I couldn't get the mechanism between my fingers. I flung my body over the edge of the seat, forcing the stun gun into my thigh, and reached for the unlock button.

Nothing.

"Locks don't work." Startled, I looked up and found Frank and Lenny staring at me through the passenger window.

Immediately, I backed up and wedged myself onto the console. "Move it!" The cat jumped gingerly into the floorboard with a great show of indifference. Having learned my lesson, I went straight for the unlock button on the driver's side. Nothing. The whole freaking thing refused to cooperate.

Frank, with Lenny in his arms, meandered from the passenger side, across the front of the van, and over to the driver's side window. "Life sucks, right?"

Some folks might panic in a crisis—like when you realize that the guy you thought was just a loner is actually a dangerous, unhinged creeper. But this lunatic was going to give me back my dog or lose his left kneecap when I slammed it with one of his mortar rockets. I turned away from the window and pulled out my phone. I'd waited to use it because once I saw I had zero bars I'd forgotten all about it. Plus, I didn't want Frank to see me with it and take it away. Now that I knew his first priority wasn't to hurt my dog, I was willing to try our spotty cell service. Lenny, my canine friend, would thank me. I unlocked the screen and dialed 911.

Chapter 18

From Bad to Worse

"Turn it off." He stroked Lenny's head. "Or I'll silence your dog." Frank Fillmore didn't raise his voice, but still it reverberated through my brain.

I lowered my phone, careful not to disconnect. Even though coverage was spotty out of the city limits, it might connect any second.

"Yip," Lenny cried.

My heart was suddenly in my throat. "Don't hurt him. Please."

"Disconnect the phone, Josie."

My screen was dark. I could leave the phone on, hoping he wouldn't notice if and when the call went through or I could roll the dice. But could I live with myself if Lenny came to harm? My options flashed before my eyes. I'd lost my parents to an oncoming car. I'd lost my fiancé to the Great Barrier Reef. I'd lost my dream job at the *Gazette* to a bunch of greedy losers and a thing they called the housing crisis and the great recession.

My choice was clear. I lifted the phone so Fillmore could see it and pushed the power button.

"Remove the battery." With his left hand, he continued to squeeze Lenny's small muzzle closed. Slowly he placed his right hand at Lenny's neck.

"Okay, okay!" I removed the battery and held it up to the driver's window. As I did, I dropped my flashlight between the seat and the console and said a prayer it would stay on.

"Now turn around and throw both parts of it as hard as you can against the rear doors."

I swallowed hard. This had to look convincing if I wanted him to think I was complying. I took a deep breath, drew back my arm, and aimed for the box just inside the rear doors—the same place I'd stowed the missile earlier.

"Let him go!" I yanked violently on the driver's side door handle. "I did what you asked." I took a shaky breath and changed tactics. "What's this all about, Frank?" I needed to convey genuine concern. If I could just get him talking, I could think of a way out. I might be able to appease an angry Tex-Mex customer, but this was life or death. "How can I help?"

"I tried replacing the fuses for the electric locks, but that dang near broke me." He removed his hand from Lenny's neck, answering my question as if he hadn't dognapped my closest companion and trapped me inside his van. "Eventually I was replacing them every other day."

"Don't you have the key?" I smiled. "Let me out so I can tell the mayor and Mrs. Cogburn that the fireworks are about to start." Probably not the smartest suggestion.

Lenny started wriggling in an attempt to get down. "Look," I said. "So you don't like dogs. Please let me hold him, and we'll walk away without mentioning this to anyone. I'll even talk to Mrs. Cogburn about increasing your fee."

"That so?"

I shrugged. "My uncle Eddie is on the town council."

Fillmore tightened his arm, and Lenny's black eyes grew wide.

Everything in my mind slowed. I could still remember when Lenny came to me—a young and scrappy version of the intelligent, supportive friend and cowriter, not to mention sidekick, he had become. All tiny legs, minuscule steps, and fast-beating tail. So anxious to thank me for adopting him from his previous owner—who'd married into a cat family with no desire for an immature, affectionate, and long-haired dog. So anxious he'd lick my hand for hours on end.

"Hey, you don't have to scare him to force me to leave. And if you don't start the fireworks show, someone's going to come over here and find out why."

"Answer the question, Josie. What are you doing in my van?"

"Huh, what was that?" I asked, suddenly as deaf as my old Granny Callahan.

He yanked Lenny close and whispered in his ear.

My canine friend whined.

"Whoa now. That. Is. Enough. I haven't done anything to you or your cat."

With an odd smile, he kissed the top of Lenny's head. "I don't want to hurt him. In fact I'm very fond of animals."

I tried to laugh, but it came out like a whimper.

"Oh, goodness. Don't be scared." He ran his right hand over Lenny's head. "I won't hurt you, but I have to make sure your owner didn't steal anything from my van." His gaze traveled briefly over the boxes and crates behind me. "What you see inside is all that I have to my name."

Suddenly his eyes widened and he checked his watch. "Showtime." He move Lenny carefully from one arm to the other, untangling his leash from my Chi's back legs. Then Fillmore lowered him to the ground and led him none too gently by his leash toward the fireworks launching platform. He was in the dark with my Chi for a heart-stopping minute until I witnessed the first flicker of flame, followed by a loud, high-pitched whistle. The fireworks show had finally begun.

My hope sank. Soon the audience would all be looking up into the brilliant night sky ablaze with beautiful lights and explosive sounds, not down on the ground level where Lenny and I were in nasty trouble.

Time to think logically and not like a dimwit blonde out of a horror movie.

One. Frank could hurt me. Okay, that was nearly impossible. I had all the stun guns. In fact, as soon as he opened the freaking door, I was going to charge him and see how he liked being stunned up close and personal.

Two. Before I hit Frank with a stun gun, I had to make sure Lenny was safe. It would be too easy for Frank to incapacitate or kidnap all six pounds of long-haired Chihuahua. I swallowed hard. That scenario was too awful to imagine. But my canine sidekick was tough. He'd chased down two crazy murderers. If anyone could escape or do damage to a grown, healthy psycho, it was Lenny.

What I needed was leverage.

"Meow." The orange tabby, Tabitha, rubbed against my legs, finally marking me as part of her territory.

Three. The cat. The fact that Frank was a cat owner definitely worked in my favor. I suspected that he was—as he claimed—honestly an animal lover as well. Otherwise, why not hurt Lenny from the get-go? As long as I had the cat, I could bargain for Lenny's return. And once I had Lenny, we'd bust out of this van like the Incredible Hulk on steroids.

Four. The phone. Without a battery, it was useless. No one would be able to track it or me. My only hope was that my aborted call to Emergency Services had connected before I hung up. Living in Broken Boot often felt like living on the moon. Cell service was sketchy outside of town, and in town too. If the winds were howling, or we had a dust storm, or the governor decided to play bingo on Monday night, our cell service would suffer. Still, I knew roughly where the pieces had gone. Now to find them, hopefully in one piece, and put the device back together again.

Five. The tire iron. Every van had to have one along with a spare tire. I'd been itching to find his and bust out his precious van's window with it since the moment he held Lenny's tiny muzzle in his big brutal hand. I found it very suspicious that Frank hadn't demanded that I pass a tire iron, the cat, and my phone through the window. Perhaps he'd remembered those stun guns after all. Or, and this rattled my nerves more than an angry rattler about to strike a hiker's boot, he knew he had no tire iron inside the van to worry about.

I tried the door again for good measure. It had no lock mechanism that I could reach with my fingers, and forget fingernails—I had none. Brilliant ribbons of light rippled through the sky until it was a dark umber, and still he lit fuse after fuse. Suddenly a rocket whirled and whizzed. Above me a shower of lights fell down around the van, pops and sizzles grazing the top.

Maybe he'd left me in the van, knowing it would catch on fire.

Yes, by now my subconscious had put it all together. He had to be crazy. Mr. Crazy had taken a stun gun out of this van and helped Lucky to a heart attack by blowing the circuit of his pacemaker. I sighed in frustration. No, Ellis had said it was a computer programming malfunction. My brain was working so hard, I expected smoke to come roaring out of my ears. Frank told me he programmed the fireworks display. He also said that he'd had a number of careers. What if he'd programmed the interruption to Lucky's pacemaker? What if he'd used the stun gun to scare Lucky into a heart attack?

A missile exploded directly above the van, and I hurled myself into the cargo area. If I hid behind his gear or, heaven help me, made it out the back of the van before he returned, he might hesitate before killing or hurting Lenny. I had stun guns at my beck and call. This joker had better watch his butt.

I crawled into the back of the van with my flashlight, determined to find the phone and managed to wedge one of my legs between a large crate labeled EXPLOSIVES and my other fat thigh between the explosives crate and a roof-high stack of cases of a popular red soda. Too much soda. Maybe that was this guy's problem. Too much food coloring? Too much caffeine? Fear was slowing me down. I shoved with all my might and gained nothing. There was silence.

Was the show finished? Would he be back any minute? Did he have to stay with the show in case something went wrong? I prayed I was right.

The back doors of the van creaked open. He reached up and unscrewed the cabin light, dashing my hopes of attracting someone's attention. Who was I? A wimpy scary movie heroine? No.

I froze, praying he wouldn't see me where I crouched behind the cases of red soda, my head fully exposed.

"I bet you're wondering why I'm holding your dog in my arms like a watermelon I'm about to crush?"

I refused to answer, hoping beyond hope that he was bluffing, that he hadn't actually seen where I was in the van. I let my gaze roam the corners of the van that I could see. No phone. No tire iron. Not yet.

He rubbed his hand over his face. "Most people, they

never see it coming until it's too late." He waited. "My wife, Felicia. All sunny and bright eyed one day, and dead from cancer three months later."

"Oh, Frank. I'm so sorry. Felicia is a beautiful name."

"I always thought so."

"How did she die so suddenly?"

He rubbed a hand across his eyes. "She'd lost a lot of weight. Had no appetite. I tried to get her to see a doctor, but she refused. Blamed her stomach discomfort on food allergies and indigestion."

"Was it pancreatic cancer?"

He ignored me. "We didn't have any money to speak of, what with my layoff and all."

"Surely the county hospital would have taken her."

"And I was never home—always traveling across the state with my fireworks, trying to make ends meet." He stroked Lenny's head. "I'd come home and ask her how she was feeling, but she always said she was fine. Or that the new medicine the doctor gave her was making her sick to her stomach."

"Did she ever see a doctor?" Poor woman. What a painful way to die.

"She lied to save my pride!" His eyes became those of a madman. "She didn't want me to feel bad or blame myself. Stupid woman wouldn't go to the doctor if it meant I'd have to do without."

Puzzle pieces began to fall into place. "Were you laid off from Texas Power?"

His fevered gaze turned toward me. "Lucky Straw never cared for anyone but himself. Didn't matter that I'd given my life to the power company. Didn't matter that I'd worked long hours and never saw my wife. Heck fire, it didn't matter that I was too old to be offered another job in my line of work. All that mattered to that SOB was that his budget sheets looked good when he presented them to the board. His bonus was the only thing he cared about in his entire life." A slow grin spread across his face. "That and making Lucky's Naked Chili."

Should I prod him to confess outright? Or will I drive him away?

His manner changed abruptly. "If you're not going to tell me the real reason you're snooping around my personal belongings, I'll go back and check on my fireworks. The show's a real humdinger." And then he laughed as if all his screws had not only come loose, but had fallen to the floor and been kicked under the sofa. "Not to mention, I'm getting hungry."

I debated turning on my flashlight to draw attention to our plight, but I didn't want to lose a possible weapon. At that hopeful thought, a shower of sparkling fireworks showered down nearly on top of us. Frank wasn't fazed. Lenny tried to wriggle free. And I prayed the lights had illuminated Creepo for a second or two.

I gathered my thoughts and slowed my breathing. Enough was enough. I gripped my flashlight and tensed my muscles to run. If I could distract his captor, Lenny could either scratch or bite him, or escape the way that Toto escaped from the Wicked Witch of the West.

Then he closed the rear door and locked it.

And I lost it! I began to bang the side of the van with my fist, metal or no metal. Fireworks made no difference. I banged and screamed. Tired and spent, realizing that no one was going to hear me until the fireworks show ended, I collapsed and felt a tear try to wriggle its way down my face. Stupid tears. Not going to happen because everyone knows tears get you nowhere.

Suddenly the driver's door opened.

Chapter 19

Josie to the Rescue

"Cut it out!" His voice was still low, but heavy with fury.

I cowered from his rage.

"Comfort this flea-bitten mutt until I get back. One more sound and it'll be your last."

As a journalist, I couldn't help but notice he was speaking in clichés. Were all bad guys idiots or did they mimic other villains in movies and television shows—heck, even Saturday morning cartoons—and then come back ready to try them out on their own victims?

When I wrote about this event, and by God I was going to . . . Forget feeling afraid. Forget allowing this *estúpido gringo*, as Senora Mari would say on a very bad day when the butcher from Alpine tried to deliver bad fish, to control my life and stink it up and make me and my family sick with grief and suffering.

I gave myself a mental slap. Now who was being melodramatic?

Frank dangled Lenny inside the door and my heart

leapt. I pushed and shoved the boxes away, reaching for him. He needed me, to feel my arms around his quaking body.

"Psych." He chuckled low and smarmy. "You ain't getting him back until I'm good and ready." Quietly he closed the door and locked it.

"Yip, yip, yip," Lenny complained from the other side of the door.

I counted to thirty and then tried the driver's door. Nothing. What had he done to make it impossible to get out? Could you install a child safety lock on the driver's door? Doubtful. If he could set up a fireworks display and figure out how to kill someone with a stun gun and an extension cord, then this jackalope could keep the door from opening on the inside.

I banged my head on the driver's headrest. When would he monologue? Weren't villains supposed to start monologuing? Giving the good guys a chance to get away or talk them out of it? Or something?

My vision narrowed to hyper focus. I turned on the flashlight, praying someone would see it, but it glowed only dimly. The front of the van was parked away from the crowd. No way would they be able to see the light inside even if the full cabin lights were on.

Why? Why had Frank Fillmore, Aunt Linda's prom date, killed Lucky Straw? I couldn't imagine the frustration and despair he must have felt to watch his wife die without the proper care. But why would you do something criminal if you had proof that you would be caught, tried, and relocated to death row?

My arms and legs, even my lungs, were heavy from the long ordeal. My heart was slowing. Adrenaline was wearing off. Not good. Not going to help my flight instinct.

"Ugh." I slapped both hands to my forehead, and I did it

another eight times for good measure. I had a cell phone somewhere in the back of this van. With the help of the dying flashlight, I found the battery and finally the rest of it. The battery slipped into place. *Hallelujah!*

I crawled through the cargo, fireworks explosives, and crates full of sparklers, watching my screen for any change in service. I stood, neck and shoulders bent, moving the phone like a divining rod. If there was service in one micro inch of this van, I was going to find it.

Did I mention I prayed? I do that. And not just when I'm in trouble. Though to be honest, more fervently when I'm in trouble.

After minutes that felt like hours, I slumped back into the driver's seat. I was going to have to go for it. This loser was going to kill Lenny if I didn't get out of there. Heck, if I didn't get out of there, he was going to hurt us both. My heart dropped to my socks. If I escaped he might not just hurt my friend. He might do much more.

The screen on my phone flickered to life. I had one bar. I sat up straight and unlocked the screen. The bar disappeared. I held my breath. I slumped back into the seat, and sure enough, the bar came back. I dialed 911.

"Nine-one-one Emergency Services Big Bend County. What's your emergency?"

"I'm being held against my will in a white fireworks van at the county fairgrounds near the fireworks platform." I took a breath and realized that my voice sounded thin and reedy. The bar had disappeared. NO SERVICE displayed quietly on my screen.

I exploded into action, hitting the driver's side window with full force. I screamed like a banshee. I threw my weight into it. My shoulder ached and lactic acid began building in my underused biceps muscle and still I slammed the light into the window.

I stopped and inspected my flashlight. The lamp cover was dented in several places, but the lamp itself was intact. I was going to get out of this piece of junk. Now.

I turned the flashlight off and found a crate I could haul into the front seat. Ridiculous. I couldn't hit the window with a crate full of fuses. I reached for the stun gun. Gone. No wonder I could sit and maneuver without feeling the ripping and pinching of the stun gun in my front pocket.

I went back into the cargo bay with my wounded flashlight until I located a gorgeous tire iron, the old kind actually fashioned out of iron. I grabbed the remaining two stun guns and turned one on. Nothing. No charge. I flew back into the front seat and began hacking at the window with the tire iron. I swung and swung until with a pop the window cracked.

Success. I changed hands to give my right arm a rest. I swung at the window like I was at the State Fair of Texas and was on my way to winning a giant stuffed unicorn, complete with blue eyes and a pink tail. The crack grew. Outside the fireworks had slowed even more. There was a noticeable gap between the rockets that was longer than before. I raised my boots to the window and kicked with both feet.

Nothing.

This is what came from not working out. This was what came from missing your walk for thirty more minutes of sleeping. I kicked with both feet a few more times, my long-lost adrenaline surging back to the fore. Suddenly, my right boot heel went all the way through the upper right-hand side of the cracked pane of splintered glass.

I nearly screamed with relief until I suddenly remembered Frank.

I moved my boots to the left side of the window and kicked like a mule on speed. The window released from its moorings and fell out onto the grassy scrub beyond. Quickly I reached out of the hole where a window had once been and tried the handle. It was locked. Small shards of glass littered the window seal, but my gut told me I had seconds to spare. My gaze landed on the floorboard and I knew I hadn't misjudged the opportunity. I grabbed the floor mat and stuck it through the opening.

I had my legs through the window opening when it dawned on me my curves might get stuck. Had dancing made me flexible enough? Too late to find out.

I grabbed onto the upper window seal, too late feeling a sting in my palm. I hefted myself up, threw my head back, and slid into the opening. Now my feet dangled out the window, my, uh, curves sliding slowly, ever so slowly, downward toward the ground. The floor mat was moving with me until I felt it fall out the window below me.

My breath squashed out of my lungs and for a few scary moments I just knew I would hang there by my, uh, bra for eternity. My head thrown back. My legs dangling above the ground. Bent backwards like a wilted prawn.

Desperate to not be caught by the nutjob while I was hanging out the van window, I changed the position of my hands and surged through. I hit my back on the door handle on the way down. I fell to the ground in a puddle of relief. Despite my own heavy breathing, I heard footsteps in the scrub somewhere to my right. I slithered to the ground and rolled underneath the van. My back throbbed where I'd hit it and my palms smarted. The Maglite was still in the van. My only weapon. The stun gun too.

I inched away, slowly. The steps grew closer and came to a halt inches from my nose. I lifted my hand and felt for my phone in my back pocket. It was still there. *Yes! Thank you, God!*

The steps began again, rounding the van to the other

side. I inched back to the other side. My eyes had adjusted to the dark and the fireworks and in the distance the glow of flashlights and battery-operated lanterns. The footsteps stopped. They dropped to one knee. I tucked my head and slithered to the back of the van like a salamander.

"Josie," he whispered.

I made it to the edge of the undercarriage and skedaddled out from under the van far enough to bang my head on the bumper.

I hissed and rubbed my head as stars added to the rockets still bursting in the sky above. Before I knew it, he was on me. He grabbed me by the arm.

"Let me go, you turd!"

"Josie! Be quiet! It's me."

My vision cleared. It wasn't Frank the freak fireworks guy who had my dog. It was Lightfoot. Strong, dependable, Detective Quinton Lightfoot.

Chapter 20

On the Trail

Those nasty tears—caused only by adrenaline—trickled down my face once again, and I silently cursed them and wiped them away. "How'd you know where to find me?"

Lightfoot watched me closely. "You called Patti and she called nine-one-one."

"But I swear I didn't. I barely managed to dial nine-one-one." My voice came out high and screechy. "I called her on my way here, but she didn't answer."

Keeping a careful eye on me, he slowly surveyed the scrub around us. "You can thank your pants. They dialed for you."

"But how did she know where to find me?" I grabbed his arm.

"Breathe." He placed his hand briefly over mine. "You told her you would be here tonight with your family."

"Oh, my God." Suddenly I felt light-headed. "Give me a minute to catch my breath." I was taking deep lungfuls of air and thanking God that he blessed my cell phone connection. I must have looked as overwhelmed as I felt.

"Senora Mari was out in the parking area when I arrived." He took my arm. "Steady. Don't rush off. Take your time."

I wanted to scream with anger. "He wouldn't let me out of that stupid van!" I began to cry in earnest. I refused to look at him. I didn't want to see his reaction to Josie Callahan, reporter, losing it.

He let go of my arm and put his arm around my shoulders.

Any second, I was going to pull myself back together and go and find Lenny. Lightfoot's arm was so steady, so . . . there. I turned into his chest, laid my head on his shoulder.

"Uh, Josie?"

"Yeah." I couldn't move. I just needed to stand there with my head against his chest and share his strength.

"You sure you're okay?"

"I will be. Give me a minute."

It was time to go if I could just clear my head. "Quint?"

"Yeah."

"Would you mind putting your arms around me for a minute?"

I couldn't take it back. And I was too overwrought to be embarrassed. I was thinking that I might need to apologize if I'd embarrassed him with my emotional outburst, when his arms came around me.

"Thanks."

"You're always welcome."

I chuckled and found the strength I needed. I stepped away and his arms dropped. "Let's go get this loser."

"Take it easy, slugger. Senora Mari asked me if I'd seen you. By the time I got to your aunt and uncle, they both met me on the way."

This didn't make sense to me. Had I really been gone that long?

"Did you see Lenny?"

He held his flashlight up to make it easier to study my face. "No. Is he missing for the same reason you were hiding under this van?"

"Frank has him. Threatened to kill him if I didn't keep my mouth shut."

Lightfoot flashed the surrounding scrub and a distant mesquite tree. Only yuccas, cacti, and sand sage made an appearance. "Why would he do that?"

"Because he killed Lucky Straw and he wants to shut me up." My brain was foggy.

He frowned. "What do you know?"

I tried to open the back of the van, but it was locked. "In here are explosives."

"Okay."

My brain sputtered. "You know . . . explosives and fireworks and extension cords."

Slowly he shook his head as if acknowledging that I'd finally lost my ever-loving mind.

I hurried to the broken window. "Here's where he locked me up and I broke out." I reached inside and found the stun guns on the front seat. "And these." I shook one at him.

"A stun gun?"

"You betcha, and he's got three or four of them."

"And?"

I wanted to scream, but a guy like Lightfoot gets riled up when you lose control. "And, don't you see? He jolted Lucky with a stun gun. And he programmed the interruption in his pacemaker so the shock would scare him stone-cold dead."

In the near dark, I could still read Lightfoot's disbelieving frown by the light of his torch. He cocked his head to one side. His ebony eyes locked on mine. "Maybe." He gave a slow nod.

"Frank kidnapped Lenny and threatened to kill him." I wanted to shake the skeptical look from Lightfoot's face. "Would a sane, law-abiding citizen steal my dog?"

The fireworks ended. The crowd cheered. A coyote howled in the distance.

"Come on." Lightfoot turned away, heading toward the parking area.

"Where are you going?" I refused to budge. "He's got to be here."

"Trust me." He grabbed me by the arm and pulled me along. "I have a feeling."

We hurried through the crowd as folks gathered their belongings. Some greeted us. Lightfoot nodded once and ignored the rest. Both of us jogged through the crowd, eyes peeled for any sign of Fillmore and a feisty long-haired Chihuahua in the crowd. Finally I spied Mr. and Mrs. Cogburn up ahead.

"Mr. Mayor thought tonight's show was fabulous. Isn't that right?" Mrs. Cogburn asked.

The mayor raised his brows. "Yes, yes. Superb. Never doubted you for a minute, sugarplum."

She smiled and pinched his arm. "You did too, you big fibber."

"Ow. Stop that." He rubbed his arm enthusiastically. "Never. Except for the waiting around, it was perfect."

She pinched him again for good measure. "That built up the excitement. Didn't it, Josie?"

"Sure," I said distractedly. "Have you seen Frank Fillmore? Did he come round to get his check?"

"The man demanded cash." Mayor Cogburn looked disapprovingly over his glasses. "What does he think I am? An ATM?" He cracked his knuckles.

"When was that?" Lightfoot asked.

"Exactly five minutes ago." Mayor Cogburn turned to his wife. "Wouldn't you agree, darling?"

"Why, yes, honeybun. You are so right. It was exactly five minutes. You hit it right on the button."

"You're positive?" Lightfoot fired his question into their Chip and Dale routine.

Shocked at his tone, they glanced at each other. "Yes."

"Lenny, you haven't seen him?" I asked.

The mayor harrumphed. "Why you'd bring him into the desert beats me."

Two dogs raced by, a schnauzer chasing a poodle, barking without a care in the world. Two older women meandered after them, both in coveralls, and one wearing a John Deere cap.

"They went thataway," Mrs. Cogburn called out gaily.

"Excuse us." Lightfoot tipped his hat and we were gone.

"Where did he go?" I asked Lightfoot's back as we hurried to his cruiser.

"I think he's hit the road."

"But the fireworks just ended. Wouldn't he have to stay behind to make sure the fireworks went off without a hitch if he wanted his pay?"

"Where's your Prius?" The parking lot was already in an uproar, cars nearly backing into other cars and truck horns honking.

"Crud. My keys are in my bag!" I'd left it next to my folding chair earlier, when I'd gone to check on the fireworks.

"Where'd you park it?"

"Um, over to the far left."

"Show me."

I led him past coolers on wheels and kids in pajamas. Country music blared from nearby trucks. Tejano music floated into the air as well from a nearby Expedition as two adults loaded sleepy children into the back.

My mouth was suddenly dry as dirt. "It was here."

"You're sure?"

"Let me see that." I grabbed his flashlight and searched the empty space where I'd parked, or so I thought. The marks in the gravel and weeds could have belonged to my car. Around us, vehicles crowded the road back to town and others lined up waiting to enter the flow.

As I turned to give Lightfoot his flashlight, I caught a glimpse of something familiar at the edge of the grass. Lenny's leash. I held it up for Lightfoot to see. "Look. I was right." I wanted to find Frank Fillmore and throttle him until he confessed. I knew why he'd done it, but I needed the how. But first I needed my best friend, safe and sound.

"Come on." Lightfoot took off across the parking lot. We found his cruiser boxed in by the line of cars and trucks waiting to turn onto the road back to the highway.

I slid into the passenger seat and clipped on my seat belt. "Will I get in trouble for sitting up here with you?"

"*You* will be fine."

He snapped on his lights and hit the whoop on the siren. Behind us cars tried to move out of his way, some moving left and others moving right, but basically not leaving any room.

"Hold on." He threw the cruiser in drive and headed for the mesquite trees in front of us.

"Hey!" I covered my eyes.

A screeching sound of metal against bark filled my ears like King Kong running his fingernails down a giant chalkboard. Then we propelled out of the shoot like a bull at a rodeo, barreling through the grass, dodging large rocks and clumps of cacti until finally pitching down a shallow gulley and coming up onto the main road. He hit the siren for real this time, cut off the line of cars, whipped around the slow-moving traffic, and finally careened onto the gravel on the shoulder.

"We're going to blow a tire!" I clung to the back of the front seat like a tick to a deer.

Riveted on the road, he said, "Any sign of the Prius?"

I craned my neck, searching in all directions. "No, it's pitch-black on either side."

His eyes narrowed. His hands gripped the steering wheel until I thought his bones would pierce his skin. "Hold on!" He spun the wheel to the right and gunned it down a red clay road I hadn't even seen until we'd made the turn.

"Where does this go?"

"Tommy's Pond."

Named for the actor who'd once lived outside of Broken Boot, Tommy's Catfish Canal was a failed effort to build up the local economy. Oh, catfish and minnows still called it home, but the owner filed for bankruptcy and never came back. Locals still fished there, but they were taking their health in their hands. In the heat, algae levels would rise, making everything in the pond toxic. Or so I heard.

"What makes you think they went this way?"

He shot me a glance. "He flattened a clusterberry when he took the turn."

"What clusterberry?"

"Never mind."

The road to Tommy's Catfish Canal was as dark as the Marfa Lights pavilion on a Monday night. Stars shimmered in the sky, vibrating with a sound I could almost hear.

"If you're not so sure Frank Fillmore did this thing, why are you after him?"

He shot me a look of disbelief. "He's got Lenny, right?"

"True." Lenny wasn't best buds with Lightfoot—not like

Ryan. Lightfoot's tribal bracelet glimmered in the light from the cruiser's dash.

We were silent for a while and then he glanced my way. "He'll be okay."

Or Frank might kill him, the same way he'd murdered Lucky. I grasped for something to keep my fears at bay. "Those symbols on your bracelet . . . what do they mean?"

He hesitated so long, I thought I'd only imagined speaking the words.

"They are symbols of purity."

"Oh." I didn't know what to say. Had he taken a vow of chastity? Why did I care?

He studied my face. "It means my spirit is clean."

"Oh?"

"What did you think I meant?"

"Uh—"

"Shh."

Up ahead a split rail fence went off to the left and right sides of the road. There was no gate. Hinges, but no gate. Not anymore. A sign remained on the fence post to the right of the dirt road we traveled. NO TRESPASSING. FISH AT YOUR OWN RISK.

The headlights caught a metal building and a porta-potty off to the right. Lightfoot slammed on his brakes. What I'd thought was grass was actually the pond. I gulped. If I'd been driving we'd have driven straight into it. But then again, I'm always a much better driver behind the wheel.

"No Prius," I said. "Careful turning around. Don't get us stuck in the mud."

He turned off the engine, killed the lights, and pointed with his right hand. His bracelet and wrist caught my eye. What was it about a man's wrist that made me pause?

"Over there, Callahan."

"Oh, my great-aunt Sammie." The hood of the Prius peeked out from behind the metal building as if watching for us to arrive.

"Don't touch that door. He may be armed."

"Even if he had a knife. What's he going to do? Throw it at us?"

Lightfoot glared.

"So he's not a knife thrower in the circus. Maybe he was a SEAL or someone trained in hand-to-hand combat."

"Did he strike you as a SEAL?" I was struck by his tone of voice. Lightfoot was actually being sarcastic.

"Now that you mention it . . . no." Why would a man trained to kill other men use electronic shenanigans to kill someone? "He could have killed Lucky with electricity just to throw us off. Maybe he used stun guns and electricity to torture prisoners of war."

"Shh."

A coyote howl floated through the air, lone and spine-tingling.

"Lenny's out there." My hand flew to the door handle.

"No." He grabbed my arm and held me tight. "Wait for Fillmore to make the first move."

I counted to ten, forcing my pulse to slow. "Not a talent I'm known for."

His eyes narrowed, he scanned the area in silence.

"*Unencumbered* was the word I think you used." My eyes were focused on the Prius, the metal building, and the surrounding area, but my mind was still curious.

"Shh." He dropped my arm.

"You might as well tell me," I whispered. "I'm going to keep asking."

"Why am I not surprised?" He paused, his eyes never

leaving the scene before us. "I told you. I broke up with my lady."

I grinned. "You mean your girlfriend."

"Why people insist on using that term, I don't know. She is neither a girl or a friend."

"But she was your . . . special lady?" I wanted to giggle with relief.

"Yes."

"Ah."

Lightfoot leaned forward and I followed his gaze. At the corner of the metal building, a figure appeared at the far side of the Prius.

"Do you see what I see?" A new surge of adrenaline poured through my veins.

"Stay here."

"No—"

"It's not a request." He turned the full force of those eyes on me. "Do you understand me?"

I nodded. "Stay here."

"And I want you to get down so he can't see you."

"I could help."

"You could get yourself kidnapped again."

"Right." He had a point. Things could go sideways.

"And for pity's sake don't put a dent in her. She's brand-new."

"Um, how will I know what's going on?" There was a bright utility light shining from the corner of the metal building. "I'm not going to be able to read your lips if you should turn away from me."

He thought for a second, then he rolled down the windows an inch, no more. "That should help you follow along. Don't forget. If you can hear us, we can hear you."

He reached up and turned off the cab light, and then he locked the doors and stepped into the night. "Frank?" His pace as he walked toward Fillmore was slow and easy. "It's me, Detective Lightfoot from the Big Bend County Sheriff's Office."

"What do you want? I ain't hurting no one." I could just make out Frank's low, reedy voice. The Prius was parked between the two men.

"I'm looking for Josie Callahan's dog. She said something about you being the last person to see him." Lightfoot's voice was low and steady.

"Last time I saw him he was out in the brush chasing after another mongrel."

"That so?" One step forward was all Lightfoot took.

"Why such a big deal over such a small dog?" Fillmore glanced at the SUV, and I slumped back in my seat.

I could see Lightfoot smile, by the light from his flashlight. "Crazy as it sounds, he's a local celebrity."

"That so?"

"Writes a blog about what's going on in the town."

"Sounds like you might be a bit crazy yourself, Detective."

Lightfoot laughed again. "Not me. I imagine his owner, Josie Callahan, writes it." He stepped to the front of the cruiser. "Either way, folks read it. He's the town's mascot, you might say."

"Isn't that special."

A coyote howled and then another off to the right, closer than before.

"I'd hate for us to have to fight off these coyotes, Frank. What say you meet me in the middle so we can talk?"

After a few seconds, Frank walked slowly to the side of the metal building. "Coyotes don't attack people. You ought to know that, Detective *Lightfoot*."

"I'm headed your way. No gun." Lightfoot lifted his hands in the air.

I prayed he was lying.

The two men drew within ten feet of each other. "Aren't you tired of running, Frank?"

Fillmore turned his head left and then right as if he suspected a trap. "You ever lost someone you loved?"

"Sure." I could just make out Lightfoot's deep voice.

"Then you get why I had to rid the earth of Lucky Straw." He laughed, a sound like a squeaky gate.

"I'm trying, Frank. Help me understand."

"Who found the stun gun in the chili? Was it you?"

"No, but that was clever."

"Darn right it was. Thing is, you still don't know what killed him."

"I've got a pretty good idea." Lightfoot slowly lowered his hands a few inches. "You wouldn't be hiding any hacking abilities, would you?"

Fillmore clapped his hands. "Very good, Detective. Here's the thing. I'm a talented guy . . . one of those indispensable IT guys who's never supposed to be without a job." He spread his arms wide. "Yet here I am without work, four years after Lucky Straw fired me."

A coyote howled, Frank's head whipped toward the sound, and Lightfoot took two steps closer.

"What's the story with the blow to the head? Was that to throw us further off the scent?"

Frank's unhinged laugh cut through the stillness. "All I had to do was hack into the manufacturer's files for the know-how and Lucky's medical records for the codes."

"You programmed an interruption."

I could see Frank nod and smile. "Very, very good, Detective. The sad thing is Lucky never knew it was me."

"Not even when you whacked him in the head with his own skillet?" Lightfoot stepped closer.

"That's far enough." Fillmore stepped back, wide grin on his face. "In fact, I think I'll be going."

Off to my right, an explosion ripped through the night— like the bang of a cherry bomb only a hundred times louder. Lightfoot whirled toward the sound just as Fillmore ran at him, kicked him savagely in the knee, and made a mad dash through the brush. Lightfoot toppled to the ground.

Chapter 21

////////////////////////////

Night Moves

I had the door of the SUV open before you could say *hospital emergency room*. I hurried over to Lightfoot, keeping one eye out for Fillmore and another for Lenny. "You okay?" I whispered, keeping my eyes peeled at the place where I'd last seen Frank Fillmore as he disappeared.

"Quiet," he whispered. His face was set in a grimace, which made his normally passive expression look like a happy face by comparison.

I offered a hand.

With a frown, he reached up, and I pulled until he staggered to his feet like a drunk. "Stay here." He stumbled a step or two, gritted his teeth, and took off half running, half hobbling, with more than a little hitch in his giddyup. Frank had disappeared into the tall grass on the other side of the Prius, and without hesitation Lightfoot sprang after him.

If I'd have been born a canine, my ears would have pricked. A growl came from my left. My blood ran colder than a mountain stream. I swallowed hard. "Lenny," I whispered.

Nothing but the sound of the wind blowing the loose metal sheets on the roof of the nearby building.

Lightfoot had run off with the flashlight and his gun. I opened the cruiser door and searched the glove compartment for another flashlight or any light, for that matter. I reached under the seat and found a headlamp. When and where Detective Lightfoot used a headlamp, like a Chilean miner, I hadn't a clue. But what did it really matter?

I put it on, tightened the band. Now I could see, but I needed a weapon. Nothing was left in the cab that would help me, nor in the glove compartment, except a manual on the cruiser. It had heft, but it wouldn't hurt a fly even if I could have aimed it with precision.

A growl and a yip, weak, but Lenny, for sure.

I ran to the Prius, and as I did the moon disappeared again behind the clouds, like a shy dancer retreating to the powder room. I turned on the headlamp. Something growled closer, but off to my right. I opened the door of my Prius, searching for a weapon. Unfortunately, all I found was the crate of office supplies I kept handy. There was a stapler, some gum, and a clipboard. MacGyver I'm not, still I grabbed the stapler and the clipboard and hurried to the tall grass on the other side of the cruiser, where the yip had last been heard. Slowly, I approached the tall grass, turning my head this way and that, in order to guide the beam into the grass where a small dog might lay hurt and afraid.

"Lenny." I raised my voice to just above a whisper.

"Yip." I heard off in the distance.

"Where are you, little Lenster?" The grass whipped around my boots, the wind blowing through the juniper like so much wheat on the plains. I made a misstep and nearly turned my ankle on a rock. "Ouch," I cried, and immediately wanted to slap myself for being too loud. I kicked the rock for good measure, and a rattler set his rattles going.

"Yip, yip, yip." Lenny appeared just beyond the edge of my beam. My dear little friend was trying to protect me.

"No!" I threw the stapler at the snake's head just as it struck . . . and missed. To my right, I spotted another rock and slammed it down on the pointy head before I could doubt my abilities.

I gave the snake carcass a wide berth and scooped Lenny into my arms, thrusting the clipboard under my arm. "Oh, Lenster, I'm so glad to see you," I whispered fervently, kissing his tiny head and checking him for bites.

In return, he licked my face and his tiny body shook with joy. I walked slowly back to the cruiser, wondering where Lightfoot and Frank had disappeared to. Should I call it in? Had Lightfoot already called it in with his portable radio? And wouldn't I have heard it? I found his radio and turned up the volume from its low setting. Lenny continued to shiver as I opened the passenger door and slid inside. I placed his tiny body under my shirt; only his head remained outside, as if I'd given birth to a creature from an alien canine planet. A low growl vibrated from his throat, shaking his body with even greater force, his gaze riveted to the right of the cruiser, beyond what I could see.

"What's wrong?" I rubbed his ears and scratched under his chin.

A coyote muzzle appeared near the Prius, its owner panting and smiling as if to convince us to lower our guard. My heart leapt nearly out of my chest.

"Grrrr. Yip, yip, yip." Lenny was no longer frightened. He was downright mad. "Yip, yip. Grrrr."

Closer, maybe six feet to my right, another coyote appeared. Head low to the ground, taking small steps toward us.

Don't worry about me, he seemed to say from his posture. *I wouldn't hurt you.*

Suddenly my brain unfroze and I slammed the cruiser door. The two coyote brothers met in the front of the cruiser as if discussing a second plan of attack. They must really be desperately hungry if they hadn't run away from a human. I remembered the two coyotes from the parking lot. My gut told me these were the same ones. But were they as friendly as they seemed? I racked my brain for more information on coyotes. Just as I checked my phone for a signal so I could search *how to get rid of coyotes*, the radio crackled to life.

"Josie." Lightfoot's voice, faint and weak, came over the radio.

I grabbed the radio and couldn't figure out how to answer.

"Yip."

"You're right, Lenster. It's great to hear his voice." I took a deep breath and tried again. I removed the headlamp and positioned it so that the beam shone on the radio, but not out the window. After a bit of experimenting, I located the button to talk. "Lightfoot. Where are you?"

"I'm about a hundred yards to your east in the brush."

"Want me to call for backup?"

"I already did."

"That's great. Guess who I found?"

"Be quiet. Fillmore is headed your way. He's got a knife and a stun gun, and God knows what else."

"I'm locked in the car." My gaze darted left and right, trying to remember which way was east. "You said the cavalry is on their way."

"Look, I don't know where he is or if he's coming back. Get down in the floorboard, lock the doors, and make sure you can't be seen or heard."

I slid onto the floorboard, taking Lenny with me, forcing him behind my legs. All but my face fit beneath the dash.

"Are you *sure* the cavalry will be here any minute?"

Silence. "Yes, they're on their way. No, I think it will take longer than a minute for them to get to you."

"Oh." I calmed myself. "Are you all right? How's your leg?"

"Gotta get off this line. Quiet now. You can do it."

The line went dead. Do what? I laid my head on the seat. I could just make out the sky and the hills beyond through the driver's window. If the cavalry—read "two deputies"—was on its way, why wasn't I hearing any other radio activity? I reached out and turned a knob on the radio, and the thing screeched loud enough to deafen me in that ear for at least until the cows came home. I'd never owned cows, so that wasn't such a good analogy.

I turned it off, laying my head once again on the seat.

Behind me, Lenny made a little sighing noise and settled himself on top of my legs. I yawned. A sliver of moon slowly crept from behind a cloud, shyly peeking out just the corner of her face. A thought entered my head and bloomed into a fear. Had Frank heard the screeching radio? Had the sound carried beyond the cruiser? Maybe good ole Frank had run for the hills and was hiding out in the low trees.

I yawned again. Not. The. Time. To.

My eyes opened, heavier than if someone had weighed them down with copper pennies. Not the best of images when I was determined to stay alive. I blinked to clear away the sand of sleep. My eyes focused, and every hair on my body rose. There, pressed against the driver's window, was Frank Fillmore's face.

I knew the windows were tinted, and thank God it was dark outside. But the previously shy moon was showing not just a sliver of her face but a frighteningly bright half-moon of clear, silvery light. How could Frank not see me and Lenny with all that moonlight and the outside light on the metal building?

His gaze moved back and forth, landing first on the dash and then the headrests of both seats, where he supposed someone might be sitting. For a second he stared straight at me, where I lay, half-crouched, in the floorboard. If I moved farther down he might see me, like that dinosaur and those kids in that *Jurassic Park* movie. I slowed my breathing and cleared my mind, willing myself to disappear, to blend into the seat cushion so that he could find no trace of my body, mind, or spirit. After endless moments, he moved to the passenger window and again pressed his face to the window, desperately looking for what?

Lenny growled low.

"Shh," I uttered as lightly as I could, a mere hiss of air escaping from a bicycle tire. "Shh."

Fillmore straightened. I could no longer see him without sitting up. Slowly, I moved my chin to get a better view out the driver's window. I could just make him out as he walked away from the cruiser. I raised my head to follow his movements.

"Josie," Lightfoot whispered in a crackle over the radio.

I inched out my arm and grabbed the radio. "Shh," I whispered, quiet as breath. "He's right here."

"Watch out! He admitted he killed Lucky Straw." Lightfoot's voice was faint.

I whispered back, "Why the confession?" Nervous butterflies rumbled in my stomach. "You stay low. He's crazier than a dog in a hubcap factory."

"Said he wants to rid the world of evil."

Slowly, I raised my head a fraction of an inch and peered out the window. "Oh, shoot the moon!" I hissed.

"What?"

"He's back in the Prius."

He groaned softly. "You're going to have to come get me."

"How? You've got the keys."

"There's an extra key hidden under the driver's seat."

I watched as Frank opened the trunk of the Prius and removed a box of rockets, like the ones I'd seen on his launching platform. He bent over the box and his mouth moved as if he were crooning to his babies.

"It's not here. Someone must have taken it." I admit it— when I can't find something I always blame it on someone else. "Nothing's here."

"A small metal box connected to the spring by a magnet."

I felt around again, finally dropping my head to the floorboard so that my arm could reach farther.

"You got it?"

"No." I flung my braid out of my eyes, banging the back of my head on the steering wheel. I reached farther though I was seeing spots in front of my eyes. "Yes!" I shouted. Quickly I sat up and unscrewed the box. Inside was the key just as he had promised. "Where are you exactly? I don't want to run you over."

"Head east," Lightfoot said through gritted teeth, his voice filled with pain.

"Which way is that?"

Fillmore continued to run his gaze over the brush and grass, searching for Lightfoot. Or for me. "He's standing next to the Prius. You think he's going to let me just drive by?"

There was silence on the other end.

I stuck the key in the ignition, started the engine, and hoped Frank wouldn't hear me. No lights to warn him of my approach.

With a jerk and a roar of its four-cylinder engine, the

Prius started around the metal building, headed for the dirt road and escape.

"One, two, three!" With a gulp, I threw the SUV in gear, stomped the gas, and barreled into the passenger door of my Prius, crushing the rear driver's side door of my car, miraculously missing Frank Fillmore. I didn't have time to mourn my beloved car. My brain was rattling in my skull. Miracle or not, I'd aimed and taken Frank Fillmore down.

Frank's head rocked back and forth against the headrest as the night filled with sirens. The cavalry had arrived. Slowly he opened his door and swung his legs to the ground.

"Yip, yip, yip, yip." Lenny jumped in my lap, licking my face repeatedly, showing over and over how excited he was to have caught the man who held him hostage.

I laughed and banged the dash until my palms hurt. "We did it, Lenster! We did it."

Two deputy cruisers squealed in, neatly blocking in the Prius. Deputies Barnes and Pleasant jumped out, guns drawn. "Hold it right there," Pleasant ordered, eyes narrowed, her stance wide.

Barnes gave her a look of disbelief. "I don't think he's fit to walk as far as his toenails." He aimed at Fillmore. "Come out with your hands up."

"Lightfoot needs our help." I pointed to the stand of mesquite trees barely visible in the distance. "He's out that way, and he's hurt."

"Yip," Lenny said.

Staggering to his feet, Fillmore slowly raised his hands. "What's going on, Officers?"

"We understand you murdered Lucky Straw." Pleasant stepped closer, aiming at his heart.

"Shut it, would you?" Barnes glared at his partner.

I could see his point. If they wanted the guy to start monologuing about his crime, they had to give him some rope.

Fillmore shook his head in feigned bewilderment. "Officers, there has been some kind of misunderstanding."

"I'm going after Lightfoot while you two stay with the prisoner." I placed Lenny in a football hold and ran back to the cruiser. "I'll be right back."

"Miss Callahan, you've done enough damage."

Before they could argue, I slid under the wheel, tossing Lenny lightly into the passenger seat. "That is a government-issued vehicle." Barnes yelled loud enough for me to hear through the bulletproof glass.

"And I'm using it to find a government employee."

"I'm coming with you," Barnes said, starting for the driver's side.

I held out a hand to make him stop. "You really think you should leave only one officer here with this guy?" I gave him a pointed look. Pleasant might botch it and then she might not. Either way, Barnes's ego wouldn't let him take the chance.

"Isn't it going to take another half hour for someone from another county to make it here to go get Lightfoot? What if not only his leg is broken, but he's been electro-cuted by this guy?"

"Stun guns don't hurt you . . . much." Barnes frowned, as if trying to puzzle out the truth of what he'd said.

"His will."

Barnes's gaze fixated on Fillmore as Barnes slowly stepped farther away from their prisoner. Pleasant shook her head and gave her partner a look of disgust.

Fillmore crossed his arms and widened his stance. "She's crazy. Don't believe a word she says. Her head's all full of estrogen and cotton balls." He laughed. "Hah! Estrogen-perfumed cotton balls."

I wanted to smack him, but I knew when to leave well enough alone. I would leave any vengeance to Officer Lightfoot, the Big Bend County Sheriff's Office, and the Almighty Smiter.

With a salute to Barnes and Pleasant and a wave to the criminal element, I reversed Lightfoot's SUV into a patch of cactus, adjusted the wheel, and then promptly backed it into a utility pole. I didn't think I lost much paint since there was only a slight bump and a high-pitched scraping sound. I drove around the Prius and into the scrub and brush until I found a four-by-four trail, which took me back to the good old days in college, when we'd go mudding off-road south of Austin. I hadn't found a place to go mudding in the high desert, and I doubted I ever would. Finally I turned my high beams on and began to pick my way carefully down the trail. I called Lightfoot on the radio.

"Turn your flashlight on so I can find you." I was hoping he was still conscious. "And, by the way, you're welcome."

"You caught him?" His voice held too much skepticism for my liking.

"Me, Lenny, and a couple of deputies."

"Huh." He groaned. "That's great. Slow down. You're almost here."

"Wave your flashlight. I don't want to run you over. You'd be flatter than a fritter."

"Slow down," he ordered. "And if we're throwing around Texas sayings, you're louder than a stampede of buffalo."

I'd never heard a stampede of buffalo though I saw a herd out in Caprock Canyons State Park once on a family vacation. Lightfoot must have been all kinds of stressed out to suggest such a thing—which wasn't surprising, seeing as how he'd hurt his leg and I'd stolen his thunder by catching Fillmore.

Up ahead, I found him at the end of my high beams. He was standing on one foot, grimacing as if he'd lost the other leg in a battle with Santa Anna.

"Lenny, stay. You don't want those coyotes to come back, do you?"

My long-haired Chihuahua friend climbed into the front window for a better view as I picked my way forward with a bit more speed and threw the cruiser in park. Carefully, walking through the rocks and cacti with the help of the cruiser's headlights, I ignored Lightfoot's stern look of disapproval, took his arm, and placed it around my shoulders.

"Who said it was okay for you to drive my cruiser?" He hopped and grunted toward the vehicle.

"You did, remember?"

"What was I smoking?" Lightfoot was going into shock. I'd never heard anything halfway snarky ever pass his lips. He tried to point me toward the driver's side.

"Don't even think about it." I jerked open the passenger door and helped him into the seat, barely managing to get him inside without bumping his head.

A breath separated our faces from each other. His arm still clung around my shoulder. I stared at him, and he stared at me. "I don't kiss on a first date."

"Good thing this isn't a date." He leaned forward and so did I. He gently placed his lips against mine.

I froze, not daring to breathe, and closed my eyes.

"If you're finished taking advantage of me, I think I'm going into shock." I backed out of the car so fast I whacked my back on the door handle.

"Yip, yip, yip." Not to be outdone, Lenny jumped into Lightfoot's arms and gave him a kiss.

"Against regulations." He whined and drew in a quick breath. "You trying to get me fired?"

"Heck, yes." I ran around to the driver's side. Then it dawned on me. There was no way to turn around.

"Seriously, get out of the driver's seat. I've driven in far worse condition." His words passed slowly through gritted teeth.

"Shh. Hold on." I was in park, but the brake lights would do a fair job of illuminating our path as long as I kept watch over my shoulder. "There's plenty of light to back up with if I go slow enough."

"Hey—"

I craned my neck, held down the foot brake, and moved the clutch into reverse. Slowly, like a box turtle on Valium, I backed that cruiser down the path, taking out a barrel cactus and a sapling, which made a horrible scratching sound to the undercarriage of the SUV.

"Pull this over now." When we hit another bump, he could barely contain his groan of pain.

"Yip." Lenny tried to give him another kiss.

"Stop that," he said, and unceremoniously tossed him into the backseat.

"Watch it, buddy. He's trying to make you feel better. Service dogs, ever heard of them?"

There was silence as I continued to pick my way.

"Not in need of a service dog. If you'd bothered to examine my leg, you'd know I merely need an emergency room."

"Almost there." I focused on the Prius, at the last minute swerving around it and coming to a screeching halt.

I hopped out and gave Deputy Pleasant the keys. "Watch out, he's grumpier than an old bear."

She left Barnes beside the cruiser, reading a handcuffed Fillmore his rights. Lightfoot had managed to open his door.

"Hey, Detective, you don't look so good," Pleasant said. She studied the pain etched across his face and the way he held tightly to his leg with one arm. "You need to drive over to Marfa to the emergency room and let them check out that leg."

"He's not driving anywhere tonight." She and I exchanged a look of bemusement.

"Yes, I am." He collapsed back against the seat. "If I were a cursing man, I'd curse."

"And you'd be more than entitled." I gave Pleasant a smile. "But don't you worry. I'll get you there safe and sound." I grimaced. "Well, maybe not sound, seeing as how you're in pain."

"No. Way."

Pleasant shrugged. "Sorry, Lightfoot. The only seat we have is in the back with that Fillmore character. You don't want that?"

"No." Lightfoot and I said in unison.

"Yip."

"We'll stop by the station as soon as they've finished with me in Marfa." Lightfoot sat up straight and tipped his hat.

Lenny jumped onto the surprised detective's legs, raised his front paws onto his chest, and gave him a spectacular doggie kiss.

"Get him out of here." Lightfoot spluttered and wiped his mouth with the back of his hand.

I burst out laughing.

"Take your time." Deputy Pleasant smiled and waved.

"See you later." I retrieved my warmhearted canine friend. "You're a good boy. Yes, sir."

"Yip."

Lenny and I cruised back around to the driver's seat. "Oh, he is a very scary detective," I whispered. My long-haired Chi's bright eyes shone with mischief. "But you were very brave to kiss him."

"Yip, yip."

"And so was I."

Chapter 22

Monday, Monday

The chili cook-off had come and gone. Was it a huge hit? It was a thrill for those fortunate enough to win. It was a decent start to a tradition that I hoped would gain traction, growing and improving in years to come. A new tradition for citizens, tourists, and all who loved the high-plain desert and the simple folks who lived here.

Okay, so the publicity we received had more to do with Lucky's death and Frank Fillmore's capture than the chili cook-off itself. Still, it was something we could build on. Dani and her family, Whip and his Apache camper, and the rest of the tourists from the cook-off had packed up their knives and gone home. And frankly, if I ever ate another bowl of chili, pigs would fly across the Rio Grande on the back of a parasail.

"Where are the chile rellenos?" Uncle Eddie took off his hat and hung it on the coatrack near the front door. He found a place next to Ryan Prescott. At first, I had made a point not to invite Ryan—too afraid he'd act all weird and possessive. But Senora Mari insisted. And that was that.

"Yip," Lenny said.

"What, Lenster?" Ryan asked. "You've eaten the chile rellenos? Man, what's come over you?"

"Yip."

"See you later." Ryan said to the dog at his feet. "I'll hook you up with something for heartburn."

"Today, no chiles!" I opened the kitchen door with a flourish. "For Aunt Linda, something delicious *and* healthy." Senora Mari entered with a large tray bearing two platters of grilled snapper and peppers and onions.

Ryan's mouth dropped open. "Senora Mari, you've outdone yourself." He sniffed the air like a fox in a chicken coop. "What can I ever do to repay you?"

"Wash dishes, senor." The group laughed. "It's no joke," Senora Mari said. "I had to fire a dishwasher today. Now we're shorthanded.

"Woo-wee." He grinned. "What a treat." Ryan was acting up a storm, being kind to my *abuela*. He had a genuine and thorough disgust for any seafood that wasn't fried, except for raw oysters—he thought eating the slimy boogers a way to prove his manliness.

"I'm here. Don't count me out." Aunt Linda took her place at the end of the table. For our family's big event postmortem luncheon, we'd pushed a few tables together and invited our friends. Anthony and Lily were serving, but as soon as we all had our meals they would sit at the end table and enjoy the fruits of their labors.

"Don't start without me." My *abuela* pointed at each of us sitting around the table. "Or you will have nightmares until the apocalypse." She lifted her finger into the air, issuing a proclamation, and then hurried back to the kitchen.

"Is she kidding?" Patti asked. With one of her long black

fingernails, she hooked a piece of onion from the snapper platter and tossed it in her mouth.

"Nice manners, Perez." Ryan shook his head in mock disgust.

"In your dreams, Prescott."

"Who knows?" I asked everyone at the table. "Kidding or not, we should all be on our best behavior. What if, in addition to having prophetic dreams, she can control what each of us dreams about?"

"That would be a nightmare in itself," Uncle Eddie muttered.

"Nightmares about onions and smelly feet." Suddenly Patti looked worried.

The cowbell over the front door rang. Aunt Linda stood, ready to take control. "Sorry, we're not—"

"Am I early?" It was Lightfoot, and he was not what I expected. He wore a pair of slacks with one leg cut off above a startling white cast. A Western shirt of a fancy fabric was tucked into an exquisite tribal belt. But what really made me gawk was the fact he wore no hat over his dark braid.

I smiled and tried not to ogle. "No, no. Right this way." I gestured toward a seat at the end of the table.

"Detective, ignore my granddaughter, she is being impolite." Senora Mari set two heavy platters of shrimp fajitas on the tables.

"She comes by it honest," Uncle Eddie muttered.

Lightfoot shifted his crutches so the door could close and started clumsily for the seat at the far end.

"I was just about to switch seats when you walked in." Aunt Linda scooted out of her chair and took the seat I'd offered at the end of the table.

He stared at the seat next to mine. He stared at the tableful of guests who stared back in return. "Don't mind if I do." With a big smile, he handed me a crutch, wriggled into his seat, handed me the other crutch, and gave me a wink.

Forget the butterflies, my heart was singing "Stand By Your Man," complete with fiddles and a banjo. One wink from Detective Quint Lightfoot and I was Tammy Wynette.

I looked up and found Ryan watching me closely, his gaze filled with understanding, a lopsided grin on his face.

"Give me those before you knock yourself out with them." Patti appeared at my side, grabbed Lightfoot's crutches, and carried them into the bar. With a quick glance to ensure she wasn't seen, she locked eyes with me. "Don't let this one get away," she mouthed silently.

I folded my hands and lifted my eyes to the ceiling.

"What's wrong?" Lightfoot asked.

I nearly choked on my Dr Pepper. "Oh, nothing. I was praying you like fish."

"As long as it's not from Tommy's Catfish Canal."

"Why?" Senora Mari's eyes grew wide. "Is that against the law?"

Lenny's Little Dog Blog

❦❦❦❦❦❦❦❦❦❦❦❦❦❦❦❦❦❦❦❦❦❦❦❦❦❦

Have I Got a Fiesta for You

First things first: A big Texas howdy to all y'all from Lenny—that's me.

Next: A shout-out to all the inhabitants of Broken Boot, Big Bend County, and creatures ginormous, puny, and somewhere in between currently reading the Little Dog Blog on the World Wide Web.

Writing a blog is fun and all, but it's not what it's cracked up to be. Other folks might enjoy sharing their feelings online, but most of them have fingers. You try slapping your nose against a keyboard for an hour at a time and see how you like it. Not to mention, I have to run to the other side of the computer just to hit the backspace. My owner, spunky waitress Josie Callahan, came up with the bright idea for me to write a blog, but if you ask me, it's her way of keeping her journalistic muscles toned while saying what she really thinks about the mysterious events going on in our rustic, postage-stamp-sized town. After all, who could be offended at the scribblings of an adorable, long-haired Chihuahua?

What can I say? There's no way to explain the crazy goings-on around town. Let's review. Our debut event was the First Annual Wild Wild West Festival, full of lively music, a silent auction, tamale-eating contest, and the murder of acclaimed local jewelry designer, Dixie Honeycutt. Josie and I solved that murder with a little help from Detective Quint Lightfoot and Sheriff Mack Wallace. Our second mega event was the First Annual Homestead Days Music Festival, full of lively country music *and* the murder of country singer Jeff Clark. Josie and I solved that crime as well with a little help from Detective Lightfoot and the Big Bend County sheriff's deputies. Last but not least, and I bet you know where I'm heading with this one, the First Annual Charity Chili Cook-off and Cinco de Mayo Fiesta, full of lively music—both mariachi, my favorite, and marching bands—*folklórico* dancing, fireworks, *and* the murder of champion chili cook Lucky Straw. Josie and I solved that crime, 'cause that's what we do.

When you're planning your next Texas vacation don't forget to stop by and see us in Broken Boot. Nothing compares to the rugged beauty of Big Sky country or the mouthwatering Tex-Mex offered at Milagro on Main Street. Until then, you can read my blog. You never know what the *good* folks of Broken Boot and Big Bend County will be up to next.

Adios for now, amigos,
Lenny

Recipes

Uncle Eddie's Nontraditional Venison Chili

Serves 8–10

Prep time: 15 minutes (beans soak overnight). Cook time: 6 hours

½ pound pinto beans
2 tablespoons salt
5 cups canned tomatoes
1 medium red onion, chopped
3 bell peppers, chopped
1½ teaspoons olive oil
2 cloves garlic, crushed
½ cup chopped parsley
½ cup butter
2½ pounds ground venison
1 pound ground pork
½ cup chili powder
1½ teaspoons pepper
1½ teaspoons cumin

Wash beans thoroughly and soak overnight in water 2 inches above beans. Wash again and simmer with salt until tender (about 4 hours).

Simmer tomatoes in separate pan for 5 minutes. Sauté onions and bell peppers in olive oil; add to tomatoes, and cook until tender. Add garlic and parsley.

Melt butter in skillet and sauté venison and pork for 15 minutes. Drain off grease, add meat to tomato and onion mixture. Stir in chili powder and cook 10 minutes; add beans, pepper, and cumin. Simmer covered for 1 hour, uncovered for 30 minutes.

✒ Josie's Baked Jalapeño Poppers

Serves 8 or more

Prep time: 15 minutes. Cook time: 25 minutes

6 slices of bacon, cooked crispy
16 jalapeño chiles
1 teaspoon crushed garlic or 2 teaspoons garlic powder
3 tablespoons grated Parmesan cheese
1½ cups cream cheese, room temperature
2 cups cheddar cheese, medium or sharp, grated
Cooking spray

Preheat oven to 500 degrees F.

Fry the bacon until crisp and drain. Rinse chiles and pat dry. Remove the stems and slice the chiles in half, lengthwise. Use a small knife to remove seeds and membranes to taste. (The heat of the chiles is in the seeds and membranes. Rinse the chiles again to remove hot oils if you desire.)

In a medium bowl, add garlic, Parmesan cheese, and room-temperature cream cheese. Mix well. If you prefer a lot of heat in your poppers, you can add back the seeds and chopped membrane into the cheese and garlic mixture. Crush the bacon and add to mixture. Stir until blended.

Place the chiles under the broiler, cut side down on a baking sheet. Roast the chiles until their skin is charred a brownish-blackish color. (This yummy step is optional.)

Spray a baking sheet with cooking spray.

Using a spoon, heap the cheese mixture into each chile pepper half and top and sprinkle with cheddar cheese. Push the sprinkled cheese into the cheese mixture. Place the stuffed jalapeño poppers on the cookie sheet. Bake for 25 minutes or until the tops are a beautiful golden brown.

✎ Texas Eggs

Serves 6

Prep time: 5 minutes. Cook time: 15 minutes

3–4 jalapeños, or roasted and peeled fresh green chiles
1 large onion, diced
1 bell pepper, diced
2 tablespoons butter
1 dozen eggs
1 cup grated cheddar cheese
1 large tomato, diced

Seed and chop jalapeños. In skillet, brown onion and bell pepper in butter. Remove from skillet. Beat eggs until frothy. Pour into skillet and cook until soft and very wet. Add the other ingredients and serve.

✐ Huevos Rancheros

Serves 2

Prep time: 10 minutes. Cook time: 20 minutes

3 Roma tomatoes
¼ medium white onion
1 garlic clove
1 serrano chile (more chiles, more heat)
½ teaspoon thyme, fresh
2–3 tablespoons of water
1 tablespoon cooking oil, plus ½ cup
4 corn tortillas
4 eggs
salt to taste

Salsa

Chop tomatoes, onion, garlic, and serrano chile. Add thyme and 2–3 tablespoons of water. Blend until smooth. Heat 1 tablespoon of cooking oil in a saucepan until hot. Pour tomato mixture into the hot oil. (Be very careful, liquid may spatter.) Simmer until salsa is deep red and slightly thick.

Salt to taste.

Tortillas

Pour ½ cup of cooking oil into a small-to-medium-sized frying pan—about ¼ inch deep. Heat oil to medium hot. Fry tortillas in oil for 20 seconds on each side, 1 at a time. Do not allow tortillas to get hard. Drain excess oil.

Sunny-Side Up Eggs

Using the medium-hot oil from the fried tortillas, add 2 eggs to the oil. Tilt the pan so the eggs are close together. Cook until whites of the eggs are cooked through and yolks are runny.

Serving

Place 2 tortillas on serving plate. Carefully place eggs on tortillas. Spoon warm tomato salsa over eggs. Serve immediately.

✒ Senora Mari's Chicken Quesadillas

Serves 8–10

Prep time: 10 minutes. Cook time: 25 minutes

2 chicken breasts
½ teaspoon oregano
½ teaspoon garlic powder
¼ teaspoon cumin
salt and pepper to taste
vegetable oil or your favorite cooking oil
½ cup onion, chopped
butter for sautéing
1 cup shredded Manchego or asadero cheese
1 cup shredded pepper jack cheese
1 dozen flour tortillas

Season chicken breast with oregano, garlic, cumin, and salt and pepper to taste. Fry in small amount of oil over medium heat. Cook until browned and cooked throughout. Shred the chicken, using 2 forks.

Brown and caramelize onions in butter.

Spoon 2 tablespoons of each cheese on one side of tortilla. Add some chicken and caramelized onions. Fold tortilla in half. Fry in butter over medium-low heat until cheese is melted and tortilla is golden brown.

✐ Pecan Pralines

Makes 20 pralines

Prep time: 5 minutes. Inactive: 10 minutes. Cook time: 15 minutes

2 cups white sugar
4 cups pecans
2 cups light-brown sugar
1 heaping tablespoon unsalted butter
2 teaspoons vanilla extract
⅔ cup whole milk
6 tablespoons light corn syrup

Stir together all ingredients in a large saucepan. Be sure to stir well. Bring mixture to a boil over medium-high heat. Cook, stirring often, until mixture reaches 234 degrees F on a candy thermometer. (Candy may resemble a softball at this stage.)

Remove mixture from heat and stir 2 minutes, or until the mixture loses some of its shininess. Quickly spoon candy onto trays lined with wax or parchment paper. Let candy cool for about 20 minutes.

About the Author

Rebecca Adler lives in Texas and writes mysteries set in far West Texas, filled with sweet, Southern-fried flavor, delicious suspense, and scrumptious Tex-Mex recipes. She is the author of *Here Today, Gone Tamale* and *The Good, the Bad, and the Guacamole* (books one and two in the Taste of Texas Mystery series). Visit her online at AuthorRebeccaAdler.com.